Warning!

Violence and the Supernatural

The fictional Worlds of Palladium Books® are violent, deadly and filled with supernatural monsters. Other dimensional beings, often referred to as "demons," torment, stalk and prey on humans. Other alien life forms, monsters, gods and demigods, as well as magic, insanity, and war are all elements in this book.

Some parents may find the violence, magic and supernatural elements of the game inappropriate for young readers/players. We suggest parental discretion.

Please note that none of us at Palladium Books® condone or encourage the occult, the practice of magic, the use of drugs, or violence.

The Rifter™ Number Nine
Your guide to the Palladium Megaverse®!

First Printing — January, 2000

Palladium On-Line **www.palladiumbooks.com**

The Rifter™ #9 RPG sourcebook series is published by Palladium Books Inc., 12455 Universal Drive, Taylor, MI 48180. Printed in the USA.

Palladium Books® Presents:

THE RIFTER™ #9

BRANDT-97

Sourcebook and guide to the Palladium Megaverse®

Coordinator & Editor in Chief: **Wayne Smith**

Supervising Coordinator & Typesetting:
Maryann Siembieda

Contributing Writers:

James M.G. Cannon

David Haendler

Owen Johnson

Christopher Jones

Shawn Merrow

Mark Sumimoto

Todd Sterrett

Kevin Siembieda

Jason Richards

Nathan Taylor

Knights of the Dinner Table: **Jolly Blackburn**

Proofreader: **Julius Rosenstein**

Cover Painting: **Simon Bisley**

Interior Artists:

Apollo Okamura

Ryan Beres

Wayne Breaux Jr.

Michael Dubisch

Paulo Parentes Studio

Ramon Perez

Scott Johnson

And other Palladium Madmen

Rifts® Comic Strip: **Ramon Perez**

Cover Logo Design: **Steve Edwards**

Credits Page Logo: **Niklas Brandt**

Keylining: **Kevin Siembieda**

Based on the RPG rules, characters, concepts and Megaverse® created by Kevin Siembieda.

Special Thanks to the folks at Mirage Studios, and to all of our contributors. Our apologies to anybody who got accidentally left out or their name misspelled.

Contents — The Rifter #9
— January, 2000 —

The Cover

The cover to **The Rifter #9** is by the British master of dynamic action and vein-popping heroes, *Simon Bisley*. We thought it would be a shame if this outstanding piece of artwork never saw print. The folks at *Mirage* agreed. The painting was originally commissioned by Palladium as the cover to the (now cancelled) **TMNT RPG, Second Edition**.

A word about this issue

Hmm, somehow the focus of this issue became **Rifts®**. Part of the reason was editor Wayne Smith didn't know Mr. Siembieda planned on including the Bio-Borg™ material. Some issues just take on a life of their own — and this was one of them. Readers can count on future issues of **The Rifter™** turning its attention on non-Rifts® role-playing games, like *Heroes Unlimited™, Palladium Fantasy* and others.

Optional and Unofficial Rules & Source Material

Please note that most of the material presented in **The Rifter™** is "unofficial" or "optional" rules and source material. They are alternative ideas and things one can include in his campaign or enjoy reading. They are not "official" to the main games or world settings. For example, the story, *Siege Against Tolkeen*, is likely to be very different than Kevin Siembieda's "official" World Books coming in 2000. As for optional tables and adventures, if they sound cool or fun, use them. If they sound funky, too high-powered or inappropriate for your game, modify them or ignore them completely.

All the material in **The Rifter™** has been included for two reasons: One, because we thought it was imaginative and fun, and two, we thought it would stimulate your imagination with fun stuff that you can use (if you want) or which might inspire you to create your own wonders.

This issue, the **Bio-Borgs™** are approved as an "official" addition to the **Rifts®** role-playing game.

www.palladiumbooks.com — Palladium On-Line

Congratulations to Forjx the Maniac (I probably spelled it wrong) for being the "official" individual to make the one millionth "hit" on Palladium's web page. In honor of this momentous occasion, he received a $100 gift certificate for Palladium Product. Palladium's web page offers visitors the opportunity to access up-to-the-minute news, scheduling changes, sneak previews, meeting other gamers in our chat rooms, special on-line events, on-line RPG source material and more. Come by and visit, maybe you'll become our two millionth visitor.

Coming Next Issue ...
The Rifter™ #10

From the Desk of Kevin Siembieda

Good-Bye, Ninja Turtles®

Saying good-bye to the Ninja Turtles is like saying farewell to an old friend. So it is with a touch of sadness that I must announce Palladium Books' decision to let go of the **Teenage Mutant Ninja Turtles®** role-playing game license.

I know this news will disappoint many fans, particularly those who have been anxiously anticipating the release of the Second Edition of the **Ninja Turtle® RPG**. There will be no Second Edition or any new TMNT product from Palladium.

A tiny handful of distraught fans on-line, have suggested Palladium does not care about our fans, because if we did, we would come out with **TMNT, 2nd Edition** no matter what. If only it were that simple and easy. What these folks do not understand is that Palladium and Mirage (the TMNT people) have been keeping the game-line afloat for the last several years because we *care*.

At its peak, Palladium Books was selling over 4,000 copies of the TMNT game every month! Nearly 200,000 copies of the basic rule book, alone, have been sold since we first released it in the fall of 1985. The late 1980's also saw the black and white *comic book* outselling many color comics, with sales (I believe) of over 100,000 copies an issue. In fact, the explosive success of the TMNT comic book helped give birth to the "independent" comic book publishing industry, as hundreds of other creators began to "self-publish" their own comics and form new companies. The success of the Ninja Turtles encouraged hundreds of new entrepreneurs to take a chance, and it created a level of excitement that the comic book industry had not seen in decades (at the time, other than a few tiny, independent publishers, there was only Marvel and DC).

Meanwhile, role-playing was experiencing its own "boom" time, and with carefully executed licenses like the **Ninja Turtles®** and **Robotech®**, Palladium Books was quickly recognized as one of the top publishers of RPGs.

The mass market exploitation of the Turtles created hundreds of licensed products worldwide. That was cool, and made the original creators, Kevin Eastman and Peter Laird, some serious money. Toy manufacturers, the film studio, the TV cartoon people and scores of others made millions of dollars as the Ninja Turtles became a pop culture phenomenon — the *Pokemon* of their day. There were three movies, a long-running TV cartoon, a zillion action figures and toys, comic books, coloring books, and clothes for little kids, to name just a few of the 150+ licenses that once existed. A huge success by any standard. And it could not have happened to two nicer guys, 'cuz *Kevin Eastman* and *Peter Laird* are the best!

Ah, but you know how you always hear how everything (especially fame and success) comes with a price? Well, it is true. On one hand, the TMNT folks got to see their creation become

an international mega-hit, with millions upon millions of children falling in love with the Ninja Turtles, bringing joy and fun to them all.

On the other hand, the successful "mass marketing" killed the **Teenage Mutant Ninja Turtles®** in the *comic book* and *role-playing game* markets where they first took off. Weird, but true. You see, the Turtles were what I refer to as, "kiddified." The once gritty, satirical, hard-hitting Turtles became cuddly, fun-loving, pizza-swirling heroes to little kids — ages 3-10 — and joined the ranks of *Mickey Mouse, Donald Duck* and the *Smurfs*! While this made them a viable mass market property, it hurt them in the small, specialized market of role-playing. Basically, no self-respecting teenager or pre-teen wanted anything to do with the Ninja Turtles. Why? Because they had become "little kid stuff." It didn't matter that the role-playing game (and b/w comic book) was the same gritty, butt-kicking, imaginative and fun game it had always been. The Turtles were taboo to the teen market.

Role-playing sales plummeted overnight, from 4000+ copies a month to 1,200. A short time later sales fell to less than 100 copies a month. And sourcebooks ... forget about them.

No matter what we or Mirage did, nothing helped the RPG sales. We kept delaying the **Second Edition TMNT game** in a futile attempt to promote, hype and build excitement. We spent over $20,000 on promotional advertisements that appeared in

imaginative, helpful and cooperative even after they became millionaires. I'm telling you, these guys are the best!

I want to make it clear that the good folks at **Mirage Studios** were willing to renew our license for another two years. It was Palladium Books who declined and asked to terminate the license. Sad and disappointing as it may be, it is just time for us to let the Ninja Turtles go and pursue other, new realms of adventure. Sorry.

We wish Kevin Eastman, Peter Laird, Gary Richardson, Jim Lawson and all the fine people at Mirage a bright and happy future. Thanks everybody, it has been a grand 15 years working with you. I guess we'll just watch the next 15 years of the Turtles' success from the back seat instead of the front.

Oh, and for all you "Charlie-Come-Latelies," Palladium has till the end of 2000 to liquidate its remaining stock of TMNT products. In cooperation with Mirage, Palladium Books is offering some amazing *liquidation* specials, effective immediately. So get 'em before these gems are gone forever!

— Kevin Siembieda, 2000

Marvel Comics and offered the first 600 people to respond, a free copy of the current TMNT game. We sent out 600 copies, but saw no increase in sales. We hyped it up on-line, in The Rifter™, at conventions, etc., to no avail. After nearly three years of hype we had 30 advanced mail orders for the Second Edition compared to 300 for **Rifts® Canada** after only six months of hype. To make matters worse, half our distributors were not interested in carrying the Second Edition, and the other half were only willing to "try" a tiny amount. Despite our best attempts and advertising dollars (not counting the few thousand spent on the cover and interior artwork, some of which appears in this issue), few seemed to want it. To do **TMNT Second Edition** was throwing good money after bad. For Palladium Books, at least, the day of the Ninja Turtles had come to an end.

What drives me crazy is that to this very day I hear from gamers everywhere who first discovered role-playing games because they *tried* the **Ninja Turtle® RPG**. Even more maddening is the fact that most of them absolutely love the game, and many still even play it! And why not?! It was (is) a truly GREAT game and loads of fun!! I think it's one of game designer/writer, **Erick Wujcik's**, crowning achievements. Not to mention the fact that it helped spread Palladium's universal game system (one set of basic rules, a Megaverse® of adventure) to thousands of new gamers. Well, we had plenty of good years, got to know a couple of great guys in Kev and Pete (Gary, Jim, and Eric too). Furthermore, I'm proud to know that the **Teenage Mutant Ninja Turtles® & Other Strangeness RPG** ranks as one of the best selling role-playing games of all time. And we had a blast doing it. Eastman and Laird recognized our expertise and let us run with it. They were always friendly,

Palladium News, Info, & Coming Attractions

By Kevin Siembieda (the guy in the know)

News

Palladium Books Inc. — Strong and Healthy

1999 was very good to Palladium Books: Sales exceeded 1998 figures, the Christmas Surprise Package was a huge success for the third year in a row (lots of work but worth the smiles and good feelings), we convinced Bill Coffin to come work for Palladium full time, and we got several promising freelance writers on board to support *ALL* of Palladium's product lines.

Good news for the year 2000. Palladium is as strong and resilient as ever. We have no plans to raise prices, we have no desire to sell to a bigger company, and expect to release more great product for all game lines. 1999 already saw an increase in quality product, but 2000 should mark the beginning of a more even and regular release of exciting products for **Rifts®**, **Heroes Unlimited™**, **Nightbane®**, **The Palladium Fantasy Role-Playing Game®**, and maybe even **Ninjas & Superspies™**, along with some surprises.

Bill Coffin joins Palladium full time

This is great news, not only because Bill is a heck of a writer, imaginative and wonderful to work with, but because Bill's full attention on writing *should* help Palladium meet its deadlines.

Bill has already been helping with the development of what we believe to be the truly epic **Rifts®** series: **Coalition Wars™: Siege on Tolkeen**. We have some exciting stuff planned for that series: The Cyber-Knights divided, The Dragon-Kings united, plots and sub-plots galore, tons of world information about Tolkeen and the places around it, intrigue, suspense, betrayal, treachery and, of course, SURPRISES and WAR! Whew, every time I stop to think about this project I get excited.

Bill will also continue to write new books for **The Palladium Fantasy Role-Playing Game®**, including a few books that delve into the *Great Northern Wilderness* and *Land of the Damned*. Probably some **Heroes Unlimited™** sourcebooks too (check out his first HU2 book, *Century Station™*, in stores soon).

Mark Sumimoto leaves Palladium

Yes, people are coming and going at Palladium. Due to strong creative differences, Mark Sumimoto and Palladium Books have mutually agreed it is best to go our separate ways. Mark is a freelance writer who wrote **Splynn Dimensional Market™** (a cool world book full of Bio-Wizard items, magical stuff, and a companion to **Rifts® Atlantis**) and frequent contributor to **The Rifter™**. The Bio-Borgs that appear in this issue were cut from the Splynn manuscript due to space limitations. Palladium promised these monstrous characters would appear in **The Rifter™**, so here they are. Enjoy 'em.

We wish Mark continued success in all of his endeavors and hope he fulfills his dreams.

New faces in *The Rifter*™

Mr. Editor-in-Chief, Wayne Smith, seemed to have forgotten that part of the fun and excitement of **The Rifter™** is giving "new" people a chance to share their ideas and see their stuff in print. Oh sure, **The Rifter™** has been dynamic and fun to read these past eight issues — Wayne does *do* a very good job. However, even he admitted he fell into the trap of using several people over and over again. Well, from now on, each issue will try to offer more new faces. Not just *writers*, but *artists* too.

So all you would-be **writers** out there, and G.M.s who can write a decent sentence, send in those 8-25 page stories, source material, characters/villains/heroes, new gizmos, and adventures for Wayne's consideration. You can write for most of Palladium's RPG lines, particularly **The Palladium Fantasy RPG®**, **Heroes Unlimited™**, **Ninjas & Superspies™**, **Beyond the Supernatural™**, **Nightbane®**, **Systems Failure™**, and of course, **Rifts®**.

Meanwhile, you would-be **artists** should send photocopies (NEVER original artwork) of 6-12 different examples of your artwork for possible assignment consideration for **The Rifter™**. In the alternative, if you have just one or two cool pieces of artwork (quarter page, half page or full page) that you think looks cool, near-professional quality, or just plain butt-kicking, send us a xerox copy. Maybe we will agree and want to print it in an upcoming issue. You never know. Hey, funny cartoons too. **Note:** Make any Rifter™ art samples *"Attention Rifter Art Review"* to get a quicker response. Oh, and please, please, PLEASE do not be offended or discouraged if your artwork is rejected. Personal taste is involved in picking art and artists, plus there are only four issues a year, and ... well, we are looking for better than average, dynamic and funny art even for **The Rifter™**. Remember, the only way to improve is to keep at it. Keep trying new things and keep learning.

Shameless Plugs

This may become a new section as Palladium artists, writers and friends continue to branch out to try business ventures on their own.

Mike Dubisch is a Weirdling™

Er, I mean ... Mike Dubisch is a weirdo. No, that's not it. Mike Dubisch is self-publishing a limited edition, black and white, comic book series called **Weirdling™**. Yeah, that's right!

I would describe **Weirdlings™** as "Lovecraft in Space". It definitely has a Lovecraftean C'thulhu kinda feel — intriguing and disturbing at the same time. If you like Mike's artwork (and/or horror), you'll probably enjoy this strange offering.

The series was originally scheduled to appear in **Kitchen Sink's "Death Rattle"** anthology comic book, but the title was cancelled before **Weirdling** saw print. Being an intrepid soul, Mike decided to self-publish it as a four-part (I think) series.

Note: There is a bit of nudity and the violent story line makes it best suited for "Mature Readers" — 18 years old and up.

Weirdling #1 — Limited Edition Comic Book

- 48 pages
- 8 1/2 x 11 magazine format.
- Limited to 200 copies. (So it may be destined to become a collector's item. I've got my copy!)
- Written and illustrated by Michael Dubisch.
- If you tell him: "Palladium sent me and please autograph my copy," Mike will be glad to do so.
- $8.00 — postage and handling included.
- Available only while supplies last from:

  Fantastic Visions Studio
  15 Sieber Road
  Kerhonkson, NY 12446
  Fanvision@AOL.com

Hey Mike, you asked readers to send you comments, so here's mine. You better finish the darn series and get Weirdling #2 out soon 'cuz I want to see what happens next! Oh, and you'd better autograph each issue you send me if you expect to see any more work from Palladium Books! Seriously, good luck, pal. **Note:** Before any rumors get started, yes, Mike Dubisch will continue to do freelance art for Palladium Books.

The Other Side (store) is open for business

Those of you in the Portland, Oregon area who haven't checked out **The Other Side (book and game shop)** might want to give it a look. Palladium artist, *Mike Wilson* and his partner, seem to have launched a successful game and book store. Mike tells us they are doing better than they hoped and will continue to expand their offerings as time goes on.

Palladium fans can be certain to find (or special order) Palladium RPG products from the store as well as science fiction books, specialty items, Star Wars stuff, toys, and other good things. Mike tells us they may expand into comic books in the future too.

The Other Side
1236 Lloyd Center
Portland, Oregon 97232
(503) 288-1485

Siembieda's Top Ten Lists

With the coming of the new Millennium, everybody and their brother seems to be doing lists. So just for grins and giggles, here are some Top Ten Lists Palladium fans might enjoy.

Palladium's Best Selling
Role-Playing Game lines of all time!
1. *Rifts®*
2. Teenage Mutant Ninja Turtles® & Other Strangeness
3. Robotech®
4. Palladium Fantasy Role-Playing Game®
5. Heroes Unlimited™ (hot on the heels of Palladium Fantasy)
6. After the Bomb® (a sub-line to Heroes Unlimited™)
7. Nightbane®
8. Ninjas & Superspies™
9. Beyond the Supernatural™
10. RECON®

Note: The original *Weapons & Armor* series would fall in at number seven except it's not a role-playing game, but a sourcebook/reference for "all" fantasy and historical role-playing games. *Systems Failure™* is too new to make the list.

So just how many copies of *Rifts®* have sold to date? Approximately 140,000 copies of the basic game alone. Add in all the **Rifts®** related world books, sourcebooks and other **Rifts®** products and we have sold over 1.3 million units! This makes **Rifts®** one of the top ten (probably #3) best-selling "role-playing games" of all time! **Rifts®** sales are still going strong and we have a ton of new, great products planned for years to come. The *TMNT® RPG, Robotech®* and maybe even *The Palladium Fantasy Role-Playing Game®* might make that top ten list too.

Kev's "guess" at the best-selling RPGs of all time

1. D&D/AD&D®
2. Vampire the Masquerade®
3. Rifts®
4. Traveller®
5. Champions™
6. Call of C'thulu®
7. TMNT®
8. GURPS®
9. Robotech®
10. Runequest™; or perhaps Dark Sun® or Shadowrun®

Note: This list is based entirely on my "impressions" of the best-*selling* role-playing games in the USA and are not meant to indicate how fun or easy to play they may be. New games like *Deadlands* and *Legends of the Five Rings RPG* are too new to compete with these older titles. D&D is the hands down winner. In its hey-day it was selling zillions of copies and seemed to have an endless stream of supplements.

FASA's *Battletech* is not included because it is not, strictly speaking, a "role-playing game." If it was included it would probably be number four (and bump everybody else down one).

Kev's Personal Favorite Palladium RPG's to run

1. The Palladium Fantasy Role-Playing Game®
2. Rifts®
3. Heroes Unlimited™
4. Robotech®
5. Beyond the Supernatural™

The Palladium Fantasy RPG® is my all-time favorite. Playing it is second nature to me. The Palladium Fantasy RPG® is what encouraged me to launch Palladium Books and I've been playing it off and on for something like 23 years now. Don't really play many other RPGs. Many moons ago I played D&D and Champions a bit.

Kev's Personal Favorite Board Games of all time

1. Acquire® (the original version)
2. Risk®
3. SJG's Illuminati
4. Chess
5. Battleship®
6. Broadside®
7. Iron Clads™
8. Monopoly®
9. Dog House; an unpublished game my Dad created when we were kids.
10. Trivial Pursuit (I'm terrible)

Personally, I believe **Acquire®** (the original version at any rate — I haven't seen *Hasbro's* redo) is one of the *unknown* greatest games of all time. Every **Acquire** game is quick (under an hour, often under 45 minutes), fun, and ALWAYS different. It combines both luck and strategy and is loads of fun (we tend to horse around and be silly while we play, adding to the fun). WARNING: Acquire seems to be one of those games that people either love or hate.

Risk is another long-time fave, unfortunately, I'm so good that nobody wants to play me (or they deliberately gang-up to destroy me before going on to conquer the world).

Unfortunately, I don't find much time to play games, and when I do it is either Palladium role-playing or physical games like ping-pong, air hockey, basketball, pin ball, or fooz-ball/table soccer and so on.

Coming Attractions

Note: The dates provided here are the estimated time the products *should* appear on store shelves (ships early to distributors).

January

- **Aliens Unlimited®; Revised (HU2)** — January 3rd.
- **The Rifter™ #9** — you're holding it in your hands!
- **Rifts® Novel #3: Treacherous Awakenings** — January 21st.

February

- **Rifts® Free Quebec™** — February 2nd
- **Century Station™** for **Heroes Unlimited™** — February 25th
- **Nightbane®: Tribes of the Moon™** — February 28th

Note: *Anarchy Unlimited™* for HU2 has been cancelled.

March

- **Palladium Fantasy RPG®: Eastern Territory™**
- **Rifts® Australia Two**

April

- **Rifts® Australia Three**
- **Rifter #10**
- **Heroes Unlimited™: Mutant Underground™**
- **And a surprise of two.**

May

- **Coalition Wars™: Siege on Tolkeen, Book #1**
- **Nightbane®: In the Deepness of Night (sourcebook)**
- **And perhaps one or two other titles.**

Summer

- **Rifts® Scotland**
- **Rifts® Dimension Book: The Anvil Galaxy™**
- **The Coalition Wars™: Siege on Tolkeen epic series**
- **Hardware Unlimited™ for HU2**
- **Land of the Damned** for Palladium Fantasy RPG®

Note: As stated last issue, the year 2000 promises to be truly amazing for fans of Palladium Books Inc.. There are 3-5 new books planned for **Heroes Unlimited™**, **Nightbane®**, **Palladium Fantasy RPG®**, maybe one or two for **Systems Fail-**

ure™, and a dozen for **Rifts®**! Plus, we have a few things in the works that may surprise everybody.

Ask for
"Z-eye-tick-icks Invasion"

That's how to pronounce the name of **World Book 23:**

Xiticix Invasion™. Apparently, some stores, distributors and gamers are having trouble asking for this hot selling **Rifts®** title. Heck, even my own father who works in the Palladium warehouse called the book, "Icky-Dicky Invasion" and then later called it "Zit Bug Invasion" or something to that effect. At least my Dad doesn't read the books, but as for you gamers — come on, we have included the pronunciation every time the Z-eye-tick-icks have appear!

Okay. I admit it is a weird name. Looking back with hindsight, I probably should have changed the name to something much easier when *Kevin Long* first suggested it (Long originally designed, drew and "named" these aliens). Yeah, well I didn't.

I'm glad to report that despite the fact that nobody can seem to pronounce the darn name of **"Xiticix" Invasion™**, the book has been selling like crazy. Initial feedback is that the "Z-eye-tick-icks" are presented in delectably gruesome detail, make cool monsters, people love to see/hear more about the Kingdom of Lazlo, and welcome a book full of adventures and adventure ideas. Everybody also seems to love the cover by *Dave Dorman*, as well.

Xiticix Invasion™ (along with *Free Quebec™* and *Rifts® Canada*) is part of Palladium's efforts to define North America, resolve some story plots and build excitement for the new millennium. It offers ...

- An in-depth look at the Xiticix.
- Xiticix society and their threat to all life.
- The City of Lazlo's quest to quell the Xiticix and save the world!
- The Coalition States and their role against the Xiticix.
- Notable Xiticix Hive Networks, CS and other outposts.
- Fun, suspense and adventures as more of North America is described and mapped.
- Art by Perez, Wilson, Breaux, Okamura, Beres and Burles.
- Written by Kevin Siembieda, with Wayne Breaux and Bill Coffin.
- $16.95 for 160 pages! In stores everywhere.

Rifts® Trilogy is complete

The last book in the *Adam Chilson* **Rifts® Trilogy** of novels should be hitting store shelves as you read this (should ship around January 18th). At the printer's now.

Conflict, treachery, magic, the Splugorth, Mel Gibson(?!), and more than a few big battles all culminating into an explosive grand finale.

- Cover by John Zeleznik.
- Written by Adam Chilson.
- $8.95 — 500+ pages.
- In stores by the end of January.

Century Station™
For Heroes Unlimited™, 2nd Edition

Bill Coffin strikes again, this time creating a sprawling, vibrant, yet sinister and dangerous city brimming with superheroes, supervillains, trouble and intrigue.

Century Station™ is presented as a place to visit, stage adventures or to set one's campaign (i.e. local heroes who see the city as "their" home).

- Over two dozen new superhuman heroes and anti-heroes.
- Over two dozen new villains.
- The complete city described and key locations mapped.
- Adventures and adventure ideas.
- Illustrated by Perez, Wilson, Johnson & others.
- Written by Bill Coffin.
- $20.95 — 224 pages.

Tribes of the Moon™
For Nightbane®

There is more to the Earth of **Nightbane®** than the *Nightlords* and their monstrous minions and the freakish *Nightbane*. This tome takes a look at another group of night-creatures — the werebeasts. And how they fit into the world of **Nightbane®**.

- Werebeast R.C.C.s and special O.C.C.s.
- The werebeasts' secret society and tribes.

WILSON '99

- The werebeast's agenda and how they view the Nightbane, Nightlords, and world after Dark Day.
- New powers, magic and abilities.
- Adventure and adventure ideas.
- Illustrated by Beres, Breaux, Perez, & others.
- Written by Steve Trustrum.
- $20.95 — 224 pages.

Rifts® Coalition Wars™:
Siege on Tolkeen™!

Six pulse-pounding sourcebooks ranging from 96 to 200+ pages. Each tells a different part of the story of the **Siege on Tolkeen**.

Each describes some new place, conflict and/or event — complete with avenues of adventure.

Each progresses the story and the war, bringing the reader one step closer to the *final conflict*.

New villains, heroes, magic and monsters are introduced as the face of North America is forever changed, and an entirely new set of problems and subplots are set into motion.

A few fans have asked if we aren't stretching this story out too long. No way! Just wait until you see what Bill and I are cooking up for you. We honestly believe there has never been anything like it. A truly epic war saga with surprising twists and turns, all culminating in an earth-shattering conclusion.

- Written by Kevin Siembieda and Bill Coffin.
- Art by Ramon Perez, Mike Wilson, Wayne Breaux, Beres and others.

Siege on Tolkeen™

Chapter One: Sedition

The first book will set the stage with data on Tolkeen's defenses, weapons, magic, and notable leaders, as well as the Coalition Troops and war plans. This book will launch the all-out, winner-take-all war. It will probably be 160 pages ($16.95) and should hit store shelves in May.

The next four books will present one key adventure, and more war data with subplots and ideas for other adventures (maybe even some Hook, Line and Sinkers). Each key adventure advances the war and the story. Each adventure-sourcebook will be 96-112 pages ($12.95). The first will appear one month after the first book. Each of the others will come out every other month.

The final book is the big, grand finale in December, 2000!

Rifts® World Book 22:
Free Quebec®

Despite our best efforts, **Free Quebec** could not meet its December release date. I won't bore you with the many circumstances for its delay, but cheerfully report that it should hit store shelves any day now — i.e. by early February, 2000. I don't think you'll be disappointed either. The book sets the stage for the Coalition States' war to force Free Quebec back under its control. Free Quebec is defined as a nation and people. Key figures and places are presented as well as its very formidable army. An army with modified CS equipment and a surprising number of "new" weapons of war (well, at least the CS was surprised).

Highlights will include:

- The people and society of Free Quebec.
- Key leaders and strongholds.
- The armies and war plans of both sides.
- New types of Glitter Boys, SAMAS and other equipment.
- Art by Perez, Beres, Breaux, Wilson and Johnson.
- Written by Francois DesRochers and Kevin Siembieda.
- 200+ pages — 20.95
- In stores early February.

BY JOLLY R. BLACKBURN
BASED ON A STORY BY ANDREW WHELAN

AS YOU *SPUR* ON YOUR HORSES TO *SPEED* THROUGH THE CAMP ONE OF THE *ORC CUBS* PICKS UP A TURNIP AND *HURTLES* IT AT *KNUCKLES!*

I'M GOING TO RULE THAT THE *TURNIP* DOES *1D8* POINTS OF DAMAGE.

ROLL!

SORRY BOB. LOOKS LIKE YOU TAKE *SIX* POINTS OF *DAMAGE* TO THE *BACK* OF YOUR HEAD. YOU ARE MOMENTARILY *STUNNED* AND *DISLODGED* FROM YOUR HORSE WHICH CONTINUES TO *GALLOP* ON *WITHOUT* YOU!

GAAA! BUT I WAS WEARING A HELMET

IT DOESN'T MATTER!

AS YOU SLOWLY REGAIN YOUR SENSES AND STRUGGLE TO GET TO YOUR FEET YOU REALIZE YOU ARE *SURROUNDED* BY A *GAGGLE* OF FEMALE ORCS AND YOUNG CUBS BRANDISHING STICKS AND SMALL STONES. THEY *QUICKLY* BEAT YOU TO DEATH BEFORE YOUR COMRADES CAN RETURN TO EFFECT A *RESCUE!*

IS THIS SOME KIND OF *SICK* JOKE? YOU TRYING TO TELL ME I GOT *BEANED* WITH A FRICKIN' *TURNIP??!!* YOU'RE KIDDING *RIGHT??!!*

A TURNIP DOING *1D6?* WHERE'D YOU GET *THAT?*

FOWL!

HEY, ACCORDING TO *"APPENDIX R: IMPROVISED WEAPONS"* IN THE *HACKMASTER GM'S GUIDE* THE *GM* CAN, AND I QUOTE, "ASSIGN *ANY* DAMAGE RATING TO AN IMPROVISED WEAPON WHICH SEEMS *REASONABLE* TO HIM."

HMMMM... LOOKS LIKE A *GOOD* CALL, B.A. AS LONG AS YOU HAVE THE *RULES* TO BACK YOU UP I CAN'T REALLY FAULT YOU.

WHAT THE? YOU TAKIN' *HIS* SIDE, *FATHEAD?* WHAT'S WITH YOU?

SORRY BOB, AS AN *IMPROVISED WEAPON* THAT *TURNIP* IS TECHNICALLY CLASSIFIED AS A *MISSILE WEAPON!* ALTHOUGH I'D ARGUE *1D8* IS A BIT *HIGH*, I THINK B.A. IS ON *SOLID GROUND* AS FAR THE *RULES* GO.

BRIAN'S RIGHT! LET'S *MOVE ON!*

MOVE ON??!! THAT'S *EASY* FOR *YOU* TO SAY. YOU WEREN'T JUST *KILLED* BY SOME FOUR HITPOINT *PUNK ASS KID* WIELDING A PIECE OF *FRUIT!*

ACTUALLY IT WAS A *VEGETABLE*, BOB!

B.A.'S BEING A *JERK!*

C'MON B.A.! WE *WASTED* ALL THE *COMBATANTS* IN THIS *ORC CAMP!* YOU'RE JUST USING SOME *STUPID* RULE TO GET BACK AT ME. A SMALL ROCK OR A STICK - *THAT* I COULD ACCEPT BUT A *TURNIP?*

THIS *BLOWS* BIG TIME, B.A.! SHOW ME *WHERE* ON THE *WEAPONS TABLE* IT HAS *FRUIT AND VEGETABLES* LISTED! WHAT NEXT? ELVES BRANDISHING *BREADFRUIT?* DWARVES ARMED WITH *PEQUOTS?*

HEY I THINK IT'S *PERFECTLY* LOGICAL THAT THE *ORC CUB* WOULD PICK UP *ANYTHING* WITHIN ARM'S REACH TO *THROW* AS A WEAPON. IT JUST HAPPENED TO BE A *TURNIP*. OKAY?

GUYS, YOU'RE GOING ABOUT THIS THE *WRONG WAY!!!* THERE ARE *BETTER* WAYS OF FIGHTING THIS.

A BETTER WAY? WHAT ARE YOU TRYING SAY?

YOU SEEM TO BE FORGETTING SOMETHING THAT I'M CONSTANTLY REMINDING YOU. THE RULES WORK BOTH WAYS! B.A. JUST DID US A HUGE FAVOR.

HUGE FAVOR? BUT HE KILLED BOB!

KNUCKLES WAS NOT KILLED IN VAIN.

B.A. HAS JUST ESTABLISHED THAT A HURTLED VEGETABLE IN HIS CAMPAIGN WILL DO 1D8 POINTS OF DAMAGE.

NOW THEN, CONSIDER THE FACTS!

A STANDARD ARROW ONLY DOES A MERE 1D6 DAMAGE. ALSO, B.A. POINTED OUT THAT IT "DIDN"T MATTER" THAT KNUCKLES WAS WEARING A HELMET AS FAR AS DETERMINING DAMAGE. THAT MEANS A HURLED TURNIP FOR A NON-MAGICAL WEAPON IS INCREDIBLY LETHAL NOT TO MENTION READILY AVAILABLE.

UH OH!

HEY.... I DIDN'T THINK OF THAT.

THAT'S AWESOME!

AND THEY CAN DOUBLE AS EMERGENCY RATIONS IF YOU FIND YOURSELF IN A TIGHT SPOT.

THIRTY MINUTES LATER...

OKAY, I WALK UP TO THE GATE GUARD AND THROW A TURNIP RIGHT BETWEEN HIS EYES. THEN I'LL TURN MY ATTENTION TO HIS MOUTHY LITTLE FRIEND WHO WAS BACK-SASSIN' ME.

UH...SORRY, BOB. BUT THE GUARD SHRUGS OFF YOUR TURNIP ATTACK.

WHAT??!!

HEY WHAT GIVES? THAT GUARD TOOK THREE TURNIP HITS. HE MUST BE DEAD.

FOUL! FOUL!

I'M SORRY BUT THE TYPE OF TURNIPS YOU GUYS PURCHASED ARE A MUCH SMALLER AND LESS LETHAL VARIETY THAN THE ONE THAT ORC CUB BEANED KNUCKLES WITH.

IT WAS A MORE RESILIENT STRAIN OF TURNIP WHICH IS ONLY CULTIVATED IN THE ORKIN HIGHLANDS OF TRAX! EXTREMELY RARE OUTSIDE THAT REGION!

FINE! YOU WANNA PLAY GAMES? NO PROBLEM! WE'LL SADDLE UP AND RIDE TO THE FRICKIN' ORKIN HIGHLANDS AND TRADE FOR SOME TURNIP SEEDS.

UH...ER...THAT WON'T WORK. THE TURNIP SHAMAN ARE VERY PROTECTIVE OVER THEIR SECRET STRAIN.

OH YEAH! THEN WE BUILD AN ARMY AND GO TAKE IT BY FORCE!

FORGET THE SEED WE'LL RAID THEIR TURNIP FIELDS AND TAKE WHAT WE NEED!

TWO HOURS LATER...

DID YOU HEAR WHAT I SAID? I'M BUYING ANOTHER TEN ACRES OF BOTTOM LAND AND PLANTING MORE HIGHLAND TURNIPS!

HEY DUDE, CAN I BORROW YOUR CART? MY FIELDS ARE ALMOST READY TO HARVEST!

YOU KNOW THE TURNIP IS A BIENNIAL HERB FROM THE MUSTARD FAMILY! I WONDER WHAT KIND OF DAMAGE RATINGS A RADISH WOULD HAVE?

I HAVE NO IDEA.

WHY DO I NEVER SEE IT COMING UNTIL IT'S TOO LATE! WHY??!!

GUESS, I'LL HAVE TO LOOK INTO IT.

Knights of the Dinner Table™ © kenzerCo 2000 • Internet: http://members.aol.com/relkin/kenzerco.html
Send story ideas to jollyrb@aol.com or KODT, 1003 Monroe Pike, Marion, IN 46953

BEYOND BETWEEN THE SHADOWS™

An Optional Rules Expansion and Additional Material For Nightbane® and Other Palladium Games

By Todd Sterrett

Foreword

Much of this article is based on material from **Nightbane®** World Book One **Between the Shadows™**. Several places, spells, psychic powers, P.C.C. powers, and concepts discussed in this article are unique to that book. This material can easily be converted for use in **Rifts®**, The **Palladium Fantasy RPG™**, **Heroes Unlimited™**, and other Palladium games. It is a great source book and if you don't have it I highly recommend buying it. Material from **Nightbane®**, the **Palladium Fantasy RPG™**, **Rifts®** Sourcebook 3 **Mindwerks™**, **Rifts®** World Book 12 **Psyscape™**, and **Rifts®** World Book 16 **Federation of Magic™** is also referenced in this article. I recommend these books to Palladium fans as well.

The Astral Plane

Regions of the Astral Plane

The basic concept of the Astral Plane is given in the description of the Astral Projection psychic power (**Nightbane®** page 70-71). This description is vastly expanded upon in **Between the Shadows™** (page 37-79). In summary there are 4 basic "layers" of the Astral Plane.

The first is "coexistence with the material world." This layer of the Astral Plane overlaps with the physical world. Things and beings that exist in the physical world can be seen, but not touched by a character in this layer. The character can fly and pass through most solid objects, and can be affected by only a few weapons, spells, and powers. Time passes at the same rate in this layer as it does in the physical world.

The second layer is called the "Outer Layer." This is the classic area of white clouds and confusion. It is useful mostly to get from one place to another. A week spent in this layer is roughly equivalent to one minute in the physical world. Keep in mind what this means for navigation through the Astral Plane. The character may roll to navigate three times per melee round of real world time. This translates into once every 14 hours of Outer Layer time! While the Outer Layer is a great shortcut to get places and to find people, it can take a lot of subjective time to find what you are looking for. The psychic sensitive power of Astral Navigation will help tremendously with this time factor. Using this power the character may make a navigation roll once every subjective hour.

The third layer is the "Inner Plane." This is the most inhabited area of the Astral Plane and seems to connect multiple worlds. Time passes at the same rate in this layer as it does in the physical world. It is impossible to find your way to a desired destination without the power of Astral Navigation.

The fourth and final layer is the "Void." It is a dangerous and largely uninhabited plane. Time has little meaning here, but for game purposes could be said to pass at the same rate as that of the physical world. This plane exists largely outside of normal time and space.

Astral Domains can be built or found in any layer except the first, coexistence with the material world.

Nightbane®

How to get there

Astral Projection
(psychic sensitive ability; **Nightbane® RPG**).

Using this ability the character meditates for a few minutes and then projects his spirit or consciousness out of his body. No equipment comes with the character unless it has been Astrally Reconfigured. He will appear above his body and is anchored to it by the "silver cord." From here the psychic can go where he wills. A bit of concentration will take the character to the Outer Layer, and from there, if he knows it exists (and most psychics do not) he can even go to the Inner Plane. Any character that

foolishly projects into the Void will die, as entering the Void will sever the silver cord.

At the end of this power's duration the character will not "snap back" to his physical body. He must locate it first as per the power's description. Each time the duration of the power elapses the character must spend an additional 8 I.S.P. Astrally Projecting psychics do not recover I.S.P. normally unless they are in an Astral Domain. The duration of this power is based on the time that passes for the physical body, not the Astral self. If the character runs out of I.S.P. before he finds his body he will "snap back," and he must make a saving throw against Coma/Death or fall into a coma.

Psychics may use Astral Projection to move into the Inner Plane, but it can be dangerous for them to do so. Unless they are lucky enough to also possess Astral Navigation, or have a guide who does, they have no ability to find their way around this area of the Astral. This means that they will be unable to leave since it is impossible for them to find their way back to their bodies. The only way out is to project until the psychic runs out of I.S.P. and "snap back" to the physical body with all the attending penalties.

The power of Astral Projection may also be used to project from one area of the Astral Plane to another if one's physical body is already in the Astral Plane. The psychic may project from the Inner Plane into the Outer Layer, or even into coexistence with the physical world. Because of the time differential, it is very dangerous to Astrally Project from the Outer Layer to any other location. The psychic will quickly use up all of his I.S.P.

Astral Transference
(super psionic ability; **Between the Shadows™**)

Like Astral Projection, the psychic must meditate for 4D4 minutes to transfer his physical body into the Astral Plane. Because the physical body is not left behind to serve as an anchor, the character will appear in a random location in the Outer Layer. As with Astral Projection, no equipment comes with the character unless it has been Astrally Reconfigured. This means that the character will arrive buck-naked when he comes back to the physical world, unless he has thoughtfully had his clothing Astrally Reconfigured by an Astral Lord. And don't forget that the average set of clothing weighs 5 pounds, meaning that it costs that Lord 5 I.S.P. permanently for each set of configured clothing!

While using this power the character is unable to recover I.S.P. naturally (unless he makes it to an Astral Domain), and without his body in the physical plane the transferred character expends I.S.P. based on the rate of time of the layer he is in. This subjective time, however, does not apply to the character's attempts to find his way through (or out of) the Outer Layer. While it takes a mere 5 seconds in the physical world (or the Inner Plane) for each "navigation" attempt, this is 14 hours in the Outer Layer! The power must be maintained for the entire 14 hours for each navigation attempt. The psychic sensitive power of Astral Navigation makes navigation much faster. With it, the character gets to roll once every *subjective* hour.

After successfully navigating out of the Outer Layer, the psychic may coexist with the physical world, but the character's body naturally tries to be wholly in the physical or wholly in the Astral since it has no anchor in the physical world. It takes extra power to counter this natural tendency, costing the psychic 1 I.S.P. per minute to stay coexistent with the physical world. This will limit the character's "flying range."

If the character runs out of I.S.P. while he is in Astral space the consequences will depend on where he is. Running out while coexisting simply means that the character pops back to his natural state, meaning the physical world for most characters. If he is moving in Astral space when this happens, he will be moving when he appears in the physical world, at the same rate of speed. Materializing at mach one is not a pretty site for most S.D.C. beings, even in open air, so it's a good idea to stop mov-

ing and get to the ground before this happens. In the Inner and Outer Layers, running out of I.S.P. means that the character must immediately make a saving throw vs Coma/Death. If he fails he is dead – scattered across the Astral Plane. If he succeeds he lives, but has become a permanent resident of the Astral Plane, like the Millek. He must now use Astral Transference if he wants to visit the material world. Of course, his I.S.P. will no longer regenerate there, only in the Astral Plane. Luckily, in the physical world his attempts to return to the Astral Plane only take 5 seconds, not 14 hours, because if he runs out of I.S.P. while in the physical, then there is no saving throw. The character is dead. Period.

As an example, Sosa, a 3rd level **Mind Master** with 95 I.S.P., decides he needs to get from Los Angeles to Paris ASAP. He has just learned to Transfer his body to the Astral and is using the power by himself for the first time. He does not posses the power of Astral Navigation. Sosa concentrates for 4D4 minutes, spends 15 I.S.P. and Transfers his body to the Astral Plane. He finds himself surrounded by the clouds of the Outer Layer. Wasting no time, he starts trying to find his way. Three hours into his search he must spend another 15 I.S.P. to keep this power active. "This never happened when I was Astrally Projecting," he thinks to himself. Three hours later, beginning to sweat, he spends 15 more I.S.P. By the time he is fourteen hours into his search and gets to make his FIRST navigation attempt he has spent 75 of his 95 I.S.P. He will not have the I.S.P. for another chance. Good luck on that navigation roll. If Sosa was at 14th level and still had not learned the Astral Navigation power, he would only spend 15 I.S.P. for each normal navigation attempt since the duration of the power at this level is 14 hours. Low level characters without Astral Navigation will find that this is a dangerous power to use.

Sosa's mentor Mark, an 8th level **Mind Master,** has both Astral Transference and Astral Navigation. When he was teaching Sosa he would spend 15 I.S.P. to Transfer his body into the Astral Plane. Then he would spend 4 I.S.P. to activate Astral Navigation. This would give him 8 navigation attempts before either power's 8 hour duration ran out. In all likelihood he could move from one side of the Earth to the other by expending 19 I.S.P. Even if he did not find his way after 8 rolls, he could expend 19 more I.S.P and try 8 more times. When combined with Astral Navigation, the power of Astral Transference can be a very powerful psychic ability for any level character.

Astral Travel
(a natural ability of **Astral Lords** and **Astral Mages; Between the Shadows™**)

This power is nearly identical to standard Astral Projection. It takes less time and power to activate and has the additional advantages of letting the character choose to appear beside his body, in the Outer Layer, in the Inner Plane, or directly in his Astral Domain. The psychic may also bring other characters with him as passengers. If the passenger is separated from the psychic who brought him to the Astral Plane and is abandoned there, he must pay 1 I.S.P. per hour himself and find his own way back to his body. Running out of I.S.P. will snap the character back to his body, where he must make a saving throw against Coma/Death or fall into a coma.

Astral Transference
(a natural ability of **Astral Lords** and **Astral Mages; Between the Shadows™**)

This is a more powerful version of the super psionic power. It costs no I.S.P. to use, has no maximum duration, and takes but one minute to activate. Coexistence drains the character of 1 I.S.P. per 5 minutes. Unlike the super psionic power, the character can choose to appear coexisting in the physical world in the exact spot where he activated this power, or at a random spot in the Inner Plane. In addition, Astral Lords and Mages have an ability equivalent to Astral Navigation that uses no I.S.P.

Astral Avenger
(a side effect of some **Rifts®** psi-implants; **Rifts®: Psyscape™**)

This power is nearly identical to standard Astral Projection. Its advantages include nearly instant activation (1 melee attack/action), the fact that it costs no I.S.P. to use and most importantly that the character can affect the physical world with all of his psychic powers, including the kinetic ones. The power's downsides include the fact that the character is berserk, he is limited to coexisting with the physical world and so cannot enter other layers of the Astral Plane, and the fact that the character has no control over the duration or occurrences of this power. Running out of I.S.P. will snap the character back to his body, where he must make a saving throw against Coma/Death or fall into a coma.

Astral Self (Nightbane talent; Between the Shadows™)

This power is very similar to the Astral Lord's Astral Transference power. It costs 8 P.P.E. to activate and it must be used each time a Nightbane transfers from one layer of the Astral to another. It has no maximum duration and takes only two minutes to activate. Coexistence drains the character of 2 P.P.E. per 5 minutes. The Nightbane appears coexisting in the physical world in the exact spot where he activated this power and can quickly move to other layers if he so desires. Nightbane may not have psychic powers and have no power that mimics Astral Navigation, so although they can venture into the Inner Plane, it is very dangerous for them to do so without a guide who does posses an Astral Navigation ability of one sort or another.

Astral Projection (4th level spell; Nightbane® RPG)

This spell is nearly identical to the psychic sensitive power of the same name. The main difference is that the spell does not automatically drain more P.P.E. from the spell caster if the duration has ended and he is not yet back at his body. If the spell is not cast again before it expires the mage will "snap back" to his body as described in the Psychic power of the same name above, with the same penalties. Mages have no spells that mimic Astral Navigation, and unless they are lucky enough to also be a psychic and possess this power, or have a guide who does, they have no way to find their way around the Inner Plane. This means that they will be unable to leave if they find their way here. The only solution is to let the spell's duration end and "snap back" to the physical body with all the attending penalties.

Like the psychic power, the Astral Projection spell may be used to project from one area of the Astral Plane to another if ones physical body is already in the Astral Plane.

Astral Portal (7th level spell; Between the Shadows™)

As the spell description states, it creates a dimensional doorway between the Astral Plane and the physical world. The caster must know the "exact location" to where the portal will lead. This means that portals may only be created when they lead from the physical world to Astral Domains or Kingdoms that the character is aware of or from Astral space to locations that he knows in the physical world. Portals leading to other places may not be created. Casting this spell grants no ability to navigate between layers of the Astral Plane. In essence the caster is stuck in the Domain he appears in unless he has another Astral power or spell. Physical objects that have not been Astrally Reconfigured do not travel through the portal unless the portal leads to an Astral Domain where the physical laws are the "same as Earth."

This can be a powerful spell, as it allows the caster to cast this spell at any spot on Earth, move to an Astral Domain, cast it again, and appear anywhere on Earth he is familiar with. Essentially, unlimited distance teleportation, at a far lower P.P.E. cost than Teleport: Superior.

Plane Skip
(10th level spell; Rifts®: Federation of Magic™)

On a roll of 21-25, the caster of this spell will end up in the Astral Plane. Roll again to determine exact location. 1-70 indicates that the character is in the Outer Layer. 71-95 indicates that the character is in a random area of the Inner Plane. 96-00 places the character in the Void. A third roll is made to determine the fate of the character's equipment. On a 1-75, all of the character's equipment will come with him whether it has been Astrally Reconfigured or not. On a 76-00 no equipment will come with the character that has not been Astrally Reconfigured! This spell grants no ability to navigate between layers and unless the character has some other method of escaping the Astral Plane he is trapped there. Astral Projection may be used to communicate with people in other layers or in the physical world, but will not directly help the character escape.

Astral Hole
(11th level spell; Rifts®: Federation of Magic™)

As the spell states, a mage who is Astrally Projecting can enter the Astral Plane through this portal, and use it as a beacon to automatically find his way back to the physical world. The same is true for Astral Transference. However, the duration of the Astral Hole is only one melee round per level of experience, and if it elapses, the portal closes, and the mage is on his own when trying to find his way back.

Note: The time differential mentioned in this spell is incorrect. One melee round in the physical world is the same as 42 hours in the Outer Layer of the Astral Plane, not 5 minutes.

Dimensional Portal and Dimensional Teleport
(15th level spells; Nightbane® RPG and Palladium Fantasy RPG®)

The character's physical body and any equipment teleported will come with him whether it has been Astrally Reconfigured or not. These spells grant no ability to navigate between layers and unless the character has some other method of escaping the Astral Plane or can cast the spell again, he is trapped there. Astral Projection may be used to communicate with people in other layers or in the physical world, but will not directly help the character escape.

Dimensional Rift
(Power Circle; **Palladium Fantasy RPG®**)

This Power Circle has the same effect as the Dimensional Portal spell. The advantage to this magic over the spell is that, as long as the circle exists, the Rift can be re-opened from the circle for a mere 50 P.P.E.

Astral Domain Portals

Permanent portals leading to and from the physical world may be part of an Astral Domain. If the Astral Domain has the physical laws "same as Earth," then physical objects may be taken there without needing to be Astrally Reconfigured. Ectoplasmic objects that are part of an Astral Domain must be Astrally Reconfigured to be taken from the Domain to the physical world, and even then will vanish if they are not returned to the Domain within 24 hours.

Astral Domain Transportation

Some Astral Domains allow their creators to teleport into them at will. Only equipment that has been Astrally Reconfigured will travel with the character.

Natural Dimensional Rifts

Some random Rifts will end up in the Astral Plane. Roll to determine exact location. 1-70 indicates that the character is in the Outer Layer. 71-95 indicates that the character is in a random area of the Inner Plane. 96-00 places the character in the Void. A second roll to determine the fate of the character's equipment is made. On a 1-75 all of the character's equipment will come with him whether it has been Astrally Reconfigured or not. On a 76-00 no equipment will come with the character that has not been Astrally Reconfigured! The character will be granted no ability to navigate between layers and unless he has some other method of escaping the Astral Plane he is trapped there. Astral Projection may be used to communicate with people in other layers of the Astral Plane or in the physical world, but will not directly help the character escape.

Coexisting with the material world

Sooner or later if you use any of the spells or powers above in your game you will have an Astral character trying to affect the physical world, or a character in the physical world trying to affect an Astral being. So the question arises: Who can do what to whom?

Astrally Projecting characters affecting the physical world

A character using Astral Projection may only use psychic sensitive powers to affect the physical world. As above, powers that require touch cannot be used. The greatest danger in using psychic powers is that the character may use all of his I.S.P. before he can find his body or return to the physical world. Of course, as long as the character doesn't go further into the Astral Plane, finding the body is easy as long as it hasn't been moved.

A few Super Psionic powers may be used as well, including Empathic Transmission, Hypnotic Suggestion, Psionic Invisibility, and Radiate Horror Factor.

Spells may be cast while coexisting with the material world, but only those that affect the mind and spirit. Physical spells, such as fireball, may not be cast even against other Astral targets. A mage may also use spells of detection and perception to gain information about the material world while Astrally projecting.

Weapons that have been Astrally Reconfigured will not affect the physical world while in Astral form. Astral characters may engage each other in hand to hand combat, but cannot affect the physical world this way.

Exceptions to normal Astral Projection include those affected by the Astral Avenger syndrome, and Ecto-Travelers, who are able to create strange, ectoplasmic "bodies" that do affect the physical world.

Astrally Transferred characters affecting the physical world

A character using Astral Transference or some other power that sends his body into the Astral Plane can do all the things an Astrally Projecting character can and more.

They may use any psychic powers, including physical, healing, and super psionic powers, except for powers that require touch or physical strength to function. They can use Telekinesis to move objects in the physical world, Electrokinesis to turn on lights, etc.

Prohibited psychic powers include, but are not limited to: Telekinetic Punch, Psi-Sword, Healing Touch, Psychic Surgery, Mind Wipe, Mentally Possess Other, and Mind Bond.

Any spell may be cast while coexisting with the material world, but only those that affect the mind and spirit or are used by the mage for sensory perception will affect physical targets. An energy bolt cast in Astral form will affect other Astral creatures, but will have no effect on the physical world. In fact such spells will not even be visible to observers in the physical world.

These rules also hold true for characters affected by the Astral Avenger syndrome.

Physical characters affecting an Astral opponent

Rune Weapons, Nightbane Artifacts with the Astral Slayer power, and any object that has been rendered Astrally sensitive by the Astral Reconfiguration power will affect Astral beings. However, normal magic items and physical attacks from most supernatural creatures will not affect the Astral character.

Any psychic power that affects the mind will affect Astral beings, but kinetic attacks, including Psi-Sword, Bio- manipulation and others will not. The one class of kinetic powers that will affect Astral beings is ectoplasm powers (including the new ones listed below).

Many spells will affect the Astral character. While immune to physical attacks like lightning bolts and fireballs, spells that affect the mind or spirit, including illusions, will have full effect. Useful spells include:

See the Invisible (1st level spell; **Nightbane® RPG**)

Can be used to see Astral beings and characters.

Charismatic Aura (4th level spell; **Nightbane® RPG**)
Charm (5th level spell; **Palladium Fantasy RPG®**)
Horrific Illusion (5th level spell; **Nightbane® RPG**)

Spells like these will work just fine against Astral characters.

Mental Blast (5th level spell; **Rifts®: Federation of Magic™**)
Deathword (10th level spell; **Rifts®: Federation of Magic™**)
Soultwist (12th level spell; **Rifts®: Federation of Magic™**)

These are some of the rare spells that will cause damage to an Astral traveler.

Call Ectoplasm from Others (6th level spell; **Nightbane®: Through the Glass Darkly™**)

This spell can immobilize Astral characters. The ectoplasm generated by this spell can be used to affect the original target or other Astral entities.

Circle of Concealment (7th level spell; **Palladium Fantasy RPG®**)

One of the few ways to hide something or someone from an Astral character.

Constrain Being (7th level spell; **Rifts®, Palladium Fantasy RPG®**)

This will work against Astrally Projecting characters.

Mental Shock (7th level spell; **Rifts®: Federation of Magic™**)

This spell can cause the Astral traveler to forget how to use his powers or what the limits of his powers are.

Commune with Spirits (8th level spell; **Rifts®, Palladium Fantasy RPG®**)

A great way to communicate with Astral travelers.

Exorcism (8th level spell; **Rifts®, Palladium Fantasy RPG®**)
Banishment (10th level spell; **Nightbane® RPG**)

These spells will affect Astral beings of all varieties, driving them away.

Negation/Negate Magic (8th level spell; **Nightbane® RPG**)
Anti-Magic Cloud (11th level spell; **Rifts®, Palladium Fantasy RPG®**)

These spells can break the spell version of Astral Projection, sending the character back to his body as though he had run out of P.P.E.

Curse: Phobia (9th level spell; **Nightbane® RPG**)

A phobia of the material world will drive most Astral beings away into a deeper layer.

Realm of Chaos (9th level spell; **Rifts®: Federation of Magic™**)

This spell will affect Astral travelers. While in this realm they become physical beings, lending credence to the theory that this is an Astral Domain of some sort.

Protection Circle: Simple (9th level spell; **Nightbane® RPG**)
Protection Circle: Superior (13th level spell; **Nightbane® RPG**)

Astrally Projecting characters will be unable to approach either circle, but those using Astral Transference can only be held at bay by the superior circle.

Control/Enslave Entity (10th level spell; **Nightbane® RPG**)

Works just fine against Astral characters.

The Finger of Lictalon (11th level spell; **Palladium Fantasy RPG®**)

Weapons enchanted by this spell will affect Astral beings.

Sanctum (13th level spell; **Nightbane® RPG**)

This spell will prevent Astral navigation to the protected location. Must make a saving throw against magic to enter the sanctum.

Barrier of Thoth (spell of legend; **Palladium Fantasy RPG®**)

Astral beings may not pass through the barrier, but may move around or under it.

Circles and Wards from the Palladium Fantasy RPG®

Circle of Protection from Ghosts, Spirits, & Entities

Astral characters will be unable to enter the circle.

Other Protection Circles

Astral travelers will be unable to enter circles that defend against them. For instance an Astral Demon will be unable to enter a Circle of Protection from Demons.

Summon Spirits Circle

This will afford some protection against Astral beings.

All Seeing – Power Circle

Astral characters coexisting with the material world can be seen and tracked with this circle, but Astral characters in other layers cannot.

Command, Domination, Insanity, Knowledge, Pain, Passion, Power Leech, and Wonder – Power Circles

These circles will affect Astral beings normally.

Wards

Astral beings do not normally disturb wards, but can be affected by some area effect wards that are disturbed or activated by others. Agony, Burning Pain, Blind, Charm, Confusion, Death, Despair, Evil, Fear, Good, Hate, Knowledge, Magic, Mystic Energy Drain, Sleep, and Undead can affect Astral beings.

M.D.C. and S.D.C. in the Astral Plane – Cosmology 101

Each material world, **Rifts®**, **Nightbane®**, **Heroes Unlimited™**, **Palladium Fantasy®**, etc., has its own Outer Layer; whether or not they are connected directly is a matter of debate among the Astral community. There is only one Inner Plane and it does connect all the Outer Layers. Likewise, there is only one Void and it touches everywhere and everywhen.

In a magic rich world like **Rifts®** Earth, much of that power leaks over into the Outer Layer of that world. Spells cast in the Astral Plane at Astral beings can do Mega-Damage. Creatures of magic, supernatural predators, and other M.D.C. beings are still M.D.C. in the Outer Layer of this world. Instead of doubling their H.P. and S.D.C., they simply double their M.D.C. while in Astral space. Supernatural strength does Mega-Damage as normal in **Rifts®** Earth's Outer Layer. This holds true for coexistence with the material world in Rifts Earth also.

The Inner Plane and Void are a different story. These are relatively magic poor places compared to **Rifts®** Earth. They are roughly equivalent to the magic level in the **Palladium Fantasy®** world and the world of **Nightbane®** Earth. M.D.C. beings revert back to S.D.C. Magic, and supernatural strength, do S.D.C. damage.

Mega-Damage items that make it into the Inner Plane are converted into S.D.C. items. Rules for this are given in several books. I suggest that you convert the M.D.C. into S.D.C. and double or triple it. Only when inside Domains with the "Supports Mega-Damage" physical law will these weapons do M.D. in the Inner Plane.

Vibro-swords and rail gun rounds can be Astrally Reconfigured and will inflict Mega-Damage when used against Astral travelers who are coexisting with the material on **Rifts®** Earth. Reconfigured energy weapons will not be able to harm Astral beings from the material world except when used a crude clubs — it is impossible to Astrally Reconfigure an energy beam. However, they can be taken into Astral space and will work fine there, subject to the rules above. Keep in mind that taking M.D. weapons and armor into S.D.C. settings can imbalance most games.

Astral Domains
Creating an Astral Domain

Creating a private Astral Domain is an intensely personal undertaking. The Astral Lord permanently expends personal energy to create a place limited only by his imagination and power. Astral Mages must build a Domain as part of establishing their connection to the Astral Plane, but Lords are free to wait if they so choose. They could build a Domain at the beginning of their careers, or wait until they have traveled widely and gained experience.

Creating a shared Domain is a slightly different experience. The Astral Lord or Mage may end up not spending any personal energy in the creation of the realm. Even if he does, the Domain will reflect the imaginations and prejudices of any other beings that share in its creation. While bigger and more powerful Domains can be built this way, the Lord or Mage usually does not have quite so intimate a connection with his creation.

The process of creation varies from Lord to Lord. Some meticulously plan how their Domain will look and what laws it will obey. Other Lords let their subconscious run wild, creating a realm based on their inner desires and imagination. Still others will copy other realms or places from everyday life while creating their Domains. Also keep in mind that most Astral Lords and Mages gain their powers early in their teen years. Imagine what kind of realm a 13 to 15 year old would build! Astral Inhabitants that look like that classmate the Lord has a crush on, TV star he drools over, and similar things would be quite common. Modern Lords and Mages will likely have bottomless soda machines, pizza delivery at all times, and other such sources of food. Forbidden things would be common. Who is going to stop you from drinking as much as you want in your own Domain? Many will build very idealized realms, places where the world is like they wish is was, and where they are well liked by all. Lords who wait to build a Domain or Mages who come to their power late are much more likely to worry about strategic things like Domain defenses, accessibility, and advantageous placement of portals than most teenagers.

Also remember that unless the Astral Lord specifically alters his Domain otherwise, he will never age while he is there, just like he does not age while in the Astral Plane. This life extension becomes more important the older the Lord gets, but can have an impact on teenage Lords as well. Many Astral Lords will look younger than they actually are. A 16 year old may look 13 or 14. A 21 year old could look only 16 or 17. This can have an impact on social situations in the Material world ranging from getting a driver's license to buying a movie ticket, getting a date, buying beer, etc.

In any event, the mechanical process of creating an Astral Domain is largely the same every time. While in the Astral Plane the Lord chooses a spot to build on. While he concentrates fiercely, ectoplasm begins to gather around him, growing thicker and thicker. The landscape begins to form and details slowly become clearer. Finally, the Lord creates the Domain's outer defenses, possibly walling it off, hiding it in clouds, or shifting it out of sight all together. Any gateways or portals are usually created at this time. It takes 1 hour per 20 P.P.E. spent to create a Domain.

Astral Lords are rarely attacked or molested while in the act of creating a Domain. First off, the Lord is difficult to reach. The swirling ectoplasm offers 200 S.D.C. protection and regenerates at 10 S.D.C. per melee round (this protection is M.D.C. in **Rifts®** Earth's Outer Layer). more importantly, if the Lord's concentration is disturbed at this point, the results are likely to be fatal to both the Lord and whoever is attacking him. Roll on the table below. Many Astral creatures and permanent residents are aware of the dangers of attacking a Lord in the process of creating a Domain and tend to avoid doing it if possible. (Note that S.D.C. damage is converted into M.D.C. in Rifts Earth's Outer Layer and in Domains where the "Supports Mega Damage" physical law is already active.)

1-10 Astral Vortex: The Astral Lord, and everything within 1000 feet (305 m) or twice the radius of his Domain, whichever is greater, is sucked into a vortex that leads to the Void! The Astral Lord loses all P.P.E. spent to that point.

11-50 Astral Explosion: The Astral Lord and everything within 1000 feet (305 m) or the radius of the Domain he was building takes 6D6x10 S.D.C. Those within 2000 feet (610 m) or double the radius take 3D6x10 S.D.C. Those within 3000 feet (914 m) or triple the radius take 1D6x10 S.D.C. Should the Lord survive, he will lose all P.P.E. spent to that point.

51-80 P.P.E. Feedback: The Lord and his attacker lose control of their P.P.E. as it is converted into pure energy. These two take 1D6 S.D.C. per point of P.P.E. both of them have added together, minus whatever has already been spent on the Domain. The good news is that the Domain is undisturbed, and if the Lord survives he may continue building it when he has recovered his P.P.E.

81-100 Lucked Out: Nothing happens!

What Astral Domains Are and look like

So what exactly is an Astral Domain? The short answer is that it is a collection of ectoplasm shaped by a powerful mind. However they are much more as well. Because of the fantastic ability of Astral Lords to shape the physical and magical laws of their Domains, they are creating much more than mere globs of ectoplasm, they are creating their own small sub-dimensions. Sometimes their dimensions overlap entirely with a layer of the Astral Plane. These are the Domains that are open, hidden, or walled off by ectoplasmic barriers from the Astral layer where they are created, but still quite visible. A walled Domain, containing a tower surrounded by a small rocky plane, may look like an opaque cylinder from the outside. Domains with free ac-

cess are clearly visible in their exact shape from the Astral layer where they are created. Large sections of places that are Rifted in look this way. One might see a floating island in the Outer Layer, or leaning tower attached to a misshapen hunk of earth lying on a dragon road in the Inner Plane. With Restricted, Controlled and Forbidding Domains, the creator can choose one of two looks from the outside. The first leaves the Domain looking like a walled Domain. An opaque barrier defines the shape of the realm, but unlike an ectoplasmic barrier, no amount of outside force will penetrate the wall. In the alternative, the Lord can have his realm be all but invisible. Beings able to sense dimensional anomalies will sense the point where the Domain was created, but it will be otherwise undetectable. The Domain, while created in a layer of the Astral, and still connected there, exists as a totally separate dimension.

Clarifications and New Domain Characteristics

Accessibility

7. Impassible: The Domain can only be entered by one of the Transportation Domain Characteristics, and Astral travel powers used by the Domain's creators. If the Domain does not have one of the advanced Transportation Characteristics, or if the Domain builder does not have dimensional travel magic, the creators will be stuck there. The Astral Portal spell and Astral Transference abilities will not work to enter this Domain, but will enable someone to leave it. The Dimensional Teleport spell and other dimensional travel magic can be used to leave the Domain or enter it. Creation Point Cost: 90 points

8. Sealed: The Lord who creates the Domain is completely sealed off, and is unable to leave once the Domain has been created. Only the Two-Way Transportation characteristic, Dimensional Teleport spell, Dimensional Portal spell, Dimensional Rift Power Circle, and other powerful magic may be used to enter or leave the realm. If none of these are spells or powers are available, the Lord is stuck in his Domain. Creation Point Cost: 150 points.

Size

7. Gigantic: 1000 cubic miles (1600 km). Creation Point Cost: 65 points

8. Immense: 10,000 cubic miles (16000 km). Creation point cost: 80 points

9. Planetary: 100,000 cubic miles (160000 km). Creation point cost: 95 points

Portals or Gateways

3. Physical World Portals: If the Domain is in the Inner Plane on a Dragon Road Nexus, or in the Void, these portals can lead to any dimension that the Astral Lord is aware of and has visited. These portals may *not* lead to different times. So portals from current day **Nightbane®** Earth to the past or future are not possible, but portals from **Nightbane®** Earth to **Rifts®** Earth, Phase World, the **Palladium Fantasy RPG®** world, **Heroes Unlimited™** Earth, etc., are.

4. Movable Portal: If the Domain is in the Inner Plane or on the Edge of the Void, these portals can be moved to other dimensions and will still function. If the Domain is in the Outer

Layer, these portals will only function in the physical world the caster came from, as well as in the Outer Layer. **Nightbane®** Earth and the Nightlands are unique. The same Outer Layer surrounds both worlds. If one of these portals is taken into the Domain that it leads to (via another portal or spell), it will temporary cease to function. As soon as it is moved to a new location, it will again function. Creation point cost: (+10 points to make an M.D.C. structure into a portal. +15 points if the portal has other enchantments, e.g. a Cloak of Invisibility as a portal.)

7. Instant Transportation: Same as number 5, but only takes 1 melee action of concentration. Creation point cost: 150 points

8. Two-Way Transportation: Same as number 5, but the power may be used to teleport out of the Domain as well as into it. The character can only teleport out of the Domain to the last place where he teleported in from. So if the character teleported in from a back alley in the Nightlands, this is where he will teleport out to the next time he uses this power. Creation point cost: 90 points

9. Near Instant Two-Way Transportation: Same as number 8, but the power takes only 1 melee round to activate. Creation point cost: 150 points

10. Instant Two-Way Transportation: Same as number 8, but takes only 1 melee action of concentration to activate. Creation point cost: 225 points

Special Defenses

7. Time Differential: Intruders find that time passes differently for them than for other inhabitants of the Domain. Intruders lose half of their normal attacks per melee round (round down), are at -10 to initiative, and −3 to all attack rolls. They move at half their normal speed. Creation point cost: 50 points. (+5 points to allow the Astral Lord to mentally "designate" guests who are not to be affected.)

8. Spatial Distortion: Intruders find that space is badly distorted to them, as compared to the Domain's normal inhabitants. Victims are at −6 to strike, parry, and dodge. They are also at -40% to all skills, and -60% for those that require precise spatial measurements. Creation point cost: 40 points. (+5 points to allow the Astral Lord to mentally "designate" guests who are not to be affected.)

9. Ghost Effect: Intruders find that they are not able to physically affect anything in the Domain! The effect is the same as Astrally coexisting with the material world. Intruders may use some psychic and magic powers, but cannot physically touch anything. Victims with Astral Transference may try to materialize fully, but must make a saving throw at 16 or better to succeed. Characters with this power gain +1 to this saving throw per every 5 levels of experience, and get to add their M.E. bonus. Once fully materialized, the intruder must pay 1 I.S.P. per 5 minutes that he is in this state. Creation point cost: 100 points. (+5 points to allow the Astral Lord to mentally "designate" guests who are not to be affected.)

Physical Laws

8. Supports Mega-Damage: M.D.C. items and weapons work normally in this Domain. Creatures of magic and others become M.D.C. beings as per the various **Rifts®** books. Magic, psionics, and super powers do Mega-Damage as described in

Rifts®. Domain defenses are converted from S.D.C. damage to Mega-Damage. The Domain must be built on a dragon road or nexus to support this power. Creation point cost: 50 creation points.

9. Limited Time Control: This power allows the Domain's creator to control the rate at which time flows in his Domain, in a very limited way. He may set two rates of time flow, and switch between them at will. This control affects the Domain as a whole, and cannot be used only on individuals or portions of his Domain. This power is commonly used in Astral Domains in the Outer Layer, where the lord usually sets one rate of time equal to the flow of time in the Outer Layer, and another the same as time in the material world. Creation point cost: 20 creation points.

Living Conditions

3. Food and Water: For 60 creation points, the Domain can create tasty food with no cooking roll needed. Be sure to note how the character's Domain generates the food. Examples include a never empty refrigerator, a mindless construct pizza delivery boy, fried chicken trees, etc.

Remodeling or Changing your Domain

When creating an Astral Domain, the Astral Lord or Mage permanently expends his own P.P.E. or that of others. This energy is used to lock the ectoplasm into a particular form or to fix the laws of the Domain. Rules for upgrading an existing Domain are given on pages 53 to 55 of **Between the Shadows™**. But what happens when the young Astral Lord decides that he is tired of having "Any Surface is Down," and just wants to get rid of this, or any other feature, and perhaps add a different one? Also, the rules for creating a Domain and developing it later are a bit strange mathematically.

When building a Tiny, Small, Large, or Greater Domain, the Astral Lord gets 2.5 creation points per 1 P.P.E. spent. However when building an Average Domain, he gets 3.75 creation points per 1 P.P.E. spent. When upgrading an existing Domain, you only get 1 creation point per P.P.E. spent unless you increase the "Size" of the Domain, in which case you get one of the ratios above. This is confusing and can hinder role-playing by encouraging characters to make 80 point Domains, the cost of an "Average" Domain, time and time again. Instead of the above rules, I would recommend just using a flat 2.5 creation points per P.P.E. point permanently expended, both when creating a Domain and when upgrading it.

Domains can be changed after they are created, but there is a cost for doing so, and energy once spent cannot be regained by the Astral Lord. To change a feature costs the Lord additional permanent P.P.E. He must spend $1/10^{th}$ of the P.P.E. he used to build the feature in the first place. This will negate the feature and free up the creation points used to build it. There is a minimum cost of 1 P.P.E. per change.

In the example of the Lord who gets tired of "Any Surface is Down," he would have to spend 1 P.P.E. permanently to negate this feature (20 creation points = 8 P.P.E. Then divide 8 P.P.E. by 10 and round up to 1). After spending the 1 P.P.E., he can then use the 20 creation points that had been consumed maintaining this physical law, in any way he chooses. Creation points that are not reinvested at this time are lost.

Location is the one feature that cannot be changed in this way.

Creation points are not gained back when a feature is destroyed. If your mobile portal is blown up, or your bound Astral entity is slain, you get no points back.

Multiple Domains

An Astral Lord or Mage can build more than one Domain. They can build tiny Domains that serve as extra-dimensional pockets, like a magician's hat (mobile portal that leads to a 3x3x3 foot/1x1x1 m Domain where he keeps his rabbits), and still have a larger Domain that they go home to at the end of the day. A cautious Lord may have several Astral "Bolt Holes." The only limiting factor is the Lord's own supply of P.P.E., and that which he can gain from other people by friendship, threats, bargaining, or con-artistry. Creating Domains for others is one of the most valuable abilities that an Astral Lord or Mage has. While some Lords may build Domains "free of charge" for their friends, most drive a hard bargain when they create for others. They may demand magic items, P.P.E. for their own Domains, a period of servitude, or even hard cash. This will vary from Lord to Lord.

Most Astral Lords are considered arrogant or greedy by other characters that frequent the Astral, because of this propensity for charging dearly for their power. It is not unusual for Lords to demand periods of servitude, spent either guarding the Lord's Domain, waiting on them hand and foot, or doing some other menial task. Few Astral Lords possessed much status or power in the material world before gaining their abilities, and because of this it is not uncommon for them to abuse what they have in the Astral. People who pay this kind of price, or suffer this kind of abuse, naturally resent the person responsible.

"Look what I found!" — the fate of all Domains

While Astral Lords and Mages do not age in the Astral Plane, neither they nor their creations will last forever. Astral Lords do age while in the material world and some Astral Kingdoms. However, few die of old age. The Astral Plane is a dangerous place. Lords and Mages usually have high amounts of P.P.E. and I.S.P., making them tasty morsels for Astral predators. Without ambient power from the Dragon Roads, many Astral entities must hunt for other sources of "food." Astral thieves powerful enough to break into a Domain are powerful enough to be dangerous to its creator. Politics and rivalries between Lords also take their toll. These and other like reasons are why few Lords live much past a few hundred years, despite not aging.

So what happens to a Domain when its Lord dies? After all, he and any co-creators spent permanent P.P.E. building it.

The answer is that when the Lord dies, his Domain starts to die, too. The Domain is not a permanent structure. As long as at least one person who contributed P.P.E. to the Domain lives, it is fine. But it is the will and belief of the creators of a Domain that keeps it from fading. After they die, the Domain starts to loose 5 P.P.E. per week. As the Domain loses P.P.E., a corresponding number of Creation Points must be turned in. A little bit at a time, the special characteristics of the Domain will fade and it will start to shrink until nothing is left.

It is possible for a character to stop someone else's Domain from fading, but it is not easy. The character must have the Astral Domain ability, and must spend temporary P.P.E. equal to the entire P.P.E. cost of the Domain, each week, to keep the Domain from losing any P.P.E. and Creation Points that week. The character will be unable to alter any of the Domain characteristics, or repair any losses the Domain has already suffered due to deterioration.

Fading Domains are dangerous places. As the barriers and protections fail, scavengers often take up residence. Astral entities living off of any remaining P.P.E. and I.S.P. sources in the Domain, lesser psychics seeking refuge, and other even more menacing creatures can be found in these places.

The true power of Astral Domains

The existence of Astral Lords and Astral Mages can have a tremendous impact on the game you run. Your players will most likely try to use their Domains as bolt holes, places to heal up, storage places for loot, and occasionally a means to travel quickly. Creative players will have movable portals that they use for ambushes, quick escapes, and the like. However, since they tend to operate in small groups, they will barely scratch the surface of what a Domain can do in the context of a gaming world.

Just imagine for a moment that Astral Lords existed in our own world and were accepted by business and government, much like they would be in some **Heroes Unlimited™** games. By building a restricted Domain with only physical world portals, your Domain is safe from almost all Astral creatures and influences. Astral Domains would revolutionize many businesses. In the computer industry, for example, companies with offices in remote locations have to have cable run between them, and the speed which information flows over these long cables is limited. With an Astral Domain, the company could put all of its servers in one place, and have many small portals leading directly to the various offices. Most of the portals would only need to be the width of a cable. Also, the Domain properties could be built such that a cool temperature was maintained and that free electricity was available. The cost savings would be tremendous. Similarly, Domains that generate electricity could be used to power just about any business, freeing them from one of their major expenses. This would especially benefit manufacturing companies and universities, two major consumers of electricity. Manufacturing companies could also take advantage of Domain features like time differential and psychic constructs. Raw material would be brought through one portal to a Domain in the Outer Layer. There, constructs could manufacture a finished product in seconds of real world time. Then the product could be "shipped" instantly via another real world portal. Governments would have Domains linking their various embassies. Diplomats and couriers could quickly be gotten from one side of the globe to the other. The delivery of sensitive messages would be made much faster and more secure. The military would have Domains with mobile portals to quickly move troops to trouble spots. All it would take is a plane and a small team of soldiers to get a portal behind enemy lines to let the military perform a flanking maneuver. The rich would have Domains to suit their whims, and would sleep there to reduce aging. Athletes could go to recovery facilities located in Outer

Layer Domains, and take advantage of the time differential to get back on the field again quickly after injuries. Astral Domains could even allow RPG writers and editors to finish their projects on time or ahead of published schedule! And these are only a few of the many uses that Domains could be put to.

Now with all this in mind, picture what the Coalition States in Rifts would do with just ONE Astral Lord. Emperor Prosek would have a large command center / living quarters area in a Domain, with two portals that lead to rest of the imperial suite. By sleeping and working there part of the time, he could easily double or even triple his remaining life span. Think what the Coalition military would do with mobile portals, and the effect that this would have on the siege at Tolkeen. Trade with Triax would be easy and safe, with but one Domain that had large portals connecting secured warehouses in both countries. Astral robot and power armor factories would be created to quickly manufacture these items for the Coalition War Machine. Be sure that the Coalition would make the maximum use out of a resource like an Astral Lord. They would have no trouble finding "volunteers" to donate P.P.E. for the creation of whatever they deemed necessary...

Astral Mages and Lords would have a similar impact on the Palladium Fantasy world. Travel time is one of the greatest barriers to effective communication and movement of armies. Astral Projection, Magic Pigeons, and Teleport – Power Circles have an impact, but not like an Astral Domain does. Anyone can assist in the creation of a Domain, and then is free to use it without having to burn more P.P.E. or use resources like Faerie wings. Astral Domains could short circuit the dangers and limitations imposed by distance. Smaller Domains could be used to make great "magic" items. Cloaks that are mobile portals, allowing travelers to sleep safely at night. Bags that are mobile portals, and allow storage of great amounts of treasure, can be created for anyone.

In **Nightbane®**, a world where magic and psychic powers are kept hidden, the effects of Astral Domains are limited. But in worlds where people accept the supernatural and even embrace it, they can have quite an impact. Astral Lords will be able to acquire wealth and power very easily, and will probably have less reason than ever to "adventure" in the material world.

Translating existing Astral O.C.C.s to other games

Astral Lords and **Astral Mages** fit well in most Palladium games that feature magic and psychic powers of some sort.

In **Heroes Unlimited™** they need not be changed at all. In fact, they make great heroes and better villains! Tracking down an Astral thief could make an awesome mystery, leading to a dangerous battle in his Astral Domain – perhaps a place where no super powers work! If you are using the **Heroes Unlimited** skill system, few Lords and Mages will have an education level beyond High School or "On the Job Training." In any event, almost all Lords will take the Technical skill package and choose Lore: Astral as one of their selections. The very few who do not, would always take Lore: Astral as a secondary skill.

Palladium Fantasy RPG® Lords and Mages fit in easily. For Lords and Mages from PFRPG, simply replace the skills listed in **Between the Shadows™** with the Psychic Sensitive skills for Astral Lords, or Psi-Mystic skills for Astral Mages, and then substitute Lore: Astral, with a +20% bonus, in place of one O.C.C. Related skill. His ability to easily travel the length of the Palladium world in seconds should be taken into account before letting someone play such a character, however. If this sort of thing starts to become a problem, don't hesitate to "remind" the character that he is not the only one who uses the Astral Plane. A tough encounter or two at the right moment can be a factor in changing the player's behavior. Also, giving their enemies a similar advantage can be devastating. Role-playing opportunities as scouts, explores, and messengers abound.

In **Rifts®**, Astral Lords gain an additional 1D4x10 I.S.P. and +2 to their saving throws vs Horror Factor and Possession. This additional I.S.P. may not be spent on Astrally Reconfiguring objects. Their Ectoplasmic Armor also provides M.D.C. protection. **Astral Mages** gain an additional 4D6 I.S.P. and P.P.E. This P.P.E. may not be used to build or add to an Astral Domain. They also gain +2 to their saving throws vs Horror Factor, Magic, and Mind Control. They gain +1 Spell Strength at levels 6 and 12. As with Palladium Fantasy campaigns, these characters may unbalance things by being able to travel anywhere in the world quite easily. Characters should also be aware that many of the supernatural creatures they encounter while Astrally coexisting or while in the Outer Layer will be M.D.C. beings and have attacks that do Mega-Damage.

Astral Lords can be interesting characters in the **Ninjas & Superspies™/Mystic China™** or **Beyond the Supernatural®** settings. No changes need to be made. Astral Lords and Mages have no special Chi abilities or unusual defenses against Chi attacks, except for the usual Mind Block (see **Ninjas & Superspies™** for rules for interaction between Chi, Psionics, and Magic). Chi powers work normally in the Astral Plane, but there is NO background Chi, either positive or negative. Domains can have Chi sources and Chi powers built in. Treat the same as P.P.E. sources and spells.

New Astral P.C.C.s

Astral Knight P.C.C.

Astral Knights are psychics with powers that are very similar to those of an Astral Lord (**Between the Shadows™**, pages 49-51). However, instead of focusing their powers on building elaborate Astral Domains, these wanderers focus their power inward. While some do join Lords or Mages in building a Domain, many spend their lives traveling through the various layers, kingdoms, and Domains of the Astral Plane. Others spend their time on Earth, doing good where they can, or using their power in other ways to satisfy their own interests.

While Astral Knights do have above average P.P.E., most of this energy has been permanently expended on rendering their bodies permanently Astral to some degree. They have, in effect, used a variant of the Astral Lord's ability to Astrally Reconfigure objects, on their own bodies! While this does grant them some unique abilities, it also has its drawbacks.

Many Astral Knights tend to follow a very loose code of honor. They rarely attack other Astral Knights without some sort or warning. They prefer to avoid ambush and rear attacks. Almost all will obey their word of honor. Some individuals may live by a much stricter code, others may ignore honor all together. All but the most evil of Knights are appalled by the conditions some of the Astral Junkies (see below) live in, and try to act as a check against unscrupulous Astral Lords and Mages.

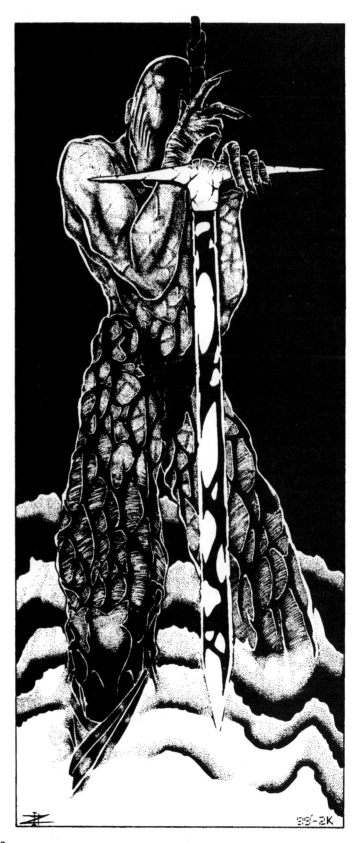

Many Astral Knights suffer from wanderlust and seldom stay in one place long.

Astral Knight P.C.C. Abilities and Bonuses

Astral Senses: (as per the Astral Lord, **Between the Shadows™**, page 50)

Astral Reconfiguration: (as per the Astral Lord, **Between the Shadows™**, page 50)

Astrally Active: The character's body exists both in the Astral Plane and in the material world, at all times. The advantages of this include the natural doubling of the character's H.P. and S.D.C. as if they were fully Astral. If he stays in the material plane, the character will find his life span tripled, and of course he will not age during any time he spends fully in the Astral Plane. He will bio-regenerate 1d6 H.P./S.D.C. per hour, but will not naturally re-grow limbs or other damaged organs. He can also attack Astral beings and travelers with his bare hands and damage them! However, the reverse is true as well. Astral beings can attack the Knight with bare hands, or other Astral objects that would have no effect on normal solid characters. Another disadvantage is that the Astral Knight cannot use any form of Astral Projection. While he can transfer his body without undue problems into the Astral Plane, by rendering himself Astrally Active the Knight forever ties his body and Astral spirit.

Astral Transference: This power is very similar to the Astral Lord's power of the same name, however due to the Astral Knight being Astrally Active, there are some important differences. The Astral Knight can use this power to fully enter the Astral Plane. This takes a full melee round of concentration, but costs no I.S.P. Once there, the Knight can stay coexistent with the material world, or choose to move into the Outer Layer, and from there to the Inner Plane if he wishes. The Knight can also use this power to temporarily shunt himself fully into the material plane. When he does this, he loses all bonuses gained from being Astrally Active, but also is no longer vulnerable to many Astral attacks. The Astral Knight must spend 1 I.S.P. per 5 minutes when either coexisting with the material plane or using this power to stay fully material. It costs no I.S.P. to stay in the deeper layers of the Astral Plane.

Ectoplasmic Armor: (as per the Astral Lord, **Between the Shadows™**, pages 50-51)

Ectoplasmic Weapon: The Astral Knight can create a powerful melee weapon, from both ambient ectoplasm and that within his body. Any ancient hand to hand (no missile weapons) implement of war may be chosen, but most (80%) Knights chose some kind of sword. Damage is 4D6 S.D.C. (M.D.C. in Rifts), +2D6 at 3rd level, and +1D6 at levels 6, 9, 12 and 15. It takes 2 melee actions to summon the weapon and costs the Astral Knight 15 I.S.P. Duration is 10 minutes per level, unless the weapon leaves the Knights hand, which will cause it to immediately dissipate.

Ectoplasm: As per the normal physical psychic power, but +50% range and duration. This power costs the Astral Knight half the normal I.S.P. to use.

Other Psionic Powers: The Knight can choose one other Ectoplasm power of choice, and a total of 3 powers from among the Healing, Physical, and Sensitive categories. He may choose one additional power from among these three categories, each level thereafter.

I.S.P.: The Astral Knight starts with M.E. + 1D4x10 I.S.P. He gains an additional 2D6 I.S.P. per level.

P.P.E: 3d6 at first level. Gains an additional 1d6 P.P.E. each level.

Other Bonuses: The Astral Knight is immune to possession, and gains an additional +2 to Strike and Parry with the W.P. associated with his Ectoplasmic Weapon. They are +4 to saving throws against Horror Factor.

Attribute Requirements: M.E. of 13 or higher. An above average P.S., P.E., and P.P. are recommended, but not required.

P.C.C. Skills:

Language: Native (98%)

Lore: Astral (+20%)

One Technical skill of choice (+10%)

One Piloting/driving/riding skill of choice (+10%)

One Domestic skill of choice (+10%)

One W.P. of choice

Hand to Hand: Basic (can be upgraded to Expert at the cost of one P.C.C. related skill, or either Martial Arts or Assassin for two)

P.C.C. Related Skills: Select 11 other skills. Plus select one additional skill at levels three, six, eight, ten and thirteen. All new skills start at level one proficiency.

Communication: Any (+5%)

Domestic: Any (+5%)

Electrical: Basic Electronics only.

Espionage: Any (+5%)

Mechanical: Basic Mechanics only.

Medical: First Aid and Paramedic only.

Military: Any (+5%)

Physical: Any (+5%)

Pilot: Any (+10%)

Pilot Related: Any (+5%)

Rogue: Any (+5%)

Science: Math only.

Technical: Any

W.P. Any

Wilderness: Any

Secondary Skills: The character also gets to select 5 secondary skills. These are additional areas of knowledge that do not get the bonuses listed in parentheses. Also, skills are limited (any, only, none) as previously indicated on the list.

Standard Equipment: Typically starts with 3D6x100 dollars worth of equipment, and may own an old beat up car or similar vehicle.

Money: 1D6x100 dollars; may be adjusted to represent the character's background.

Experience: Use the chart given for Necrophim in **Between the Shadows™**.

Astral Junkie P.C.C.

Astral Junkies are the lower class of the Astral Plane. They are minor psychics that have discovered the Astral, and have actively explored parts of it. However, unlike the Astral Lords these psychics cannot build Domains, and very few of them can actually transfer their body into the Astral.

For whatever reason, many of these psychics tend to either suffer from poverty, abusive family situations, or lack of self-esteem. When they have jobs, the employment is usually

dull, menial, or in inhumane conditions. These psychics are usually poorly educated.

Many of them are looking for an escape from their everyday lives, and Astral Projection can give them just that. They can visit any place in the world that they want to. Most of them have seen the Great Wall of China, the Pyramids, the Castles of Europe, and many, many others places via Astral Projection. But many tire of this and find the greatest escape in the Outer Layer of the Astral Plane. It is the time differential between this layer and the material world that make Domains and kingdoms there so seductive to the Astral Junkies. Most beginning Junkies spend less than one "perceived" day out of 6 in the material, or so called mundane, world. More experienced Junkies spend even less subjective time in the mundane world.

Many of these psychics come to live for their Astral escapes from their mundane lives. Almost anything would seem better to many of them, and the unique and varied places in the Astral seem far more exciting than what they live in during their non-Astral hours. Many of these characters seek out Astral Lords to help them build Domains, or try to join existing Astral Kingdoms. Often times, due to their relatively low P.P.E. they must band together to build a reasonably sized Domain. Unscrupulous Astral Lords and Mages frequently take advantage of these individuals. Junkies desperate to escape the material world make easy prey.

Junkies are often forced to serve an Astral Lord long and hard before being granted full membership in an existing Kingdom or Domain, and must often make even more sacrifices or pay a higher price to have a Domain built for them. These Astral Junkies are often called "Astral Commoners" or "Astral Serfs" by other Astral residents.

The Dream of most Astral Junkies is to have their own Domain, or one shared with a few others of their kind, with a portal that will allow them to physically enter the Astral Plane. This dream can and does happen, just not very often. Unfortunately, the promise of never having to go back to their mundane lives can entice even the most experienced Astral Junkie to extreme acts or degrading servitude.

There are confident and capable Astral Junkies, but these are in the minority. A few have become activists, trying to protect the rights and lives of other Astral Junkies. In spite of the reputation of most Astral Junkies, one who is reliable and trustworthy can make excellent guardian for an Astral Lord's Domain, and can even contribute valuable P.P.E. towards creating or expanding it. A competent and experienced Junkie can sometimes name his price, as several Lords or Mages will in all likelihood desire his services and abilities.

Astral Junkie P.C.C. Abilities and Bonuses

Astral Projection: As per the normal physical psychic power, but with twice the normal duration and half the normal I.S.P. cost.

Other Psychic Powers: Astral Navigation and one Sensitive power of choice.

I.S.P.: The Astral Junkie starts with M.E. + 2D6. He gains 1D6 I.S.P. per level.

P.P.E: 4d6 at first level. May or may not increase with level; see below.

Additional Powers: At levels 5, 10 and 15, the character can choose to gain one psychic sensitive power of choice, an additional 2D6 P.P.E, or an additional 3D6 I.S.P. Alternatively, the character can forego any of the above choices at any TWO of the above levels and gain the super psychic power of Astral Transference instead. Choosing how they develop their abilities is one of the most wrenching choices an Astral Junkie will ever make. They can gain more I.S.P so they can use Astral Projection longer. They can choose to gain more P.P.E. and hope that the increased power will tempt an Astral Lord into making them a co-creator of a Domain. They can develop another psychic power to better their survival chances or to increase their usefulness to an Astral Lord. Or they can risk quite a bit and shoot for the Astral Transference ability. However, few junkies survive long enough and are adventurous enough to reach 10th or 15th level.

Astral Gossip: Astral Junkies tend to talk about various Domains, Kingdoms, and Lords. An Astral Junkie has a base 5% chance, +2% per level after the first, to know at least a little about a given Astral Domain or Lord. They have a base 15%, +3% per level after the first, to know explicit details of large Astral Kingdoms and their rulers. Famous subjects grant a bonus of +10% or more to this roll.

Attribute Requirements: M.E. of 13 or higher. An above average P.S., P.E., and P.P. are recommended, but not required.

P.C.C. Skills:
Language: Native (98%)
Lore: Astral (+15%)
One Technical skill of choice (+10%)
One Piloting/driving/riding skill of choice (+10%)
Two Domestic skills of choice (+15%)
Hand to Hand skills must be bought as P.C.C. Related skills (Basic costs one skill, Expert two, or either Martial Arts or Assassin can be obtained for 3 P.C.C. skills)

P.C.C. Related Skills: Select 8 other skills. Plus select one additional skill at levels three, six, eight, ten and thirteen. All new skills start at level one proficiency.
Communication: Any
Domestic: Any (+10%)
Electrical: Basic Electronics only.

Espionage: Wilderness Survival only.
Mechanical: Basic Mechanics only.
Medical: First Aid and Paramedic only.
Military: None
Physical: Any, except Boxing or Acrobatics.
Pilot: Any (+10%)
Pilot Related: Any (+5%)
Rogue: Any
Science: Math only.
Technical: Any
W.P. Any
Wilderness: Any

Secondary Skills: The character also gets to select 4 secondary skills. These are additional areas of knowledge that do not get the bonuses listed in parentheses. Also, skills are limited (any, only, none) as previously indicated on the list.

Standard Equipment: Typically starts with 1D6x100 dollars worth of equipment, or may own an old beat up car or similar vehicle.

Money: 1D6x10 dollars; may be adjusted to represent the character's background.

Experience: Use the chart given for 'Kinetics, Geniuses & Naturals, and Psi-Mechanics in **Between the Shadows™**.

High Lord P.C.C. (Mega Hero)

Note: High Lords are the Mega Hero equivalents of Astral Lords. These are extremely powerful beings and can unbalance most campaigns. Godlings, Cosmo Knights, and Mega Heroes are on par with this character class. With amazing amounts of P.P.E. they can build fantastic Domains. These beings make excellent archenemies for player characters. High Lords are not an appropriate O.C.C. for most campaigns and are not recommended as player characters.

High Lords are some of the most powerful beings in the Astral Plane. They are as far above the typical Astral Lord as that Lord is above an Astral Junkie.

High Lord P.C.C. Abilities and Bonuses

Astral Domain: (as per the Astral Lord, **Between the Shadows™**, page 50)

Astral Senses: (as per the Astral Lord, **Between the Shadows™**, page 50)

Astral Reconfiguration: (as per the Astral Lord, **Between the Shadows™**, page 50)

Astral Transference: (as per the Astral Lord, **Between the Shadows™**, page 50)

Astral Travel: (as per the Astral Lord, **Between the Shadows™**, page 50)

Astral Reconfiguration: (as per the Astral Lord, **Between the Shadows™**, page 50)

Ectoplasmic Armor: The same as the Astral Lord (**Between the Shadows™**, pages 50-51), with the following differences: The armor has 150 S.D.C. + 30 S.D.C. per level in the Astral Plane, and 30 S.D.C. + 30 S.D.C. per level in the material world. These are M.D.C. in **Rifts®**. The duration is 15 minutes per level, or until destroyed. The armor costs 10 I.S.P. to activate. The armor also magnifies the High Lord's strength, making it Supernatural.

Ectoplasm: As per the normal physical psychic power, but double the range and duration.

Other Psionic Powers: (as per the Astral Lord, **Between the Shadows™**, page 51)

I.S.P.: The High Lord starts with M.E. + 2D4x10 I.S.P. He gains an additional 2D4 I.S.P. per level. He may permanently convert P.P.E., both his initial amount, and what is gained at each level, into I.S.P. at a 1 to 1 ratio.

P.P.E: P.E. + 1D4x100 at first level. Gains an additional 1D4x10 P.P.E. per level.

Other Bonuses: Immune to possession. Bio-Regenerates 4D6 H.P. / S.D.C. per hour while in the Astral Plane. Has Extraordinary Strength in the Astral Plane.

Mega Power:

1-20 Magic: Gains spells as per the Astral Mage.

21-50 Psychic: In addition to the powers listed above, the character starts with an extra 4 powers from any of the three lesser categories and 1 super psionic power. Gains 3 lesser powers and 1 super power at level 2. Two minor powers may be selected each level thereafter instead of one per level. Gains an additional super psionic power at levels 3, 6, 9, 12 and 15.

51-75 Astrally Active: As per the Astral Knight. Bio-regenerates and has Extraordinary Strength at all times. Loses his Astral Travel ability. Has the Astral Transference ability of an Astral Knight, instead of an Astral Lord. Gains +6 Spd, +3 P.S., +1 P.P., +2 P.E., and +1D4x10 S.D.C.

76-90 Elemental Link: Gains all the abilities of a Warlock except for spell casting. This includes the brotherhood and summoning of Elementals. Gains 1 elemental spell, of half his level or lower, from his chosen element, every even level. Two elements can be chosen by the character if he meets the requirements for a normal Warlock doing so. He then gains the Warlock abilities of both elements and can summon both types of Elementals, but gains no spell casting ability.

91-100 Alternate Physical Form: Ectoplasm: The High Lord can transform his body into ectoplasm. In this form, he may float at half his normal running speed. He may not float higher than 50 feet (15.2 m). The High Lord can flatten and distort his body to pass under doors, through keyholes, etc. The High Lord has no need to breathe, drink, or eat in this form. He receives an automatic dodge against all attacks that he is aware of, by unnaturally stretching out of the way of the attack, creating holes in his body, or suddenly flattening. His physical statistics, H.P. and S.D.C. remain unchanged. The High Lord's natural Bio-Regeneration rate is doubled, and he may Transfer into the Astral Plane in just one melee action while in Ectoplasmic form.

Mega Weakness:

1-10 Vulnerable to magic: -4 to all saving throws against magic, and suffers double damage/effect from spells. The character takes triple damage from enchanted weapons.

11-20 Vulnerable to psionics: -4 to all saving throws against psionics, and takes double damage/effect from all psychic powers. The character takes triple damage from psychic weapons (like the crystal swords that can be found in the Palladium Fantasy world).

21-50 Lord of all syndrome: Character believes that he is superior to normal beings. He expects obedience from everyone,

except for other High Lords, gods, dragons, Godlings, and those that directly serve such beings. The character can go into a rage when "lesser" beings do not obey him or pay him his proper respect.

51-80 Isolationist: The character is not afraid of people, but instead has no desire to leave his personal Domain. He may live there himself, or rule many other beings who live there with him. The character insists on being the undisputed lord of his Domain. He will only leave his place of power in rare and dire circumstances (He must make a saving throw vs insanity to leave).

81-100 Ectoplasm Dependence: The High Lord requires high levels of ectoplasm in his environment to maintain his powers and his life. Such levels are only found naturally in the Outer Layer and Inner Plane of the Astral Plane. It can be artificially maintained in the physical world, by use of the Ectoplasm power by 2 or more psychics for a full hour. If deprived of ectoplasm, the character will loose 5 P.P.E. per hour. When that is exhausted, he will Loose 5 I.S.P. per hour. And when that too is gone, he will loose 5 S.D.C / H.P. per hour. This lost P.P.E., I.S.P., and damage cannot be recovered by normal rest or bio-regeneration until the High Lord is again in a high ectoplasm environment. The High Lord is particularly vulnerable to the spell Call Ectoplasm from Others. This spell will drain all of the High Lord's P.P.E., and then go on to drain his I.S.P., S.D.C. and H.P. until he is down to 1 H.P., at which point the spell will

end. He will be at -4 to his saving throw against this spell while he is in the material world.

Attribute Requirements: M.E. of 16 or higher. An above average P.S., P.E., and P.P. are recommended, but not required.

P.C.C. Skills:
   Language: Native (98%)
   Lore: Astral (+20%)
   One Technical or Science skill of choice (+10%)
   One Piloting/driving/riding skill of choice (+10%)
   One Domestic skill of choice (+10%)
   One W.P. of choice
   Hand to Hand: Basic (can be upgraded to Expert at the cost of one P.C.C. related skill or either Martial Arts or Assassin for two)

P.C.C. Related Skills: Select 8 other skills. Plus select one additional skill at levels three, six, eight, ten and thirteen. All new skills start at level one proficiency.
   Communication: Any
   Domestic: Any (+10%)
   Electrical: Any
   Espionage: Any
   Mechanical: Any
   Medical: Any
   Military: Any
   Physical: Any except Acrobatics and Boxing.
   Pilot: Any (+5%)

Pilot Related: Any
Rogue: Any
Science: Any (+5%)
Technical: Any (+10%)
W.P. Any
Wilderness: Any

- **Secondary Skills:** The character also gets to select 2 secondary skills. These are additional areas of knowledge that do not get the bonuses listed in parentheses. Also, skills are limited (any, only, none) as previously indicated on the list.
- **Standard Equipment:** Typically starts with 4D6x100 dollars worth of equipment, and may own any type of car or similar vehicle.
- **Money:** 1D6x1000 dollars; may be adjusted to represent the characters background.
- **Experience:** Use the chart given for Morphiomoths and Living Nightmares in **Between the Shadows™**.

More Dwellers of the Astral Plane

The Builders R.C.C.

"So we have a bargain." Tom did not like the being in front of him. It was ugly, for one thing. It vaguely reminded him of a starfish. A starfish covered with slimy wisps of pinkish-gray ectoplasm, and with a huge, gaping carnivorous mouth. The being's telepathic 'voice' also disturbed him. It felt sticky even though it superficially sounded somehow smooth and deep.

But in spite of all this he replied, "Yes, we do." Raymond had allied with Elaine, and the two of them had built one of the most amazing Astral Domains that he had ever seen or heard of. He did not have the power to create anything on that scale. Not without help, he didn't.

Even if Elaine had deserted him, leaving him for the man he had already despised more than any other, he still had to impress her. Humiliating Raymond was also a large consideration. So he had searched for the legendary Builders. And here he was speaking with one. And really, the price was not all THAT high...

The enigmatic Builders are a legend in the Astral Plane. Nearly all ancient and great Astral kingdoms are rumored to have been built by them. Their creativity in shaping ectoplasm is said to be unmatched, and their raw ability to do so unequaled. There are a hundred stories about what they look like, and a thousand more about what they have built. Legend on the Inner Plane tells that most of these creatures died in the invasion of the Locust Horde. They were at the forefront of the effort to rid the Astral Plane of these vicious predators. Most tales portray the Builders as champions of all that is good and beautiful, however some few others claim that they are all part of some insidious conspiracy.

The truth is both more and less than the legend. The builders do have an amazing ability to shape ectoplasm. They are more adept at building Astral Domains than most Astral Lords. At one time, they were fairly numerous in the Inner Plane and acted as helpers and guardians of the other good races. But all that started to change when the Locust Horde swarmed through the Astral landscape. For some reason, the Builders' Domains and kingdoms were ravaged far more frequently than those of the other races. On top of that, the vast majority of the race perished in the defeat of the Locust Horde. Their best, brightest, and most honorable were suddenly gone. The heart of the Builder race perished that day, leaving only a handful of them alive. For the most part, only the evil and cowardly survived, along with a very few of the less powerful and young ones.

In the centuries that followed, the majority of the Builders became convinced the Locust Horde had been an attack aimed specifically at their race. They became bitter and convinced that they were the target of some vast conspiracy of the other Astral races. No one remembers how it started, but someone decided that it was time to strike back. Lacking the strength of numbers, they would use stealth and cunning. Soon the idea spread, and an active "counter-conspiracy" was born. They looked to the natural political bickering and animosity among the Astral community, and encouraged them whenever possible. They build realms for others when they think that these realms will be used to increase political tensions, or for outright conflict between the other races. They never hint at their motives, however. Instead they either hide behind a mask of greed, demanding powerful magic items, P.P.E., or other things of value to build a Domain, or else they pretend to have altruistic motives and help "out of the goodness of their souls." Regardless of how the builders present themselves when they create a Domain for someone else, they almost always demand that the recipient join some sort of pre-existing political alliance, and that the person never reveal that the Builders helped create the Domain. Oddly enough, by encouraging these alliances, the builders encourage widespread and destructive conflict.

There are very few Builders left, and your typical Astral Lord is unlikely to meet one in the course of his long lifetime, but their political power and influence on events in the Astral Plane

cannot be underestimated. There are still a few Builders who don't believe there is a conspiracy out to get their race. These few naturally good natured Builders act as protectors and altruistic Domain makers. However, the vast majority of this race act to destabilize the other races in the Inner Plane, creating much pain, misery, and death in the process. Even the actions of the super rare good Builders further the ends of their evil and selfish brethren. The altruistic Builders' good deeds serve to keep alive the race's ancient reputation as champions of good that can be trusted by all.

The Builders are Astral creatures, and while they can coexist without problem, if they transfer their body to the material world they weaken and eventually die. In any event, they have little interest in the material world. The only time they bother is when they need to gather information to further one of their schemes. They mostly concentrate their efforts on the Inner Plane and its inhabitants.

Alignment: Miscreant (33%), Diabolic (25%), Anarchist (25%), Aberrant (12%), other (5%).

Attributes: I.Q. 3D6+4, M.E. 4D6, M.A. 3D6+2, P.S. 4D6, P.P. 2d6+3, P.E. 2D6+3, P.B. 1D6, Spd 1D6. Strength and Endurance are supernatural.

Size: Averages 8 to 10 feet (2.4-3 m) in diameter, and is about 3 to 4 feet (0.9-1.2 m) thick.

S.D.C.: 4D6x10 (Half as much in the material plane. On M.D.C. worlds, they have M.D.C. equal to their combined S.D.C. and Hit Points.)

Hit Points: P.E.x2 plus 2D6 per level (Half in the material plane).

Horror Factor: 13

P.P.E. 5D6x10

Natural Abilities: See the invisible, sense the presence of ley lines, nexus points, Astral Domains, and Astral kingdoms up to 5 miles (8 km) away, and bio-regenerate 3D6 S.D.C. per 5 minutes. They have no need to eat, drink or breathe, in spite of their fearsome appearance.

Floating Movement: Builders are incredibly slow when restricted to ground movement. They may float along at a speed of 4D6 while on a Dragon Road in the Inner Plane. This power is only half as fast when used anywhere else.

360 Degree Vision: Builders are able to see equally well in all directions. They have many small eyes located over their entire bodies.

Create Astral Domain: This is nearly identical to the Astral Lord's power of the same name. The primary difference is that the Builder is far more efficient in converting P.P.E. into creation points when building a Domain. The Builder gets 3.75 creation points per P.P.E. spent.

P.P.E. Transfer: the Builder can permanently transfer P.P.E. from a willing target to his own P.P.E. base. The range is a mere 10 feet (3 m). This transfer is permanent and cannot be performed against an unwilling target. Permanent transfer of P.P.E., above and beyond what is needed to create a Domain, is a common price named by these creatures when building for others.

Ectoplasmic Armor: This is identical to the Astral Lord power of the same name.

Combat: Builders have 5 attacks per melee round. +1 at levels 5, 10 and 15.

Damage: As per supernatural P.S. or psychic power. Bite does supernatural P.S. damage plus 2D6.

Bonuses: +2 to Perception, +2 to Initiative, +3 to Strike, +4 to Parry, +2 to Dodge, +5 to save vs magic, +3 to save vs psionics, +6 to save vs Horror Factor. Immune to mind control and possession.

Magic Powers: None

Psionic Powers: Telepathy, Mind Block, Ectoplasm, and Telekinesis. Also select 2 sensitive powers, 2 physical powers, and 2 super psionic powers at first level. Select 2 lesser powers from any category or one super power each level thereafter.

I.S.P.: M.E. + 2D6x10. Gains 2D6 per level after the first.

Average Life Span: 1000 years

Experience Level: Varies. Player characters will start at first level. The average non-player character will be 4th to 9th level in experience (1D6+3).

Vulnerabilities/Penalties: Astral Dependency: When outside the Astral Plane, the Builder will suffer 3D6 points of damage every hour, and is at -2 to strike, dodge, and initiative. Furthermore, all skills will be at -10%. Builders without Astral Transference cannot leave the Astral Plane, except through physical world portals.

R.C.C. Skills

Language & Literacy: Dragonese/Elf (98%)

Languages: Two of choice (+20%)

Math: Basic (+30%)

Math: Advanced (+15%)

Lore: Astral (+30%)

History: Astral (+20%)

Art: Domain Sculpting (+25%)

Archaeology (+5%)

Anthropology (+5%)

Psychology (+10%)

Hand to Hand Combat: See Combat and Bonuses above.

R.C.C. Related Skills: Select 10 other skills. Plus select two additional skills at level three, and one more at levels six, nine, twelve and fifteen. All new skills start at level one proficiency. Some Builders know quite a bit about technology, while others know nothing. Their lack of hands prevents the use of most weapons.

Communication: Any (+20% to cryptography, +5% to all others).

Domestic: Any (+5%)

Electrical: Any

Espionage: Any except for Wilderness Survival (+5%).

Mechanical: Any

Medical: First Aid only.

Military: Any

Physical: None

Pilot: None

Pilot Related: Read Sensory Equipment only (+5%).

Rogue: Any (+10%)

Science: Any (+5%)

Technical: Any (+10%)

W.P. None

Wilderness: None

Secondary Skills: The character also gets to select 4 secondary skills. These are additional areas of knowledge that do not get the bonuses listed in parentheses. Also, skills are limited (any, only, none) as previously indicated on the list.

Alliances and Allies: None long term. They ally with whomever will further their twisted goals.

Standard Equipment: Typically starts with one or two minor magic items of choice.

Experience: Use the table given for Necrophim in **Between the Shadows™**.

Living Realm R.C.C.

Sarah looked around at the lush forest. Bird songs filled the trees around her. Turning her head, she saw an open field with a quaint stone castle in its center.

"Isn't it perfect?" asked Joey.

Looking directly at him, she replied, "Yes. But how did you find it? You didn't..."

"Didn't sell my soul to some Astral Lordling? No, love. I found it. I was drifting through some particularly thick clouds while I was dreaming about the kind of place I would like to call home with you and ... I found it."

"It seems almost too easy." Sarah replied, feeling a twinge of uneasiness in spite of how absolutely perfect this place was.

"Who cares? It is all ours now." Joey replied, taking her into his arms.

Living Realms are the big cousins of Ectomorphs. They are living clouds of ectoplasm that can reshape themselves. However, they are much larger than Ectomorphs, and do not change their outer shape to resemble animals or objects. Instead, when they encounter an Astral traveler, they reshape themselves into Astral Domains modeled on what the traveler subconsciously desires.

As wonderful as this sounds, they do not do this for entertainment or for pleasure. They do it to feed. They drain P.P.E. and I.S.P. from those who stay inside the Domain that they create. When this energy is drained, they absorb the unfortunate victim's body and the Domain will slowly disperse. They then wander as a could until they again encounter someone.

Living Realms possess no real intelligence. They are instinctual predators who slowly drain their prey. They are not evil, just unthinking.

Alignment: Anarchist

Attributes: Not applicable. Strength and Endurance are supernatural.

Size: Varies, depending on the size of the Domain they create and the creature's natural P.P.E. Few are smaller than 1000 feet (305 m) in diameter when they are in their unformed state.

S.D.C.: 2D6x100 when in their unformed state.

Hit Points: 1D6x100

Horror Factor: 12, but only when they are recognized for what they are.

P.P.E. 1D6x50 for the most common ones, 2D6x100 for the largest and oldest.

Natural Abilities: See the invisible, sense P.P.E. and I.S.P. by touch, sense the presence of ley lines, nexus points up to 1 mile (1.6 km) away. They bio-regenerate 1D6 per minute in the Outer Layer, 2D6 per minute in the Inner Plane, +1D6 when on a Dragon Road or +2D6 when on a nexus. They float at a speed of up to 10 miles per hour (16 km).

Create Astral Domain: Living Realms will use their own P.P.E. to create an Astral Domain. Like Astral Lords, they receive 2.5 creation points per P.P.E. spent. However, they do not permanently expend this P.P.E. Over time they siphon off energy from their victims and use this energy to return to their natural state. When their victim dies, or when he abandons the Domain, the Living Domain will convert back into its normal form and will permanently lose 10% of the P.P.E.

spent in the Domain's creation. They typically will scale the Domain to the victim's power level. A victim with little P.P.E. and I.S.P. will only have a small Domain created for him by a Living Realm. A powerful Mage or Psychic may have a correspondingly larger Domain built for them. All features of the Domain may be chosen by the victim or by the G.M., except for Physical World Portals and Transportation abilities, which the Realm will not or can not build, and location. Location is where the being is encountered. They do not move or drift while in Domain form. Also, they always have ectoplasmic barriers or better protection.

Energy Drain: Those living inside a Living Realm will loose 1D6 P.P.E. or I.S.P. per day, whichever they have more of. This may be recovered normally. Each week spent in the Living Realm will permanently drain the character of 1 point. When the higher of P.P.E. or I.S.P. is permanently drained, the other source of power will be drained. Victims are often unaware of this drain at first, and uncaring of it later on, due to the power below. The Living Realm permanently gains 1 P.P.E. per point of I.S.P. or P.P.E. permanently drained.

Allurement: When the Domain is created, the person who inspired the Living Realm must save against psionics at -2 or he will be unwilling to leave it. If he makes his saving throw, he must save again every 2 days spent in the Domain, and has an additional cumulative -1 to the roll. Other beings that choose to inhabit the Domain save normally when first entering, and their saving throws are made each week at a cumulative -1.

Limited Telepathy: Domains are able to sense what the creatures inside them want, and instinctively use this information to create an appropriate Astral Domain. There is no saving throw against this power, but it can be blocked by Mind Block or similar powers.

Combat: Not applicable in natural form. As a Domain, they may have Domain defenses.

Damage: See above.

Bonuses: Immune to transformation, disease, poison, mind control and possession.

Magic Powers: None

Psionic Powers: None

I.S.P.: None

Average Life Span: 5000 years

Experience Level: Not applicable

Vulnerabilities/Penalties: Astral Dependency: When outside the Astral Plane, the Living Realm will suffer 5D6 points of damage every minute. Normally they cannot leave the Astral Plane.

R.C.C. Skills: None

Alliances and Allies: None

Standard Equipment: None

Experience: Not applicable

New Psychic Powers

Ectoplasmic Objects

(Physical power in Nightbane®, Super in other games)

Range: Touch (to create the object. Will maintain solidity at 40 feet/12.2 m, +5 feet/1.5 m per level from the psychic).

Duration: 10 minutes per level.

I.S.P.: 20

Saving Throw: None

Prerequisite: Ectoplasm, and at least one other ectoplasm based power.

This power allows the psychic to create objects made of ectoplasm. Any type of object can be created. Clothing, weapons, tools, ropes, and other things can all be created with this power. At first level the character may create any object that normally weighs 12 pounds (5.4 kg) or less, has no more than one moving part, and does not violate any of the restrictions listed below.

At each additional level, the psychic may modify the power as follows: Add 2 pounds (.9 kg) to his weight limit, add 1 moving part, or create 1 additional object (not to exceed his total weight limit). A 5th level psychic using this power could create 1 object that normally weighs 20 pounds (9 kg) with one moving part, 5 objects with no more than one moving part each that total 12 pounds (5.4 kg) normally, one 12 pound (5.4 kg) object with 5 moving parts, or any combination of the above. Skill rolls must be made to create complex objects.

Everything created with this power will have a somewhat dull and pasty appearance, much like the disguises created by ectoplasmic disguise, or can be invisible, at the psychic's discretion when the object is created. Objects will very obviously be "strange" or "fake" unless an appropriate skill roll is made while creating the object (i.e. a Sewing roll to create realistic clothing).

All ectoplasmic objects will weigh half as much as their normal counterparts, and have half their normal S.D.C., or 40, whichever is less (multiple objects may have a total of 40 S.D.C.). Ectoplasmic melee and missile weapons do half their normal damage, but DO affect Astral creatures and beings only affected by psychic powers and magic.

In the Astral Plane, ectoplasmic objects will have their normal weight & S.D.C. Weapons will do their normal damage.

Ectoplasmic objects have none of the chemical or electromagnetic properties of their normal counterparts, so electronics, explosives, batteries, and the like may not be created, but ectoplasmic objects that only LOOK like them can.

Ectoplasmic guns CAN be created, provided that the appropriate number of moving objects can be created and an appropriate skill roll is made, but ectoplasmic ammunition cannot. Normal ammunition must be used in these weapons, and will do normal damage (but will not affect Astral travelers & those only affected by psionics and magic).

Ectoplasmic Food

(Physical)

Range: Touch (to create the food. Will maintain solidity at 40 feet/12.2 m, +5 feet/1.5 m per level).

Duration: 4 minutes per level (effect from eating the ectoplasm is permanent).

I.S.P.: 6 per wafer (3 in the Astral Plane).

Saving Throw: None

Prerequisite: Ectoplasm

This power allows the user to create "food" wafers out of ectoplasm. This "food" will nourish anyone who eats it before the duration expires. Ectoplasmic Food always appears as dull gray wafers. They are airy and light, with little taste.

There is a price to eating ectoplasm regularly, though. If a character eats ectoplasmic food only for 3 consecutive days, his stomach will start to shrink. Reduce P.S. and Spd by 3/4. After a week, reduce P.E. by 3/4. After two weeks, reduce P.B. and P.P. by 3/4. After a full month of existing almost entirely on ectoplasmic food, the person's attributes will return to normal, but he can only eat normal food again after months of work. His body will have adjusted completely to ectoplasmic food. The only way to recover from this condition is to slowly start re-introducing food into his diet. It will take a full year of gradually increasing the normal food intake for the unfortunate victim to be able to subsist fully on normal food again.

Ectoplasmic Skids

(Physical)
Range: Self
Duration: 10 minutes per level.
I.S.P.: 9
Saving Throw: None
Prerequisite: Ectoplasm

This power creates 1 or 2 small ectoplasmic clouds under the user's feet. These clouds allow the psychic to reduce friction between his feet and the ground in a controlled manner, simulating the effects of skates or a skateboard. The huge advantage of this power over traditional skates and boards is that the ectoplasmic versions work fine on uneven and rough terrain. The user will glide right over small rocks and holes that would trip up or slow down a normal skater. The maximum speed obtainable on ectoplasmic skids is three times the character's normal running speed, or 150 miles per hour (240 km), whichever is less.

It is important to note that the ectoplasmic skids do not reduce the weight of the character in any way. They do not allow "skidding" on water or any other surface that would not normally bear the user's weight.

Ectoplasmic Limb

(Physical)
Range: Self
Duration: 4 minutes per level.
I.S.P.: 12 (+6 per limb beyond the first).
Saving Throw: None
Prerequisite: Ectoplasm

This power creates one or more limbs made of semi-solid ectoplasm. The limb's appearance will be a ghostly, gaseous gray. It will function in all ways as a normal limb with P.S., P.P., and Spd of 8 (On the Astral Plane these numbers are doubled). These phantom limbs can be used to temporarily replace those lost in combat or through mischance, or can be used to create extra limbs. Tails, tentacles, wings, arms, and legs are but a few of the possible "limbs" that can be created with this power.

Ectoplasmic wings will not allow the psychic to fly, except in the Inner Plane of the Astral Plane (flying speed 8 there).

Creating 2 or more extra limbs will grant the psychic one extra melee attack per round. Creating more than 2 limbs has no additional effect in combat.

Ectoplasmic Limbs will affect Astral beings, and creatures only affected by magic or psionics.

New Spells

Create Clothing

Level: 6
Range: Self
Duration: Permanent
Saving Throw: None
P.P.E.: 20

This useful spell allows the caster to create a normal set of clothing. The caster must choose one set of clothing as a model when learning this spell. He can create this set of clothing without difficulty each time he casts this spell. Creating a set of clothing different from the one memorized, requires a successful Sewing skill roll. A failed roll indicates that the clothing is flawed in some way. The clothing may be poorly made, not fit, or even fall apart when worn, depending on how badly the roll is failed. Clothing created by this spell cannot provide protection greater than that of soft leather armor. When the spell is cast, the clothing appears either on the character's body, or neatly folded by his feet, at the character's discretion.

Build Astral Domain

Level: 13
Range: Self
Duration: 1 day per level.
Saving Throw: None
P.P.E.: 240 or more, +1D4 from Permanent base (Ritual).

Casting this spell allows the mage to create an Astral Domain, much like an Astral Lord is able to do. The primary difference is that Domains created this way are temporary in nature, and the spell is not nearly as energy efficient as the natural ability of the Lords. Casting this spell using 240 P.P.E. will allow the mage to use 40 creation points when building his Domain. More creation points can be gained by spending an additional 2 P.P.E. per creation point. For example, to create a 150 creation point Domain would take 460 P.P.E., and permanently burn 1D4 additional P.P.E. (compared to 60 permanent P.P.E. for an Astral Lord to create an identical permanent Domain).

If this ritual is made permanent by some means, the caster will find that there is another unfortunate side effect. He will continue to permanently lose 1D4 P.P.E. at the end of each normal duration period, until he has lost as many P.P.E. as he used to cast the spell. Using the above example, our mage has a Diabolist friend who uses a Permanency Ward to make the Domain permanent. Let us say that the mage is 12th level. Every 12 hours he will lose 1D4 P.P.E., until he has permanently lost 460. If this is greater than his base amount, he must make a saving throw against death/coma. If he fails, he will die. Success indicates that he lives, but loses all spellcasting ability and all but 1D4 P.P.E. permanently.

This ritual can only be used while in the Astral Plane, where no extra P.P.E is available from Ley Lines or Nexus points. Also, there are no side effects when disturbing a mage casting this spell, unlike what happens when an Astral Lord is disturbed while creating a Domain. If multiple beings participate in this ritual, and it is made permanent, they all suffer the side effects, permanently losing P.P.E. equal to what they donated as described above.

WITHIN THE BOWELS OF THE LONE STAR COMPLEX.

TELEKINESIS. WHAT A WAY TO TRAVEL...

c h a p t e r   f o u r   ☠   BY RAMÓN PÉREZ   WITH A LITTLE HELP FROM HIS FRIENDS

ELSEWHERE NEARBY.

GOOD AFTERNOON DR. HESTON

AS TO YOU DR. ALEXANDER

LEVEL A CLEARANCE REQUIRED.

JOHNNY, TAP INTO THE DATABASE AND SEE WHAT YOU CAN FIND. OJ, SECURE THE ENTRANCE.

FWOOSH

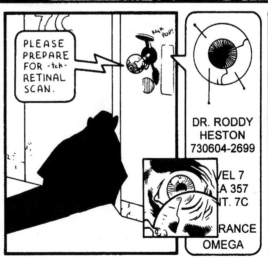

PLEASE PREPARE FOR -tck- RETINAL SCAN.

DR. RODDY HESTON 730604-2699

VEL 7 A 357 NT. 7C

RANCE OMEGA

WELCOME -tck- BACK DOCTOR HESTON. YOU MAY PROCEED.

FWOC   OOSH

FWISH
KTANG!

I SAY! WHAT'S GOING ON HERE!?

PDTTHBOF

THEY GOT CHIMPS WORKIN' FOR THEM? MAN, I GOTTA GET A RESUME TOGETHER.

ANYWAYS, I THINK I'VE FOUND SOMETHING. SEEMS WE HAVE QUITE A COOKBOOK OF GENETIC CON-COCTIONS HERE.

YOU KNOW, IF WE WERE TO MAKE COPIES OF THIS AND IT WERE TO FALL INTO THE RIGHT HANDS, FOR THE RIGHT PRICE, BRADFORD'S LITTLE FUNLAB WOULD EXPLODE IN HIS FACE.

CAN YOU DO IT?

I COULD UPLOAD IT THROUGH ONE OF THEIR RELAYS TO PETUNIA'S ON--BOARD COMPUTER.

PASS ME THE RADIO.

IS THIS THE CREATURE THAT YOU SPOKE OF?

YES, I COULD NEVER MISTAKE THE DEMON THAT PLAGUES MY WORLD, BUT THIS ONE IS SOMEHOW DIFFERENT.

OUTSIDE THE LONE STAR COMPLEX.

... NOPE, GO FISH.

E ENTERING A
RICTED AREA
SSERS, WILL BE
ROSECUTED

BIP-BIP
BIP-BIP
BIP -

YES ?

HEY SWEETS, WONDERING IF YOU COULD LEND US A HAND?

IF IT'LL SHUT YOU UP, ANYTHING.

GET PETUNIA READY TO RECIEVE AN UPLOAD ON FREQUENCY ONE- -OH-TWO-POINT- -ONE.

THEN GET READY TO RENDEZVOUS.

I'M ON IT.

OKAY BOYS, TIME TO PACK UP THIS PICNIC AND GET BUSY.

FIGURES! I WAS JUST GETTING LUCKY!

BACK INSIDE.

PLAGUES YOUR WORLD? WHAT DO YOU MEAN?

THESE DEMONS KNOWN AS THE AISHWARRA ARE NOMADIC GIANTS.

A SINGLE ONE CAN LAY WASTE TO AN ENTIRE CITY, DEVOURING ALL IN IT'S PATH. ANY WHO OPPOSE ARE SLAUGHTERED AND THOSE WHO SURVIVE ARE CARRIED OFF TO A FATE MUCH... MUCH WORSE.

THE DESTRUCTION THE AISHWARRA BRINGS PALES IN THE THREAT IT POSES TO A WORLD, FOR IT PERMANENTLY RAPES THE LAND OF IT'S MAGIC ENERGY. ONCE GORGED IT WILL SPAWN YOUNG, CREATING EGGS THAT ARE BATTERIES OF MAGIC. BATTERIES THAT MADMEN HAVE DESTROYED THEMSELVES OVER, FOR THOSE WHO POSSESS THE EGGS, POSSESS MAGIC.

BUT SURELY THAT COULDN'T HAPPEN HERE ...

IT'S A GO, AND NONE SHOULD BE THE WISER.

GROAN

IT LOOKS AS IF OUR HOST IS REGAINING CONCIOUSNESS.

THEN LET'S MAKE HIM MORE COMFORTABLE.

OOOOH OOOH OH OH

WHAT'S GOING ON HERE? UNTIE ME IMMEDIATELY OR I SHALL ...

CALM DOWN DOCTOR.

NO ONE IS GOING TO HARM YOU. WE JUST REQUIRE YOU TO ANSWER SOME QUESTIONS.

MY WORD! A GRACKLE-TOOTH! HOW RARE INDEED. I HAVE NEVER HAD THE OPPORTUNITY TO DISEC... UM ... STUDY YOUR SPECIES FIRSTHAND.

YES, "GRACKLE-TOOTH". A HUMAN LABEL. ON OUR HOMEWORLD MY PEOPLE ARE THE JIN-RO. A HOME THAT I CANNOT RETURN TO, BUT FROM WHICH SOMEHOW YOU HAVE RECREATED THIS MONSTER!

THAT THING'S FROM YOUR HOMEWORLD? REMIND ME NOT TO VISIT. EVER.

HOW HAVE YOU DONE THIS?

43

I HAVE NO IDEA WHAT YOU ARE TALKING ABOUT. THIS BEAST WAS CREATED FROM A GENETIC ENCRYPTION PROVIDED BY THE GREAT DOCTOR BRADFORD. IT IS A BEING WHOSE BENEFIT TO THE COALITION CANNOT BE MISTAKEN. ONLY FOUL CREATURES OF MAGIC NEED FEAR IT.

THEN YOU ARE A FOOL.

IS THIS WHAT YOU DECIPHERED DOCTOR?

HOW DID YOU?

IS THIS WHAT YOU DECIPHERED DOCTOR?

AHEM... WELL YES. MOSTLY THAT IS...

EMERGENCY ALARM

YOU CREATED A CREATURE THAT YOU DO NOT EVEN COMPREHEND?

WHAT WORK IS DONE HERE IS FOR THE GOOD OF THE COALITION, AND SINCE YOU ARE OBVIOUSLY ITS ENEMY, IT IS NONE OF YOUR BUSINESS.

ACTUALLY IT'S QUITE FACINATING. BY USE-ING HUMAN DNA AS A SPRINGBOARD AND SPLICING IT WITH THIS NEWFOUND INFORMA...

WHAP!

THEY ARE ALL MAD! THIS MUST END. WE MUST DESTROY THE DEMON ..NOW!.

44

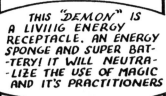

45

NEW TYPE BIO-BORGS™

By Mark Sumimoto
Additional text and rules by Kevin Siembieda

The Splugorth are always developing and experimenting with magic, in general, and Bio-Wizardry in particular. The Bio-Borgs presented in the following pages are their latest creations.

Note: This material was originally scheduled to appear in *Splynn Dimensional Market — Rifts® Atlantis Two*, but was cut out due to space limitations in order to present a larger number of vehicles and gizmos. As promised in the *Splynn World Book*, we present these unique and powerful beings here, in the pages of **The Rifter**™ for your enjoyment. These are "official" stats, rules and information provided for optional use by the Game Master. Enjoy.

Bio-Leech R.C.C.

Bio-Wizard parasites are usually used as a form of punishment or as a cheap, temporary means of augmentation. Most subjects enhanced by parasites suffer from a number of debilitating penalties and rarely last long enough to be of much value to serious buyers. Rather than limit themselves to selling parasite-infected slaves as *temporary laborers* only (the parasites kill their host within a matter of months), the Splugorth have used their mastery of Bio-Wizardry to create durable and powerful, augmented slaves. The result is a grotesquely altered human or D-Bee who survives being feasted upon by parasites by feeding on other life forms themselves. A monstrous predator with a frightening appetite for humanoids. This new Bio-Wizard monster is called the **Bio-Leech**. A fiendish creature that requires eating the flesh, blood, and brains of others to survive.

To create a Bio-Leech, the recipient is subjected to a series of parasite infections, magic transmutation, and Bio-Wizard reconstruction. First, the subject is infected with a number of parasitic organisms. Second, the *Brain Feeder* and *Lobee-Optos* are used to instill psionic powers. Third, a *Mystic Leech* prevents the subject from using any magic he may have had or using magic weapons against his master. Fourth, an *Oplos* is implanted to enhance the subject's visual acuity, and *Heart Worms* increase his strength and vitality. Finally, a *Living Armor* parasite envelops the host to make him a Mega-Damage being.

Normally, these parasites would consume the subject's brain and/or heart after a year, assuming the subject could survive the multiple infestation in the first place. Furthermore, he would suffer from numerous other penalties which would neutralize most benefits gained from the combination of hostile organisms. However, the potential Bio-Leech is subjected to Bio-Wizard transmutation within the Splugorth's magic slime chambers that compensate and transform the hodgepodge of organisms into one horrible creature. In addition to the abilities provided by the symbiotes and parasites, *Living Armor* to protect the subject's body is permanently melded to the host, becoming his new skin. Teeth become sharper and the jaw stronger. Regenerative capabilities are raised to supernatural levels and his nervous system is modified to ignore the discomfort associated with the implanted parasites. The digestive system is also altered to give the subject a very strict diet (i.e. other humanoids and raw meat). The end result is a carnivorous humanoid monstrosity with tough, gray, armored skin to protect both his body and the parasites inside of him. Were it not for the magical transmutation, these parasites would eat their host alive. Instead, the dramatically altered physiology, regenerative abilities, and melding of many into one being, enables the Bio-Leech to not only survive, but for the organisms within to breed and repopulate so they never run out (normally parasites are short-lived, not so in the Bio-Leech).

The Bio-Leech is encouraged to act on his need for the flesh of other intelligent beings and taught the arts of hunting and combat. Bio-Leeches also receive extensive training in methods of torture. Backed by their psionic power of Bio-Manipulation, they make excellent torturers and interrogators. However, the Splugorth generally view the Bio-Leech with disfavor. Parasites are generally used as a means of torture by the Splugorth or cheap form of augmentation. This means they consider those who receive parasites to be weak and contemptible. As a result,

Splugorth rarely keep Bio-Leeches as part of their own stable of slaves and sell them on the open market. Even evil Bio-Leech slaves who learn to love their new life of hunting and torture are never allowed to join the ranks of the Minions because of the disdain the Splugorth hold for them. Thus, they are forever slaves and regarded as nothing more than a dog to serve its master.

The handful of Bio-Leeches who escape their Splugorth masters tend to stay within the boundaries of Atlantis, most living in the Preserve or other remote area. Few have joined any anti-Splugorth organizations, but there are some counted among the Liberated Underground. Most prefer to live alone in the wilderness, using their skills and abilities to survive and evade the Splugorth's Minions. As many as one hundred are believed to exist along the eastern wilderness of Canada and the USA — all have escaped, been lost or abandoned (left for dead?) by their Splugorth masters. A few are also found in the British Isles and another few dozen on the continent of Africa. Others have found their way into the Magic Zone of North America, where their anti-magic capability is most helpful. In most cases, these predators make their lairs in the wilderness, preying upon tribal people and unsuspecting travelers. However, they are known to raid villages and cities, and occasionally ally themselves with or serve other powerful beings, including Necromancers, Shifters, dragons and demons.

Powers and Abilities of the Bio-Leech R.C.C.

1. Supernatural Endurance and Bio-Regeneration: The creation process gives the Bio-Leech incredible endurance and healing abilities. He becomes a Mega-Damage creature with $2D4 \times 10 + 80$ M.D.C. plus 1D6 per level of experience. If an M.D.C. D-Bee, add this to the base amount. Also, add 1D6 to the P.E. attribute. Furthermore, the character never fatigues and can function normally without sleep for four days straight before requiring rest.

The Bio-Leech has been given supernatural healing abilities in order to regenerate the tissue lost to his hungry parasites. This also allows him to heal any injury sustained in combat at the rate of 1D6 M.D.C. per melee round and survive injuries down to -50 M.D.C. below zero. Even severed limbs and destroyed organs can be fully restored within 2D4 hours. Even brain tissue can be healed, although he cannot regenerate a severed head. The only thing the Bio-Leech cannot regenerate are lost parasites. Such a loss will usually require surgery and results in the loss of any powers that parasite provided.

The Heart Worm parasites make the Bio-Leech impervious to poison, toxins, drugs and disease. Even gas attacks only do half their damage and last for half their duration. Other physical bonuses are listed under R.C.C. bonuses.

2. Enhanced Strength and Speed: Add +6 to P.S. and +20 to Spd. Overall P.S. is not considered to be supernatural, but his jaw muscles and fangs have been augmented to supernatural levels to allow him to feed on M.D.C. flesh. Bite attacks inflict 2D6 M.D.

3. Enhanced Senses: The Oplos implant provides the Bio-Leech with increased visual acuity and supernatural vision. His eyesight is improved to perfect 20/20 vision and augmented with the abilities of nightvision 100 feet (30.5 m), telescopic vision 2000 feet (609.6 m), see the invisible, see aura, and is able to see in all spectrums of light, including infrared and ultraviolet.

4. Psionic Powers: Given psionic powers by the Lobee-Optos parasite, which are further enhanced by the Brain Feeder and psionic senses of the Oplos, the Bio-Leech effectively becomes a Master Psionic with limited abilities. The creature possesses the Super-Psionic power of *Bio-Manipulation* and the lesser powers of *Deaden Senses, Empathy, Psychic Diagnosis,* and *Psychic Surgery,* plus three additional lesser powers selected from any category, except Super or Mind Bleeder. Needs a 10 or higher to save vs psionic attack.

5. I.S.P.: Initial I.S.P. is 100 plus the M.E. attribute number. Add 1D6+1 I.S.P. at every additional level of experience. Although considered to be a Master Psionic, the creature's powers (and I.S.P.) are limited, and not as great as a true Master Psychic/Mind Melter.

6. P.P.E.: None! The *Mystic Leech* parasite attached to the Bio-Leech consumes all of his available P.P.E., including extra P.P.E. provided by the other parasites. In fact, the unique bond with his parasitic partners allows him to use the draining power of the Mystic Leech on other creatures. Each time the Bio-Leech touches another being, he can attempt to drain P.P.E. from him; up to 10 P.P.E. with each touch (each draining touch counts as one melee attack/action).

Likewise, any magical effects, powers or protection provided to a character by spell or other means of magic will suffer from the draining touch. In this case, duration and potency (P.P.E. reserve, the M.D.C. of a magic force field/armor, the M.D. of a magical blade, energy blast, etc.) are both reduced by 10% per each touch. After ten touches, the magic is completely negated). However, even a few magic draining "touches" may effectively minimize the damage capabilities, threat or effectiveness of the magic.

Limitations, Exceptions & Notes:

- Spells 10th level and higher, as well as other types of powerful magic are NOT effected by the Bio-Leech's draining touch. Nor does the Bio-Leech's power have any effect on ancient dragons, Godlings, true gods, Alien Intelligences, splinted essences or Demon Lords.

- In the case of Techno-Wizard items, rune weapons and other magical weapons or devices, the range, duration and damage of any magic it may possess or can cast is reduced by 25% when that item is in the hands of the Bio-Leech. Likewise, any magic leveled against the Bio-Leech from spells, circles, runes or magic items inflicts half its normal damage on the monster. Also see the creature's R.C.C. bonuses.

- If used against a *Psi-Stalker* or other P.P.E. vampires, the touch will drain the victim's metabolism with only two touches, causing the victim to become famished and probably very angry. Reduce the victim's combat bonuses by one point until his hunger has been sated.

7. R.C.C. Bonuses: +3 to initiative, +3 to save vs magic, +3 to save vs magic illusions, +4 to save vs psionics, +4 to save vs mind control, +4 to save vs Horror Factor, +3 to save vs possession, and +12% to save vs coma/death, all in addition to skill and attribute bonuses.

8. Food and Sustenance: The constant regeneration of tissue (much of which is consumed by his own parasitic partners) places such demands on the Bio-Leech's metabolism that the monster must eat frequently. A steady diet that consists of human or D-Bee flesh and brain tissue. Humanoids and other intelligent creatures (including dragons and demons), are the Bio-Leech's primary prey — presumably, the Splugorth have programmed the creature on some level to *need* this type of "food" to survive. They will even eat their own kind, making them cannibals. Roughly 100 lbs (160 kg) of flesh and a pound (1.6 kg) of gray matter (brains) must be consumed every two days to function at peak efficiency.

Being deprived of food for a week will cause the abomination to become fatigued, losing one melee attack and -1 on initiative. Each additional week without food makes the character weaker still: -1 on initiative, -1 to strike, parry, and dodge, plus reduce speed attribute and M.D.C. by 5% for each additional week deprived of sustenance. All penalties are erased 1D6+1 hours after gorging himself.

Being deprived of brain tissue for a week or two inflicts much more serious penalties. I.S.P. is reduced by half and the character's I.Q. and M.E. will drop by one point every week until brain tissue is consumed. If the I.Q. is reduced to half, the character will suffer a penalty of -25% to all skills. If reduced to a quarter, the skills will be reduced by 50%. Losing all I.Q. or M.E. points, means the character is reduced to a mindless vegetable and will die within 4D6 hours. I.Q. and M.E. return to normal within 1D6 hours after consuming the equivalent of one, complete, human brain. I.S.P. returns after 24 hours.

9. Insanities: The Bio-Leech suffers a great deal of trauma undergoing the transformation and coping with its aftereffects. His horrifying appearance, loss of humanity/normalcy, and the sensations that come with sharing your body with other living creatures which are a constant source of torment and pain. The trauma, pain, sensations and cravings all contribute to the level of insanity.

All Bio-Leeches tend to be aggressive, violent, and anti-social characters who enjoy fighting, killing and devouring their victims. Most see themselves as monsters or freaks and are filled with self-loathing, and feel like outcasts even among friends. Moreover, the transmutation and Splugorth conditioning makes the Bio-Borg enjoy killing and crave the taste of brains and flesh. Many are sadistic and enjoy hurting/torturing others.

At every level of experience, there is a 25% chance that the Bio-Leech will develop an insanity. Roll the percentile dice upon reaching each new level. A roll of 01-25% means the character gains one of the disorders listed on the *Bio-Borg Insanity Table* in the *Splynn Dimensional Market* world book. A roll of 26-00% means no new insanity. Also see the section on Physical Appearance for other disadvantages and penalties relating to the character's inhuman appearance.

Bio-Leech R.C.C.

Also known as: Brain-eater and simply, the Leech.

Character Note: Ideal as an NPC villain or monster, but also available as an *optional* player character at the sole discretion of the Game Master. Any player character will be evil or selfish, with unprincipled being the best alignment possible.

The Bio-Leech is a sad example of the Splugorth's callousness and deliberate cruelty towards lesser beings. Once a normal person, the potential Bio-Leech is transformed into a disgusting predatory cannibal. His training and brainwashing usually suppresses any past emotions and memories, but there are a few Bio-Leeches who manage to hold on to a piece of their humanity. These few must choose between feeding on the flesh of other intelligent beings or dying from starvation (animals can not be substituted as a food source). Bio-Leeches of an Unprincipled (and in some cases, Aberrant) alignment will be torn between their former morality and the drive for self-preservation.

The typical Bio-Borg has suffered greatly at the hands of the Splugorth. His training makes him a capable warrior and ruthless killer. He has been taught to be aggressive and to take advantage of weakness. Even in social settings, he will have a tendency to be aggressive in conversations, easily provoked and is quick to anger. This is further exasperated by their inhuman appearance. The Bio-Leech knows he is a deformed monster and is not usually happy about it.

Alignment Restrictions: Evil or selfish only! Because of their dietary needs and instinct to hunt and kill other intelligent life forms and their training by the Splugorth, a Bio-Leech cannot be of a good alignment. The best alignment he can try to attain is Unprincipled. Anarchist and Aberrant are the most common alignments among Bio-Leeches who struggle to maintain some level of humanity; most are Miscreant or Diabolic.

Attribute Requirements: M.E. 12 or higher — The higher the better for M.E. A high P.E. and P.P. are also desirable, but not required. **Race Restrictions:** Humans and humanoid D-Bees only! Non-magical M.D.C. D-Bees are acceptable for transmutation, but supernatural beings and creatures of magic are not.

Physical Appearance: The body is covered in a thick, gray organic armor for skin, has a monstrous, oversized jaw, fangs and the third eye from the Lobee-Optos parasite. In addition, his facial features are twisted and obscured by the transformation. **Note:** Change P.B. to 1D6 and give the Bio-Borg a Horror Factor of 15.

Life Span: 26+3D6 years after transmutation. Death often comes to the Bio-Leech in combat, but they can also just up and "drop dead" without warning. Their magically augmented and tortured bodies just give up the ghost one day, often without warning. Note that the Bio-Leech can not procreate.

O.C.C. Skills:
Language: Two of Choice (+30%)
Interrogation Techniques (+25%)
First Aid (+10%)
Math: Basic (+5%)
Radio: Basic (+5%)
Tracking (+15%)
Wilderness Survival (+15%)
Running
Athletics (General)
W.P. Sword
W.P. Knife
W.P. Blunt
W.P. of choice (any)
Hand to Hand Combat: Assassin

O.C.C. Related Skills: Select eight skills at level one, but four must be selected from the categories of rogue and/or wilderness, plus one additional skill at levels 4, 8, and 13.

Communications: Any
Cowboy: None
Domestic: Any (+5%)
Electrical: Basic only.
Espionage: Any (+5%)
Mechanical: Basic only.
Medical: None
Military: Any, except NBC warfare, parachuting, or demolitions (any).
Physical: Any, except wrestling or acrobatics.
Piloting: Any, except robots, jets, or tanks.
Pilot Related: Any, except parachuting.
Rogue: Any, except computer hacking (+10%).
Science: None
Technical: Any, except computer skills.
Weapon Proficiencies: Any
Wilderness: Any (+10%)

Secondary Skills: Select three secondary skills at level one, plus one additional at levels 2, 5, 9, and 14 from those listed, excluding those marked "None." These are additional areas of knowledge that do not get the advantage of the bonus listed in parentheses. All secondary skills start at the base skill level.

Standard Equipment: Slaves start with very little. Usually only has a few knives, two other weapons, and a few wilderness survival items depending on the whims of their master. Ancient types of melee weapons, their modern equivalents (i.e. Vibro-Blades), and energy weapons may all be used by these characters — Kittani items are usually favored. Magic items are rarely used for obvious reasons.

Money: Slaves start with none. A small allowance may have been provided by the slave master, but not usually. Free Bio-Leeches also start with none, but may accumulate wealth as luck and the character's inclinations dictate.

Slave Market Value: Highly regarded as a torturer/interrogator, assassin, and anti-magic countermeasure warrior/defender, as well as a conventional fighter. Still not quite as in demand as the human T-Man, but the average Bio-Leech sells for an average price of 2D6×100,000 credits. May sell for two to four times that much to the right buyer, particular other monstrous beings. More powerful Bio-Leeches with higher physical attributes and/or combat experience can sell for three to five times as much.

Bio-Wizardry and Cybernetics: Starts with the parasites and augmentations listed previously, but no others. Bio-Leeches are rarely given further augmentation, but exceptions are made depending on the desires of the buyer. However, no more than two additional parasites or symbiotes are possible.

The healing powers of the Bio-Leech prevent him from receiving cybernetics and bionics. Any such implants are rejected within a few minutes and replaced by new tissue after a few hours.

Fire Eater R.C.C.

"Those flames must've been 20 meters high. The crowd was deafening. And when I saw the flesh sizzle right off the bones of that juiced-up wimp, I could feel the gold bulging in my pockets. Yeah, he got in some really good shots, but my boy still came out on top. When his flames finally caught that jumping freak, they really caught 'em! Too bad my Fire Eater had to explode to get the job done, but what the hell. At least, I made a profit! Barkeep! Another round for the house!"

*— Spoken by a drunken slave owner shortly
before spending the last of his winnings*

Through the miracle of Bio-Wizardry, the Fire Eater's entire digestive system has been removed and replaced by a strange supernatural fire-producing parasitic organism, also called the Fire Eater. Placed in the belly of the Fire Eater, the organism has a long feeding appendage that replaces the subject's esophagus. Any food the Bio-Borg consumes is taken through this appendage and is digested by the symbiote before passing any nutrients on to the host. The organism is capable of totally consuming any organic material that is swallowed and using it as fuel. Thus, the host needs to consume roughly 2-3 times more food than normal (he literally has another mouth to feed). The parasite also has a series of long tentacles that connects itself to the Fire Eater's nervous system, becoming fully integrated into the body.

To complete the transformation into a Fire Eater, the subject undergoes further magic transmutations. His flesh and bones are altered to be impervious to the intense magical fire the organism can produce, as well as all other forms of heat and fire. Then, a specially prepared Eye of Eylor is implanted in the Fire Eater's chest. This Eye is designed to combine its own magic with that of the host body and the Fire Eater organism to create a number of other magical effects. All of these other modifications must be done within 24 hours of the organism's initial implantation. After that, the parasite becomes fully integrated and, unless the host is modified to be impervious to fire, he will be completely consumed, body and all, by his own magical flames.

Once the parasite is fully integrated, the fire within will feel as if it is permeating every cell of the Fire Eater's body. The character finds the warmth both soothing and energizing. The internal body temperature will rise thousands of degrees. Smoke and flame will leak from the Bio-Borg's mouth and nostrils with every breath, and the eyes turn bright red like a fiery blaze. Meanwhile, the fire inside is contained, maintaining an external body temperature only slightly higher than normal.

As the Fire Eater adjusts to his new body, he will learn to release his flame through his mouth in a manner more similar to vomiting than a dragon's fire breath. He will also learn how to channel his flame through his Eye of Eylor implant to perform other feats. As time progresses, the fire parasite will burn hotter and hotter to vainly try to consume its host. As he becomes more experienced, this increasingly hotter flame will add to the damage of the Fire Eater's attacks.

The primal and spectacular nature of the Fire Eater's powers make him a "hot seller" in the Splugorth slave markets (pun intended). They are often sold in groups with other fire oriented beings, like Bursters, for use as slash and burn squads for defoli-

ation projects, demolitions, and combat. They also look great in arena combat, able to finish off fallen opponents with a spectacular burst of concentrated flame. They are also trained in dance and performance arts to add to their stage presence and panache. Fire Eaters assigned to arena combat often deliver consistent victories and crowd-pleasing showmanship. They in turn receive a roar of cheers from the spectators and high praise and rewards from their masters. This comparatively good treatment and star-status makes them more accepting of their life as slaves than most others. Most Splugorth, Lord Splynncryth included, maintain a small stable of Fire Eaters for their private use.

Renegade Fire Eaters are uncommon. Those few who have abandoned Atlantis are most likely to be found in hot, arid regions. A small number are found in Mexico, on either side of the vampire conflict. Central Africa also has its share of Fire Eaters who operate primarily on their own, although some have joined the ranks of small death or Phoenix cults. It is interesting to note that the Fire Eater's powers are admired by Necromancers, even though fire is harmful to zombies, mummies, and animated dead.

Powers and Abilities of the Fire Eater R.C.C.

1. Immunity to Fire: To survive the intense fires generated by the Fire Eater parasite, the subject's entire body is transmuted to be completely impervious to fire. Mega-damage plasma, magic flames, and heat and fire of all sorts do absolutely no damage to the Fire Eater. In fact, some show off by attempting to catch fire attacks directed toward them in their mouths or hands to illustrate their immunity. Eating fire provides no nourishment but is an impressive and disturbing sight.

2. Super-Fire Breath: By summoning up the magic fire burning in his belly, the Fire Eater can expel it from his mouth in a powerful destructive blast — spit out as a ball or stream of plasma.

Damage is 4D6 M.D. at level one, plus an additional 1D6 M.D. gained at each additional level of experience. Damage can be regulated in increments of 1D6 down to the minimum of 4D6 M.D. or up to full damage. Range is 200 feet (61 m), plus an additional 100 feet (30.5 m) at each additional level of experience. Bonus to strike using fire breath is +3 at level one, plus an additional +1 at levels 3, 7, and 12. No other bonuses apply. Each fire breath attack counts as one melee attack. Payload: One full meal enables the character to unleash 30 blasts. Consequently, many Fire Eaters are gluttons who consume the equivalent of 2-4 meals at any given time and snack continuously throughout the day to maintain maximum combat potential.

3. Mini-Fire Bursts: Rather than unleash the full fury of his power, the Fire Eater can spit forth comparatively tiny gouts of fire. These do only 2D6 M.D., have half the range as the Super-Fire Breath attack, and are typically used to punctuate a statement or as a warning. Payload: 90 mini-fire bursts per one full meal; three count as one Super-Fire Breath attack.

4. Flaming Fist: Rather than hurl or spit a fiery blast the character causes his fist to burst into fire. This can only occur when emotions are hot and the character desires to fight, lash out or destroy. The Flaming Fist inflicts 3D6 M.D. in addition to his or her normal punch damage.

5. Flame Aura: This power takes the Eye of Eylor's ability to create a force field around itself and its host and combines it with the Fire Eater's magic fire. The result is a fiery aura that originates from the Fire Eater's mouth and then spreads out over his face and body to completely engulf him. The fiery force field provides the character with 80 M.D.C., plus 10 M.D.C. per level of experience. The aura is continually refueled by the internal flames, regenerating damage at the rate of 2D6+10 M.D.C. per melee round. The field also inflicts 4D6 M.D. to anyone or anything the character touches and vice versa. Combustibles ignite instantly upon contact with it. Further note that, unlike the Burster, the Fire Eater has no protective aura to protect his clothing or other personal items from his own destructive flames. Thus, anything on his person at the time the Flame Aura is engaged will burn. Typically, slave owners outfit their gladiators with a special fireproof uniform, but many are allowed to wear just the flame aura.

At third level, the Fire Eater gains greater control over his flame aura, to the point that he can reshape it to appear as a swirling field around his body or to pull it away from selected parts of the body, such as the hand or arm. This enables the Bio-Borg to touch and handle things without setting them on fire, but that body part is not protected until the aura is restored to that area.

Note: A single meal allows the force field to be maintained for 12 minutes +2 per level of experience. No melee attacks are used in shaping the field, it just comes naturally to him.

6. Hellfire Scourge: The Fire Eater can draw upon his magic to project a mystical flame that invades the victim's body and attacks his spirit. Victims of this attack must save vs magic at 12 or higher or suffer from incredible angst and inner pain.

Penalties: -4 to all combat bonuses, -20% to all skills, the loss of initiative and one melee attack. This attack can only be inflicted by touch and can be used once per melee. Duration is one melee round per level of experience. This power can only be unleashed four times per hour.

7. Healing Fire Breath: In addition to being able to destroy targets with his breath, the Fire Eater is also able to heal them. By channeling his fire through his Eye of Eylor implant, he is able to change the normally lethal M.D. flames into a revitalizing life-giving energy. By breathing this flame into the mouth of an injured person, he can immediately restore to that person 4D6 Hit Points and S.D.C. or 2D4 M.D.C. If the person is in a coma, the healing warmth pervades the body, restores half the amount noted previously and gives the character a bonus of +20% to save vs Coma and Death. The Fire Eater can also direct this flame inward to heal himself with the same effect. The healing breath can only be used once per melee round.

8. P.P.E.: The Fire Eater has an available base P.P.E. of 2D6! His P.P.E. is what fuels the parasite's flames, which in turn is converted into his magical powers, consequently, P.P.E. is constantly being renewed and literally burnt up. With his P.P.E. steadily consumed by the parasite, he is prevented from using many types of Techno-Wizard devices or having it drawn off by practitioners of magic or P.P.E. vampires.

9. R.C.C. Bonuses: The Fire Eater's internal fires incinerate all foreign chemicals and microorganisms that enter his system, making him impervious to poisons, toxins, and disease. Even oxygen cannot reach his lungs, but, fortunately, he no longer needs to breathe. This energy also gives him a bonus of +20% to save vs coma/death and +2 to save vs magic. Also, add 2D4×10 to S.D.C. and +1 to P.S. All are in addition to any attribute and/or skill bonuses.

10. Penalties and Insanities: Besides having little available P.P.E., the Fire Eater also has the drawback of perpetually having smoke and flame leak from his mouth and nose. To contain it, the character must wear a specially created muzzle designed by the Splugorth Bio-Wizards. The big disadvantage to the muzzle is that it also contains all of the character's fire powers. Common practice is to sell the muzzle with the enslaved Fire Eater to enable his new owner to control him. The Fire Eater is also much warmer than normal, even with the muzzle on. This makes him easily spotted by thermo-imagers and other heat sensitive devices, including heat-seeking missiles. Sensory operators receive a bonus of +30% to their read sensory equipment skill when using heat sensors to track or locate the Fire Eater. Another downside to the internal fires is that the Fire Eater will explode into flames if he is killed. Damage from this explosion is 3D6×10 M.D., +10 M.D. per level of experience, to everything within a 20 foot (6.1 m) radius.

Having an alien creature in place of a digestive system and being transformed into a fire-breathing dynamo is traumatic for most recipients. At level one, there is a 40% chance of the Fire Eater developing an insanity. Roll percentile dice. A roll of 01-40% means the character must roll on the Bio-Borg Insanity Table. A roll of 41-00% means no insanity. Roll again at levels 4, 8, 12 and 15. Also, see the section on Physical Appearance in **Splynn Dimensional Market** for other disadvantages and penalties relating to an inhuman appearance.

Fire Eater R.C.C.

Also known as: Firebreather, Flame Spitter, and Super-Burster.

Character Note: This character can make for an excellent NPC villain or monster, but is also available as an *optional* player character at the sole discretion of the Game Master. A player character is likely to be good or selfish, and hold a grudge against the Splugorth, their minions and allies.

Like the element of fire itself, the Fire Eater can be volatile, prone to rages and often lashes out as a vicious destroyer. On the other hand, the character can be warm, comforting and offer protection or healing.

Protected by a Mega-Damage force field and armed with magic flame, the Fire Eater Bio-Borg is both fearless and devastating in combat. He rarely backs down from a challenge, but is respectful of magic and other powerful creatures. Fire Dragons, Fire Elementals, and other such creatures are immune to most of the Fire Eater's powers, but are more than capable of hurting him. Obviously, the Fire Eater watches his step around these creatures and is usually uncharacteristically humble around them.

Whether caused by some chemical imbalance involving the parasite or the character's unnaturally high temperature or some other factor, many Fire Eaters are irritable and temperamental. Many have a hair-trigger temper and will attack an antagonist at the drop of a hat. Even good Fire Eaters are easily aggravated. This can spell serious trouble in the heat of the moment, for unlike Bursters, Fire Eaters are not able to extinguish any fires they set. This means that player characters will have to be extra careful when using their powers to avoid burning down entire villages or accidentally hurting their comrades. Fortunately, the character's anger burns quickly and often ends in a short fiery outburst followed by calm and self-control. Also note that like the Sym-Killer, the Fire Eater is a living weapon who rarely uses other weapons no matter how powerful they may be.

Alignment Restrictions: None, but the majority seem to be evil or anarchist beings who use their power to dominate or intimidate others. Good characters are usually rebellious towards their inhuman masters, and are likely to try to escape.

Attribute Requirements: None. Desirable traits are a high M.E. and P.E., but just about anyone the Splugorth Bio-Wizards deem suitable can be made into a Fire Eater Bio-Borg.

Race Restrictions: Humans and S.D.C. D-Bees only. The Fire Eater parasite is not able to bond to and feed on supernatural beings, creatures of magic, or any M.D.C. being.

Physical Appearance: Except for his red glowing eyes and the smoke and flame that leaks from his mouth, the Fire Eater looks very much like he did before the transformation. The obvious elemental or demon-like fire features give the character a Horror Factor of 12 and P.B. is reduced by 30%. Note that, unlike the Kill Crazy, the Fire Eater's Eye of Eylor is implanted inside his chest and is not visible on the outside.

O.C.C. Skills:

Language: Two of Choice (+30%).

Radio: Basic (+10%)

Paramedic (+10%)

Interrogation Techniques (+10%)

Intelligence (+5%)

Performance (+10%; See **Rifts® World Book Ten: Juicer Uprising™** for this skill).

Dance (+10%)

Boxing

Body Building

Climbing (+10%)

Swimming (-5%; yes minus, the Fire Eater is uncomfortable in water).

W.P. Two of Choice.

Hand to Hand Combat: Basic; can be upgraded to Expert at the cost of one "other" skill selection, or Martial Arts (or Assassin, if evil) for the cost of two skill selections.

O.C.C. Related Skills: Select five skills at level one, plus one additional skill at levels 4, 8, and 13.

Communications: Any

Cowboy: None

Domestic: Any

Electrical: None

Espionage: Any, except forgery (+5%).

Mechanical: Basic only.

Medical: Field Surgery and Holistic Medicine only.

Military: Any, except NBC warfare or parachuting.

Physical: Any, except SCUBA (+5%).

Piloting: Any, except robots, jets, and tanks.

Pilot Related: Any, except parachuting.

Rogue: Any, except computer hacking (+5%).

Science: Math: Basic only.

Technical: Any, except computer skills.

Weapon Proficiencies: Any

Wilderness: Any (+10%)

Secondary Skills: Select three secondary skills at level one, plus one additional at levels 3, 6, 9, 12, and 15 from those listed, excluding those marked "None." These are additional areas of knowledge that do not get the advantage of the bonus listed in parentheses. All secondary skills start at the base skill level.

Standard Equipment: Usually starts with none. The character is a living weapon and has very few needs beyond food. Keep in mind that, unlike the Burster, the Fire Eater does not have an aura that protects his clothing or personal items from his flame aura, so anything he may be wearing and/or carrying on him at the time will probably be incinerated the instant he activates the Fire Aura. Consequently, most wear ponchos, cloaks and robes that can be easily discarded, along with a backpack. Many slave owners provide their Fire Eaters with gladiator garb that has been enchanted to be immune to flame, usually to enhance the warrior's appearance, not for protection.

Money: Starts with none, but Fire Eaters are among the most likely slaves to be given a small allowance. Free Fire Eaters will be able to make good money as mercenaries or arena combatants.

Slave Market Value: With both healing and destructive powers, the Fire Eater is a good value for most buyers. Their visually spectacular powers also enhances their perceived value. Average price for a Fire Eater is 5D6×100,000 credits. Slaves with combat experience, high physical attributes, and/or demonstrated showmanship can sell for up to five times that amount.

Bio-Wizardry and Cybernetics: Parasites, symbiotes, cybernetics, and bionics implanted in the body will be consumed by the Fire Eater parasite and most externally attached organisms and mechanisms will be vaporized by the flame aura. Bio-wizard additional appendages and partial reconstructions are possible, but rarely added to the Fire Eater.

Kill Crazy R.C.C.

Psychotic and murderous, the Kill Crazy is the Splugorth's version of the mentally unbalanced Crazy. The conventional Crazy is a superhuman created through the use of cybernetic brain implants which stimulate certain brain activity and chemical stimulation unleashed by the brain. This activity causes the brain to make the body perform beyond its normal capabilities. The result is enhanced strength, speed, endurance, reflexes, and healing. The conversion is called Mind Over Matter or M.O.M. for short.

Rather than use cybernetic enhancements to create this super-athlete, the Splugorth have relied on their advanced Bio-Wizardry to create a symbiotic organism to do the job. Along with this organism, they add a number of other enhancements to top of the conversion and make the subject all the more powerful. Unfortunately, the normal M.O.M. process inevitably causes its subject to lose mental stability and act wild and irrational, hence the name "Crazy." The Splugorth's Bio-Wizardry is much more advanced than human cybernetic technology, but their process also results in insanity. Bolstered by cruel treatment and physical torture, the *Kill Crazy* is even more psychotic and unstable than the normal Crazy. The result is an insane kill-ing machine with superhuman capabilities more than worthy of its name.

The root of the Kill Crazy's powers comes from a specially created symbiotic organism called the "Brain Scrambler-Enhancer." This organism is a large, bumpy thing placed atop the head of its subject, giving the individual the appearance that his brain is growing through his skull. During the Kill Crazy's creation, this brain attachment is placed on his head and slender tentacles are extended from its underbelly. These tentacles drill their way into the skull, causing unimaginable pain and severe trauma. Once fully inserted, these tentacles pull the organism very tight against the subject's head and it begins to permanently bond to its host. At the same time, chemicals are secreted through the tentacles which trigger certain parts of the subject's brain. These secretions trigger similar reactions as the mechanical M.O.M. implants do in the conventional Crazy.

One resulting effect of this process is the instilling of psionic powers. The Splugorth's Kill Crazy creation process activates much stronger psionic powers than those of the conventional Crazy. The most notable power is the ability to create a much stronger version of the Super-psionic power, Psychic Body Field. The other initial powers are in the physical category, but other psionics are gained as the Kill Crazy becomes more familiar with his abilities.

A few other Bio-Wizard enhancements are also added to the Kill Crazy for additional *improvements*. His eyes are removed and replaced by a single Eye of Eylor. This legendary component of the Splugorth's gives the Kill Crazy a wide range of vision related abilities from telescopic and magnifying eyesight to the power to see the invisible and the auras of others. In addition, the character's sense of smell and hearing are enhanced by other implants. These senses far outclass those of the regular Crazy and help to make the character more dangerous.

Despite all of its powers and abilities, the one thing that makes the Kill Crazy so dangerous is that he is totally nuts. The normal Crazy suffers from psychological disorders too, but the Kill Crazy is taken far beyond those personality quirks and bizarre fetishes. Designed from the start to be a killing machine, the Splugorth purposely cultivates the subject with predatory instincts, paranoia and unbridled aggression. This desire to kill backed by the power to carry it out makes this Bio-Borg a relentless monster, psychotic killer and an insane risk taker.

Like the Splugorth's other Bio-Borgs, potential Kill Crazies are taken from the ranks of their human and D-Bee slaves. Many are mentally acute, but physically frail before the augmentation process. A high Mental Endurance is critical to the subject's ability to survive the process with most of his intelligence intact, while his poor physical traits are raised to superhuman levels. Before the process, this kind of slave would ordinarily have sold for a very low price, but after being transformed into a Kill Crazy, the value of this once pitiful slave shoots to levels equal to that of the T-men. Thus, the Splugorth are able to increase their profits on these otherwise low quality slaves.

The dangers in purchasing a Kill Crazy are immediately apparent — they are insane killers. But the cunning Splugorth have turned this into their biggest selling point. Kill Crazies draw in big crowds in the blood sport arenas and they make ideal assassins, bodyguards and henchmen willing to kill anyone

they are pointed toward. However, their erratic behavior often leads to unexpected developments. A Kill Crazy may attack things, like trees, for no reason, and many succumb to berserker rages. Others must be watched constantly, lest they wander off to rape and pillage, or torture some unsuspecting soul or torment the house pet. They may set fires, steal, or the words "credit card" (or anything) may send the Bio-Borg into a murderous rage. Others are comparatively quiet and obedient, except they hear voices in their heads and do as they tell them to do. Owners must work their way around these problems or risk losing control of their slaves. When it comes to the Kill Crazy, one lapse of control could mean the difference between life and death.

Typically, rogues and renegades do not last long on their own. A Kill Crazy may be smart and cunning, but he is also handicapped by his insanities. Many times a freed Kill Crazy will attack his enslavers rather than flee or seek refuge, despite the odds against him. Still, a few have managed to escape captivity and prosper. Many are found in the Preserves, purposely left there to serve as hunting game and "wild cards" to make hunts more unpredictable and adventurous. Of these, a good number work their way into the Refuge every year. From there, some move on to the Demon Sea, where they are Rifted to the far corners of the planet and sometimes the Megaverse. A good number have been Rifted to South America, where they compete heavily with the Ultra-Crazies. Many are also found in Europe, where they seem attracted to the Tree of Darkness. Here, they have developed a strong rivalry with the M.O.M. enhanced creations of Mindwerks. A few have been captured and dissected by the Angel of Death, but she has made no progress in studying them.

Powers and Bonuses of the Kill Crazy R.C.C.

1. Super Endurance: Although not elevated to supernatural levels, the Kill Crazy is much tougher and resistant to fatigue than ordinary humans and D-Bees.

Base S.D.C. is 4D6×10, plus bonuses from physical skills. Also add 6D6 Hit Points and +1D6 to the P.E. attribute. The Kill Crazy can lift and carry twice as much as a normal person of equivalent strength and endurance and lasts ten times as long before suffering from fatigue. He normally requires only four hours of sleep a night, but can remain active and fully awake for up to 72 hours without any obvious signs of fatigue.

2. Increased Strength: Add 2D6 to the P.S. attribute. Minimum P.S. is 24, adjust the P.S. to 24 if lower. Note that despite the mystical nature of the transformation, the character's P.S. attribute is NOT considered to be supernatural.

3. Increased Speed: Add 4D6 to the Spd. attribute. The Kill Crazy is able to leap up to 20 feet (6.1 m) across or 15 feet (4.6 m) high after a short run. Reduce by half from a dead stop.

4. Heightened Reflexes and Agility: Add 1D6 to the P.P. attribute. Minimum P.P. is 17, adjust the P.P. to 17 if lower. Additional combat bonuses from the faster reflexes and increased agility are included in the R.C.C. bonuses.

5. Supernatural Senses: The Kill Crazy's eyes have been replaced by a single Eye of Eylor placed in the center of where the real eyes were. The Eye of Eylor provides the character with perfect 20/20 vision, nightvision 600 feet (183 m), telescopic vision 6000 feet (1800 m), and magnification to the 300th power. It also gives him the following magic and psionic senses: See

Aura, See the Invisible, Sense Magic, and See P.P.E./mystic energy. All Eye of Eylor abilities are usable without limit or P.P.E. or I.S.P. cost.

Bio-Wizard enhanced senses of hearing and smell. Sounds as soft as a whisper (10 decibels) can be heard up to 75 feet (22.9 m) away and normal conversation (around 30 decibels) can be heard 300 feet (90 m) away. Enhanced olfactory capabilities allow the Kill Crazy to recognize specific scents at 70%, track by smell at 70%, recognize poison at 80%, and detect changes in the air at 80%.

6. Enhanced Healing and Bio-Regeneration: The Kill Crazy normally heals three times as fast as normal humans and D-Bees. Furthermore, if he has suffered any injury, he can slip into a healing trance similar to the psionic power of Bio-Regeneration. During this trance, the character is restored of 2D6 Hit Points and 4D6 S.D.C. after 2D4 minutes and any open wounds are closed. An extended trance of two hours will restore all S.D.C. and an additional 6D6 hit points. The character is also nearly immune to pain. He will be able to fight at peak performance even when reduced to a mere ten Hit Points and can even ignore pain induced by magic and psionic means, suffering only half the penalties.

7. Psionic Powers: Considered to be a Major Psionic, the Kill Crazy's main power is the ability to create a personal Telekinetic Body Field. It provides protection against all forms of physical harm for 5 minutes per level of experience, but will allow magic, psionic, and gas attacks to pass through unhindered. M.D.C. is 50 plus 10 per level of experience and costs 10 I.S.P. to activate. The field cuts off the character's sense of touch, inflicting a penalty of -15% to skills that require manual dexterity, such as pick pockets, palming, demolitions, etc. This is quite a contrast from the normal Crazy's hyper tactile senses.

Other psionics include *Telekinetic Leap, Telekinesis (Super)* and a choice of three Physical Psi-Powers at level one plus one additional power selected from the Healing or Physical categories at levels 3, 6, and 12.

8. I.S.P.: Initial I.S.P. is the M.E. attribute number times three. Add 2D4+2 I.S.P. at each additional level of experience. Considered to be a Major Psychic and requires a roll of 12 or higher to save against psionic attack, plus bonuses.

9. P.P.E.: 6D6+20. The augmentation increases the character's normal P.P.E. and the Eye of Eylor adds the additional 20.

10. R.C.C. Bonuses: Add one additional attack per melee, +4 to initiative, +1 to parry, +2 to dodge, +4 to roll with punch/impact, +2 to save vs psionics, +4 to save vs poisons, gases, and other toxins, +4 to save vs Horror Factor, +6 to save vs mind control, and +4 to save vs possession, all in addition to attribute and skill bonuses.

11. Penalties and Insanities: All Kill Crazies are psychotics who suffer from mild paranoia, aggression, and a lust to hurt and kill. Also roll once on the Obsession Table, and once on the Phobia Table.

At level four roll once on the *Crazy Hero Table* listed on page 57 in the **Rifts® RPG**.

At level 9 the character begins to suffer from delusions and schizophrenia.

In addition, roll once on the Bio-Borg insanity table at levels 5, 10 and 15.

Kill Crazy Bio-Borg R.C.C.

Also known as: Bio-Wizard Crazy, Sym-psycho (as in symbiotic psycho), and K.C.'s

Character Note: Ideal as an NPC villain or monster, but also available as an *optional* player character at the sole discretion of the Game Master. The Kill Crazy is not recommended as a player character. He will always be insane and can never rise to an alignment higher than Unprincipled or Anarchist. His insanities will be a constant source of problems and may lead to unwelcome conflict or unnecessary violence. He may mistake nonthreatening bystanders for potential threats or children for hated enemies. In any event, the character will have to be kept under close watch by his comrades for their own safety, and the safety of innocent bystanders, as well as that of the character.

If allowed as a player character, the player will have to play in character and act out all of his insanities. If the other players try to keep weapons out of his reach or otherwise restrain his activities, the player should accept this as a consequence of playing such an unstable and dangerous character and not take it personally, although his character may. His allies may even be forced to shoot him down like a mad dog if they perceive him to be too dangerous a threat to be allowed to live. This should also be grudgingly accepted as a consequence of playing the Kill Crazy.

Alignment Restrictions: Selfish or evil. The most common alignments are Anarchist, Miscreant and Diabolic. Only an insanity can cause alignment reversal or ardent pacifism or goodness, turning a vicious Kill Crazy into a steadfast champion of light or a harmless kook.

Attribute Requirements: Must start with an M.E. 12 or higher, but the augmentation process will reduce that M.E. by 2D4 points. Physical attributes are usually low since they are enhanced by the symbiote anyway. Besides, slaves in good physical condition sell well without augmentation.

Race Restrictions: Humans and S.D.C. D-Bees only! The *Brain Scrambler-Enhancer* will not work on M.D.C. creatures, supernatural beings, or creatures of magic.

Physical Appearance: The character's body is a toned and muscular version of his original form with a large bulbous head that looks like his brain has expanded through his skull. He also has a single large eye in place of his two natural ones. These deformities coupled with his psychotic behavior gives the Kill Crazy a Horror Factor of 13 and his P.B. and M.A. attributes are reduced by half.

O.C.C. Skills:
Language: Two of choice (+30%)
Radio: Basic (+10%)
Tracking (+20%)
Wilderness Survival (+30%)
Boxing
Gymnastics (+10%)
Acrobatics (+5%)
Climbing (+10%)
Swimming (+5%)
Prowl (+5%)
W.P. Knife
W.P. Sword
W.P. Three of choice (any).
Hand to Hand Combat: Assassin.

O.C.C. Related Skills: Select four skills at level one, plus one additional skill at levels 4, 8, and 13.
Communications: Any
Cowboy: None
Domestic: Any
Electrical: None
Espionage: Any (+5%)
Mechanical: Basic and automotive only.
Medical: First Aid only.
Military: Any, except parachuting, NBC warfare, or any demolitions skills.
Physical: Any (+5% where applicable).
Piloting: Any, except robots, jets, or tanks.
Pilot Related: Any, except parachuting.
Rogue: Any, except seduction and computer hacking (+5%).
Science: Math Basic only.
Technical: Any, except literacy or computer skills.
Weapon Proficiencies: Any
Wilderness: Any (+10%)

Secondary Skills: Select two Secondary Skills at levels 1, 3, 6, 9, and 12 from those listed, excluding those marked "None." These are additional areas of knowledge that do not get the advantage of the bonus listed in parentheses. All secondary skills start at the base skill level.

Standard Equipment: As slaves, the Kill Crazy starts out with very little. Begins with one set of warrior garb, light body armor, a water skin, a backpack, ammo-belt, and three weapons of choice. Free ones can accumulate a large amount of equipment, although most travel light and tend to focus on weapons.

Money: Starts with none.

Slave Market Value: A hot seller despite, or possibly because, of their instability. The Kill Crazy has an average selling price of 500,000 to 1.5 million credits. Experienced warriors and/or those without serious instabilities sell for two times as much, sometimes more.

Bio-Wizardry and Cybernetics: No additional augmentation is possible because the other symbiotes and parasites interfere with the brain augmentation and powers.

Sym-Killer R.C.C.

"What do you want a Maxi-Man for? Sure, they can make magic weapons and supernatural monsters appear out of nowhere, but they're not anywhere intimidating enough. Who's afraid of a half-naked human covered with little pictures, anyway? Okay, I've seen them in action with their magic weapons and powers and the monsters they can pull out of thin air. They are versatile, all right, so I guess if you're looking for tricks and magic those human freaks are worth your money. But, when you get serious about buying a bloodthirsty killer whose very appearance will strike fear into your enemies, come back and I'll sell you a Sym-Killer."

— A "pitch" from a Bio-Borg dealer trying to keep yet another potential customer from leaving in search of a Tattooed-Man

Swift and silent, strong and rugged, the Sym-Killer is the pinnacle of Bio-Wizard technology. He is powerful enough to go toe to toe with the Tattooed Maxi-Man and, therefore, is a potent warrior. As with the Splugorth Conservators, Powerlords, and Slavers, Bio-Wizard transmutation takes the potential Sym-Killer and transforms him from a mere mortal to a supernatural powerhouse. Myriad types of Bio-Wizard transmutations, additional appendages, symbiotic unions and a grueling training regimen all serve to create a near invincible living weapon.

The potential Sym-Killer is usually selected from the Splugorth's vast stable of tame, domesticated slaves and captured children who are young enough that they can be molded into loyal slaves. These manageable human, Ogre, and D-Bee candidates for Sym-Killer conversion are put through a set of rigorous tests to see if they are able to withstand the physical and mental stress that accompanies the transformation. Roughly half of the chosen do not survive the transmutation process. The ones who do are transformed into the superhuman Sym-Killers.

Enhanced strength and speed enable the Sym-Killer to strike with powerful Mega-Damage punches and move like a whirlwind. A Chest Amalgamate symbiote transforms the subject into an M.D.C. creature and further enhances his reflexes and endurance. An Elom symbiote offers the added protection of an M.D.C. force field and built-in long-range offensive capabilities. A pair of vicious forearm blades and a prehensile tail with a retractable poison-filled stinger provide additional methods of attack in combat. The transformation is completed when the symbiote called the Sym-Killer Masque is attached. Armed with his sharp claws, venomous tail, and the power to release blasts of electromagnetic energy anywhere from his body, the Sym-Killer is able to tackle and destroy even multiple opponents to a young dragon with relative ease.

Raised into a life of slavery from an early age and subjected to years of training and conditioning, the Sym-Killer is typically highly skilled, disciplined and obedient, like a loyal and capable Special Forces Soldier. Most learn to accept the monster they have become and to enjoy the power, fear and prestige they possess as a Sym-Killer. Most remain in the service of the Splugorth and their minions as an elite slave force equal to, if not higher than, the Atorian Warrior Women. After a few hundred years of service, the most capable, loyal and long-lived may even earn their freedom and be elevated to the rank of true Minion of Splugorth. A most coveted and honored position.

The years of conditioning and training before the transmutation, combined with being well treated and highly respected or feared (more than any other Bio-Borg), the Sym-Killer is usually well adjusted to its lifestyle and is less prone to mental instability or rebellion. Consequently, rogue Sym-Killers are rare. Even those assigned on solo missions or to infiltrate a group of heroes are unlikely to turn on their masters. The few who rebel are considered dangerous renegades to be hunted down and slain on sight. Reorientation is not an option. A tiny handful of renegades are found among the Liberated Underground. Likewise, a dozen or two are scattered around the world in areas far from Atlantis, especially in combat regions and war zones. In Europe, a trio is said to fight against the Gargoyle and Brodkil Empires, although they are not allied with the NGR. A few are also said to be found in the western part of old Canada with two

individuals counted among the demons of Calgary. A dozen are said to prosper in China and other parts of Asia, although nobody knows for certain.

Powers and Abilities of the Sym-Killer R.C.C.

1. M.D.C. Transformation: Linked to the Chest Amalgamate symbiote and further enhanced by Bio-Wizard transmutation, the Sym-Killer is a tough M.D.C. creature with 4D4×10+60 M.D.C. The character's Elom symbiote which is attached to the back of his neck has 1D6x10 M.D.C. of its own (typically -4 to target and strike by an opponent even with a called shot, and often covered/protected by additional armor or shielding).

2. Supernatural Strength: The monster has a supernatural P.S. of 40+1D6; no other bonuses apply.

Damage is 6D6 S.D.C. on a restrained punch, 5D6 M.D. on a full strength punch or kick, and 1D6×10 M.D. on a power punch. A swat from the stinger also does 5D6 M.D. punch damage.

3. Enhanced Endurance and Resistance: The Chest Amalgamate and transmutation in the Bio-Wizard chamber provides the Sym-Killer with supernatural endurance. Raise the character's P.E. attribute to 21; no other bonuses apply. Additionally, he *never* suffers from fatigue and requires only two hours of sleep per night.

Heals at a rate of 4D6 M.D.C. per hour and is impervious to pain, poisons, drugs, gases, and disease. In addition, the Elom symbiote makes him impervious to all electrical attacks, including ley line bolts. It also makes him resistant to magic and prevents practitioners of magic and P.P.E. vampires from drawing on his P.P.E. Saving throw bonuses are listed under R.C.C. bonuses.

4. Enhanced Speed and Agility: The Sym-Killer has incredible speed and agility approaching the level of a Juicer. Increase the P.P. attribute to 16+1D6 and double the Spd attribute. In addition, the Sym-Killer can leap a distance of 30 feet (9.1 m) across and 15 feet (4.6 m) upward after a short run. Reduce the distances by half if leaping from a dead stop. Combat bonuses are listed under R.C.C. bonuses.

5. Electromagnetic Field and Discharge: The Elom symbiote taps into and feeds upon the character's natural electromagnetic field and provides him with Mega-Damage protection and offensive abilities. Up to 12 times a day, for periods of time no longer than 20 minutes each, the Elom can surround its host with an electromagnetic force field that protects with 60 M.D.C. Once the field's M.D.C. is depleted, another field can be generated within one melee round.

The Elom can also release this energy from its host's body in the form of M.D. electromagnetic discharges. Directed blasts inflict up to 6D6 M.D. and have a range of 2000 feet (610 m). Area discharges can be released to inflict up to 2D6 M.D. to everything within a 20 foot (6.1 m) radius around the Sym-Killer. The damage of both discharges can be regulated in increments of 1D6. The bonus to strike with the directed blast is +3 and no other bonuses apply. Two discharges can be released per melee round and count as one of the monster's melee actions/attacks.

6. Poisonous Bite Attack: In addition, the Chest Amalgamate symbiote has a monstrous maw with a *second mouth* on the end of a tentacle. Both are capable of biting attacks and can inject venom into their victims.

The tentacle can inflict 2D6 S.D.C. on a restrained strike, 1D6 M.D. on a full strength strike, or 1D4 M.D. with a bite attack plus 1D4x10 S.D.C. (or 1D4 M.D. to fellow Mega-Damage beings) from the venom.

The large mouth bites to inflict 1D6×10 S.D.C. on a restrained nip, or 2D6 M.D. with a bite, plus 1D6×10 S.D.C. from the venom to mortal beings or 1D6 M.D. to Mega-Damage creatures.

Note: The bite action counts as one melee attack, the injection of venom counts as another. Victims automatically get to roll to save vs lethal poison (14 or higher). A successful save means the victim takes only one point of damage.

7. Retractable Forearm Blades, Joint Spikes, and Prehensile Tail: Implanted within each arm of the Sym-Killer are three retractable blades. They extend from their forearm housings through the top of the hand and have a reach of two feet (0.6 m) each. Mega-Damage is 1D6 per blade, so if all three are ex-

tended, they do 3D6 M.D. plus normal supernatural P.S. punch damage. In addition, wicked spikes protrude from the Sym-Killer's shoulders, elbows, and kneecaps. 1D6 M.D. is added to punch damage from the elbow and knee spikes, while the shoulder spikes add 1D6 M.D. to the Sym-Killer's body tackle (normally 1D4 M.D. plus knock-down penalties).

Attached to his spine is a six foot long prehensile tail. On the tip of that tail is a sharp stinger capable of injecting a debilitating toxin into a victim. The tail itself is +1 to strike, +3 to dodge, +4 to entangle, and adds a bonus of +10% to climb and +5% to balance. Damage inflicted by the tail is 1D6 with a whip attack or 2D6 with the stinger strike plus one of the following toxins. Select only one for the character. Victims need to save vs lethal poison at 14 or higher to avoid damage and/or penalties.

Poison: Inflicts an additional 2D6×10 S.D.C. from the venom to mortal beings or 2D6 M.D. to Mega-Damage creatures, plus

60

the victim becomes ill and loses one attack per melee round and is -2 on all combat rolls for 3D6 minutes.

Convulsion Toxin: The victim suffers from severe convulsions for 2D4 melee rounds. He suffers 2D6 points of damage (S.D.C. or M.D. depending on the nature of the victim) and cannot attack or defend against attacks for the duration, except to crawl away. Speed is reduced by half. Note that while convulsing, the gyrations make him -2 to strike by attackers and impossible to restrain by less than two or three people.

Paralysis Toxin: The victim's nervous system is temporarily disrupted, preventing movement. The victim collapses to the ground, unable to move or speak for 1D4+1 minutes and is completely vulnerable to attack. Only psionic power (if the victim has any) can be used.

8. The Sym-Killer Masque: This is the bizarre symbiote that turns the subject into a Sym-Killer. It totally enwraps the head and face, completely wiping away all traces of the subject's former humanity. It provides its host with nightvision 500 feet (152.4 m) and protection against hostile environments, including the ability to breathe without air. This enables him to operate underwater, through magic fumes, and even in a vacuum without hindrance. It also protects the host's head, providing it with 2D4×10+20 M.D.C.

The only drawback is that it completely covers the mouth, preventing the Sym-Killer from eating normally. To sustain himself, he must rely on his Chest Amalgamate to do all the eating for him; a rather disgusting sight. The Masque is altered to look monstrous, usually skull-like or demonic, which adds greatly to the Sym-Killer's Horror Factor (and consumer appeal — the customers are monsters themselves, after all).

9. Prolonged Life: The Sym-Killer has an amazing life span of 1D6x100+500 years! This means with time and experience, these monsters can attain levels well beyond 15th. However, because they are "new" creations of the Splugorth, the typical Sym-Killer ranges from level 1-8.

10. R.C.C. Bonuses: Four attacks per melee round (includes the boxing bonus) +1 at levels 2, 4, 6, 9, 12, 16 and 20. Also add 2D6x10 pounds (9 to 54 kg) to the character's weight and one foot (0.3 m) to his original height.

+4 to initiative, +5 to strike, +6 to parry, +3 to dodge, +3 to disarm, +2 to entangle, +4 to roll with impact, +5 to save vs magic, +6 to save vs possession, +7 to save vs Horror Factor, +2 to save vs psionic attack and mind control, +22% to save vs coma/death, and the various immunities listed above. These are in addition to attribute and skill bonuses.

Combat moves include all types of kicks, paired weapons/claws, Judo-Style throw, critical strike (double damage) or knockout/stun on a natural roll of 18, 19 or 20.

11. Penalties and Insanities: The main drawback to the Sym-Killer is the fact that the subject becomes a hideous monster, with a second carnivorous monster attached to his chest (the Chest Amalgamate). The Chest Amalgamate adds 100 lbs (160 kg) to the character's weight and requires blood to feed on from time to time. Also, his Elom symbiote is a potential weak point. Killing it will destroy the Sym-Killer's electromagnetic powers and may cause permanent damage. Roll on the Surgery Penalty Table for organism attached to the body, if the Elom is killed. If either the Chest Amalgamate or Masque symbiote is

killed, don't bother rolling on the table; the host will die with it. See the section on Physical Appearance for other disadvantages and penalties relating to inhuman appearance in the **Splynn Dimensional Market™** World Book.

The Sym-Killer may also suffer from psychological problems, but these typically come later in life. To determine whether the character has an insanity or not, roll the percentile dice. At level one, there is a 20% chance of suffering from insanity. A roll of 1-20% means rolling on the Bio-Borg Insanity Table. A roll of 21-00% means no insanity. Roll again to determine any possible insanities at levels four, nine, and fifteen.

Sym-Killer Bio-Borg R.C.C.

Also known as: Sym-Slayer and Scorpion Beast because of its stinging tail and claws.

Character Note: Ideal as an NPC villain or monster, but also available as an *optional* player character at the sole discretion of the Game Master. Any player character will be evil or selfish, with unprincipled being the best alignment possible.

Trained at an early age to accept the Splugorth as their masters, the Sym-Killer is usually very loyal and dedicated towards them. Thus, it is the rare renegade who will try to escape from his masters, and even renegades regard the Splugorth and their minions with respect. Regardless of whether he is free or not, the Sym-Killer is well versed in the arts of war and has been trained to be a quick and effective warrior. His first resort will often be violence and he is merciless in combat. The character tends to rely heavily on abilities and fighting skills rather than machines. Unarmed combat is usually preferred over using weapons of any sort no matter how powerful, unless it is a magical weapon.

A renegade Sym-Killer with good friends and allies can re-adjust quite well to a life of adventure, but rarely in a civilized city environment. Most have already accepted their appearance and inhuman abilities and expect others to do the same. Even when faced with occasional prejudice, a Sym-Killer tends to regard fear of him to be a good thing — often mistaking fear for genuine respect. These Bio-Borgs are taught to be self-reliant, so a life of reclusiveness, being on the run and war will not cause any problems or emotional distress. Consequently, many renegade Sym-Killers found in the wilderness operate alone and thrive under these conditions.

Alignment Restrictions: Any, but usually evil with 50% Aberrant, 20% Miscreant, and 15% Diabolic. Good Sym-Killers do exist, but, like the Coalition soldier, this warrior may be fanatically loyal towards his leaders and masters and will carry out their bidding no matter what.

Attribute Requirements: M.E. and P.E. 12 or higher. A high I.Q. (9 or better) is strongly recommended, but not required. Physical attributes are modified by magic transmutation and the use of symbiotes.

Race Restrictions: Humans and S.D.C. D-Bees only! Supernatural beings, creatures of magic, and M.D.C. D-Bees can not be turned into the Sym-Killer.

Physical Appearance: With a giant hungry mouth on his chest with a second mouth on a tentacle extending from it, organic blades shooting from his forearms, spikes jutting from his joints, and a giant prehensile tail with a stinger on the end, the Sym-Killer is definitely a very inhuman looking "thing."

Added to that is a face totally obscured by the macabre Sym-Killer Masque and the creature looks absolutely atrocious. P.B. is reduced to 1D4 and Horror Factor is 15.

O.C.C. Skills:

Language: Two of Choice (+30%)

Math: Basic (+5%)

Radio: Basic (+10%)

Military Etiquette (+15%)

Camouflage (+10%)

Intelligence (+10%)

Tracking (+15%)

Wilderness Survival (+10%)

Boxing

Wrestling

Athletics (General)

Climbing (+10%)

Swimming (+5%)

W.P. Sword (include retractable arm blades)

W.P. Three of Choice (any)

Hand to Hand Combat: Effectively Martial Arts, but see R.C.C. bonuses from specialized combat training.

O.C.C. Related Skills: Select five skills at level one, plus one additional skill at levels 4, 8, and 13.

Communications: Any (+5%)

Cowboy: None

Domestic: Any

Electrical: Basic only.

Espionage: Any (+10%)

Mechanical: Basic only.

Medical: None

Military: Any, except NBC warfare, parachuting, or any demolitions

Physical: Any (+5% where applicable)

Piloting: Any, except robots, jets, or tanks

Pilot Related: Any, except parachuting

Rogue: Any (+5%)

Science: None

Technical: Any (+10%)

Weapon Proficiencies: Any

Wilderness: Any (+10%)

Secondary Skills: Select two Secondary Skills at levels 1, 3, 6, 9, 12, and 15 from those listed, excluding those marked "None." These are additional areas of knowledge that do not get the advantage of the bonus listed in parentheses. All secondary skills start at the base skill level.

Standard Equipment: Usually starts out with no equipment since he has very little need for armor, weapons, or other equipment. Individual slave masters may equip their slaves with whatever items they may need. Loyal minions are given whatever equipment they may need as deemed necessary by their masters and those who serve the Splugorth are likely to have at one or two lesser to mid-level magic weapon.

Money: Starts with none. Even most loyal slaves and minions do not receive an allowance. The few that do receive an allowance are usually allotted no more than 1D6×10 credits a week. Free characters can accumulate a fortune, although most Sym-Killers crave action and adventure not money.

Slave Market Value: As the most powerful and comparatively rare (the Splugorth allow only a tiny number to be sold at the slave markets), the Sym-Killer is also the most valuable. The usual price is 4-8 million credits, but experienced warriors can sell for 20 million or more.

Bio-Wizardry and Cybernetics: None, other than those gained by conversion into a Sym-Killer. Cybernetic and bionic implants are rejected by the Sym-Killer's body and expelled within an hour.

Bio-Borg™ Experience Tables

Bio-Leech

1 0,000-2,100
2 2,101-4,200
3 4,201-8,400
4 8,401-17,200
5 17,201-25,400
6 25,401-35,800
7 35,801-55,000
8 55,001-80,000
9 80,001-110,000
10 110,001-150,000
11 150,001-200,000
12 200,001-250,000
13 250,001-380,000
14 380,001-480,000
15 480,001-600,000

Fire Eater

1 0,000-2,150
2 2,151-4,300
3 4,301-8,600
4 8,601-17,200
5 17,201-25,500
6 25,501-36,000
7 36,001-52,000
8 52,001-73,000
9 73,001-100,000
10 100,001-150,000
11 150,001-200,000
12 200,001-275,000
13 275,001-350,000
14 350,001-425,000
15 425,001-525,000

Kill Crazy

1 0,000-2,200
2 2,201-4,400
3 4,401-9,000
4 9,001-19,000
5 19,001-28,000
6 28,001-40,000
7 40,001-60,000
8 60,001-80,000
9 80,001-110,000
10 110,001-160,000
11 160,001-225,000
12 225,001-300,000
13 300,001-375,000
14 375,001-450,000
15 450,001-550,000

Sym-Killer

1 0,000-2,400
2 2,401-4,800
3 4,801-10,400
4 10,401-22,200
5 22,201-34,000
6 34,001-50,000
7 50,001-80,000
8 80,001-120,000
9 120,001-160,000
10 160,001-200,000
11 200,001-250,000
12 250,001-300,000
13 300,001-400,000
14 400,001-500,000
15 500,001-600,000
16 600,001-800,000
17 800,001-1,000,000
18 1,000,001-1,250,000
19 1,250,001-1,500,000
20 1,500,001-2,000,000
21 2,000,001-2,500,000
22 2,500,001-3,000,000
23 3,000,001-3,500,000
24 3,500,001-4,000,000
25 4,000,001-4,500,000

Copyright 1997 Kevin Siembieda

Rifter Subscription

Don't become a slobbering beast driven mad because you're afraid you'll miss an issue of **The Rifter**™ Subscribe and get every issue delivered to your doorstep in a protective cardboard envelope.

One Year (four issues) — Only $25.00

That's right, only 25 bucks! Postage and handling included. That's over 500 pages of source material, fun and inspiration for an incredible bargain. Of course, every issue should be available from fine stores everywhere — and stores need your support.

Each issue will be 96 to 128 pages (typically the latter).

Published quarterly with a cover price of $7.95 (a bargain at that price).

Contributing authors will include *Kevin Siembieda, Eric Wujcik, Wayne Breaux Jr., Jolly Blackburn* and other Palladium notables.

What Exactly is The Rifter™?

Well, flipping through this issue should give you a fairly good idea, but every issue will be different.

Really, there has never been anything like it.

The Rifter is a synthesis of a sourcebook, Game Master's guide, a magazine and talent show — a fan forum.

The Rifter™ is like a sourcebook because it will include a ton of role-playing source material (optional and official). This will include New O.C.C.s, NPC heroes, NPC villains, new powers and abilities, weapons, adventure settings, adventures and adventure ideas, and Hook, Line and Sinkers™.

The Rifter™ is like a G.M.'s guide because it will include special articles and tips on role-playing, how to handle common problems, how to build an adventure and so on.

The Rifter™ **is like a magazine because** it will come out four or five times a year (we're shooting for a regular quarterly release schedule), and because it will feature Palladium news, advertisements, serial articles and continuing features.

Most importantly, The Rifter™ **is a forum for Palladium's Fans**. At least half of each issue will be text and material taken (with permission) from the Web, as well as fan contributions made especially for **The Rifter**™. We get tons of fan submissions that are pretty good, but not good enough for publication as an entire sourcebook. In other cases, the submission is something clever and cool, but only a few pages long. There's lots of cool stuff on the Internet, but you must have a computer and Internet access, something a lot of fans just don't have.

The Rifter™ will reprint some of those "Web-Works™" allowing fans (and the world at large) to get a glimpse of their genius. It is one more avenue in which fans and professionals alike can share their visions of role-playing and the Palladium Megaverse with other fans. It's a chance to get published, get a little cash, get your name in lights (well, in print) and have fun.

This also means, more than any RPG publication ever produced, **The Rifter**™ is yours. Yours to present and share ideas. Yours to help shape and mold. Yours to share.

Why call it The Rifter™? Because each issue will span the Palladium Megaverse of games, adventures and ideas. Each issue will publish features from people across the Web and beyond! But mainly because each and every one of us, from game designer and publisher, to Joe Gamer, traverses the Megaverse™ every time they read an RPG or play in a role-playing game. We travel the infinite realm of the imagination, hopping from one world to the next — building one world to the next. Time and space are meaningless in our imaginations as we *Rift* from one place and time to another.

Palladium Books Inc.   **12455 Universal Drive**
Rifter Dept.   **Taylor, MI 48180**

The Hammer of the Forge

By James M.G. Cannon

Chapter Nine
Ruminations

There are still planets in the United Worlds of Warlock that celebrate Defender's Day every standard year, including a full quarter of the Draconid Hub. The festivities are as varied as the cultures that celebrate them, from the parades and fireworks of the Hub Worlds, to the Bardic Regalia of Legolas, to the bloody arenas of Ogretopia. The one thing they all have in common is a cessation of all hostilities among the celebrants, no matter how grave or petty they might be, so that all sentient beings can engage in a thanksgiving for their present liberty.

Today, these celebrations have a festive, light-hearted and often comedic air, but a hundred and fifty years ago the festivals were spontaneous and heartfelt. The first Defender's Day was a haphazard event, begun only hours after the defeat of Quajinn Huo's fleet near the Asteroid Barrier of the Draconid Hub, a culmination of months of struggle against the tyrant wizard who had conquered and razed nearly twenty worlds in the UWW despite concerted efforts to defeat him. It took the combined might of several brave heroes, among them the illustrious Doctor Abbot, the Wolfen shaman Koguk, the dark sorceress Callista, and the then fledgling Cosmo-Knight Lothar of Motherhome, to bring a close to Quajinn Huo's bid for power. Even so, the heroes were nearly overcome until a flight of Dwarven Ironships arrived to bolster the defenders at the behest of no less a personage than Inglix the Mad himself.

By day's end, Quajinn Huo's fleet lay scattered across the Asteroid Barrier and the systems he had conquered were free. While spontaneous celebrations erupted across the quadrant, and the heroes took stock, the dread wizard himself managed to escape. He bolted for the safety of Center, and only Lothar and Koguk seemed interested in pursuing him.

— "Defender's Day," A History of the United Worlds of Warlock, Third Edition

Friar nudged the gravsledge with a boot, and the heavy unit slid forward, another meter closer to the customs station. She fingered the hilt of her energy knife, a motion Elias was beginning to recognize as indicative of anxiety. Which meant the sweat beading on her pale brow was not due to the temperature; Elias knew that coming from a frigid world, Friar was inured to cold and uncomfortable whenever the mercury climbed past 15 degrees Celsius, as it often did on Center. He also knew her black and cobalt flightsuit was wired to keep her cool, and it appeared as though her nerves were starting to fray.

Elias suppressed a grimace. Now would be the worst possible time for anything to go wrong. The last fifteen hours had been a whirlwind of activity as he pulled together the team he had assembled, purchased the last few bits of gear for the mission, and fitted the ship for an extended trip. The rest of the team, the Relogian weapons expert Hector, the Kisent pilot Orix, and the Oni martial artist Tatsuda were already aboard the ship, running a pre-flight check and securing the last of the equipment in the hold.

Elias and Friar would be the last ones on the ship. They had to be, in order to ensure Quajinn Huo made it aboard.

Elias did frown finally, and Friar straightened unconsciously. She was not the target of his ire, however, but rather the Draconid sorcerer in cold storage on the sledge.

Elias had explained the plan a dozen times to Quajinn, and the Draconid seemed wary of the risks but he also seemed to understand they were necessary. Yet, when it finally came time to put the plan in action, Quajinn had balked. Most of the last fifteen hours had been used by Elias to convince Quajinn to go through with it. It was the only way, as far as the former Guardsman could see.

A century and a half ago, when Lothar of Motherhome and Koguk the Wolfen shaman had tracked Quajinn Huo to Center, the Draconid had been able to elude them in the nearly limitless expanse of the great city. They searched for him for months, and even managed to find him on a few occasions, but after a brief skirmish, Quajinn would always escape. Always.

While Quajinn searched for a way to eliminate his pursuers, the two Wolfen, tiring of the chase, discovered a way to enforce a small measure of justice upon the wizard. Koguk cast a Curse, an ancient and powerful rite practiced by his people, fueling the magic with the almost limitless energy of Lothar's cosmically powered body. The Curse bound Quajinn Huo to Center for seven times seven hundred years, with the stipulation that no spell could free him and the only way he could pass through the gates of Center before the time was up would be as a corpse. It was much more poetic in the original Wolfen tongue, Elias had been told, but no matter what language you used, it read pretty much the same. Quajinn Huo, former trigalactic despot, was a prisoner of Center.

In one hundred and fifty years, Quajinn had not found the loophole. And not for lack of trying; he had consulted other wizards from a thousand worlds and dimensions, studied ancient tome after ancient tome, bargained with the Splugorth. Nothing he tried worked. Not surprising, in Elias' opinion. Quajinn, like Koguk the Shaman, thought like a wizard. If the Curse said no spell could save the Draconid, than no spell could save him.

There were ways around that seemingly insurmountable stipulation, though. And as Elias saw it, Friar the Klikita was the key. An aberration of her birth had gifted her with a cryokinesis, enabling her to manipulate ambient temperatures to a fine degree, even to the point of conjuring ice and snow, or freezing a sentient in its tracks. Friar would freeze Quajinn, slowing his life signs down so that he would appear dead — and if that still didn't work, she could finish him off and then revive him on the ship. A simple plan. A good plan.

But Quajinn Huo was as paranoid as a Naruni client with unpaid bills. While frozen, he would be powerless, unaware of his surroundings and unable to act. He didn't trust Elias or Friar to bring him out of the freeze at all, and claimed they would sell him to the UWW for a planet's ransom. No amount of assurances from Elias would sway him, no matter how many times Elias told him he was needed to crush Lothar. Elias made the miscalculation of presenting Quajinn with the mysterious wrist chronometer taken from the Fallen Knight. After a quick analysis of the artifact, Quajinn had declared the chron could be used to stop time, somehow duplicating the effects of the freeze but also enabling Quajinn to remain conscious.

Elias reminded him that, according to the wording of the Curse, magic wouldn't do any good. Quajinn grew sullen then, and threatened to melt Elias down with a word, but Elias reminded the Draconid that if he did, he would never get off Center. Elias remained his best chance for freedom. His only chance.

At that, Quajinn relented. But just before Friar put him under, the wizard smiled slyly. He placed his right hand on Elias' forehead, and his left upon Friar's. Before Elias could knock it away, Quajinn murmured an incantation. "You have an hour to get me onto the ship before your heads explode," he warned them in his sibilant voice. "I'll reverse the spell once I am again

mobile." He smiled like a dragon, and then laid down in the case, crossing his arms and closing his eyes.

While Elias balled his fists in impotent rage, the wizard added, "You may begin." Friar brushed her knife hilt and gave Elias a worried glance, but at his curt nod she went to work. Ice slid over the Draconid's reclining form, enveloping him in a heartbeat. Elias reached over and closed the case, checking the computer on the locking mechanism for life signs.

Weak, but still visible. "Better kill him," Elias said with a wolfish grin. "Just to be sure." Friar looked like she might argue, but she complied. A moment later, Elias had levered the case onto the gravsledge and they were on their way to the docking bay.

So Elias understood Friar's nervousness, though he felt none of it himself. He felt secure in his invulnerability, and presumed Quajinn's threat to be an idle one where he was concerned. Still, it wouldn't do for Friar to die before she could get Quajinn out of his icy prison. And time was growing short.

Elias blinked as the gravsledge slid past him, right up to the customs station. Two hulking Prometheans looked down at Elias and Friar, their stony faces betraying no emotion. One stood behind the desk, thick fingers positioned to punch keys that would activate the full sensor package built into the station, reading at a glance everything on Elias' person or in his cargo. The other Promethean stood to the side, propped up by a wickedly barbed halberd that also doubled as a blaster rifle.

Elias handed a datacard to the desk attendant, while the other one leaned over and tried to peer through the ice frosted glass window of the case. It actually flinched, tightening its grip on its weapon and turning to Elias with a stormy expression. "That is Quajinn Huo," it rumbled tonelessly, suddenly master of itself again.

Elias nodded. "As my card will inform you, I managed to kill him. Now I'm taking him to the UWW for my reward." So said the datacard supplied by Squiddy, anyway.

The Promethean behind the desk, having plugged the datacard into the terminal, nodded as well. "Your papers appear to be in order," it told Elias. Turning to its companion, it said, "Tor, ensure the wizard is indeed deceased."

Tor stepped around Friar, who gave it a wide berth, and jammed the case's computer with a thick finger. Tor glanced at Friar and at Elias, and then said, "Quajinn Huo is dead."

Elias and Friar made it to the ship in record time, though Elias had to make sure the woman didn't appear to move too quickly. The Prometheans had a long history of remaining outside the political and social conflicts of the creatures that visited Center, but for a trigalactic criminal like Quajinn Huo they might make an exception. Better to keep them from getting suspicious.

Orix met them at the airlock. Tall and spare, with skin the color and consistency of bark and leafy hair tied into corn rows, he grinned savagely as the sledge slid past him. "All systems are go, captain," he told Elias in the stage whisper that passed for his voice. "We're ready to lift off when you give the word."

Elias nodded. "Let's go." Orix spun on his heel and left for the bridge at a brisk pace. Elias turned to Friar to tell her to release Huo, but the case was already open and steaming as the ice evaporated instantly into vapor. Elias suppressed a reprimand. It went against his training in the Invincible Guard to allow an underling to act without express orders, but then he wasn't in the Guard anymore. In fact, he needed people beneath him with some measure of initiative. He would simply need to get used to having people who thought for themselves.

Quajinn Huo suddenly sat up, blinking ice from his lids. He stretched and shivered melodramatically, and then muttered a word in some arcane language. Friar instantly relaxed, exhaling a pent up breath. "Welcome back, Master Huo," she said, smiling.

Quajinn levered himself out of the case and stood up. Beneath them all, the starship hummed with power as the engines came to life and the ship began to move, guided by Orix into the stratosphere of Phase World and beyond into the reaches of space.

Quajinn's Draconian face split into a wide grin, displaying all of his sharpened teeth. "Free," he whispered. "Free!" he said again, at full volume. "After all these years, I am free finally to exact revenge." He turned to Elias with his predator's grin firmly in place. "You have gained some measure of trust at last, Harkonnen. And it will last as least as long as Lothar of Motherhome lives." The grin widened. "Which will not be long at all."

Elias Harkonnen, former Invincible Guardsman and veteran of a thousand combats, ruthless and unforgiving, suppressed a shiver at the coldness and sheer evil he saw in Quajinn Huo's features.

* * *

"So Lothar broke that poor dragon's heart, only realizing after I explained much later what had happened. He's been sore at me ever since, though I promised never to put another love charm on him without his express permission."

Kassy and Caleb stood in the galley of Lothar's borrowed starship. She was whipping up an "Atlantean delicacy" from the meager scraps of food the galley offered, while he leaned against the counter ready to assist in any way. So far he hadn't needed to do much. A little stirring, some hunting for ingredients, and the like, leaving Kassy to do most of the work. Now that the casserole was baking, they were taking a break so that Kassy could tell Caleb the story of Lothar's encounter with an amorous dragon.

Lothar himself was only a few feet away, sitting at a low table and grinding his teeth, while the shadowy Doctor Abbot sipped tea from a delicate cup and admonished the Wolfen for his behavior. Abbot's words didn't seem to affect Lothar at all, though everything Kassy said increased his agitation. Throughout the story, Caleb maintained a close watch on his mentor to make sure his temper didn't explode. Though obviously annoyed — but when wasn't he? — Lothar remained fairly stable. No growling or brandishing of emerald axes, at any rate.

Kassy paused to check on the progress of the meal, offering Caleb a quick smile, saying, "Not quite there yet, but doesn't it smell delicious?"

Caleb had to agree. It was amazing how Kassy had pulled together the meal from what they had found in the galley; Caleb had assumed there wasn't much of use besides the strawberry wafers he'd eaten before. Somehow Kassy had been able to mix up a mouth watering casserole from the wafers, some broth, and a few packets of freeze dried vegetables. A few spices, completely unidentifiable to the young man who had never been very good in the kitchen to begin with, added flavor and contributed significantly to the enchanting aroma that filled the small room. "My father taught me how to cook," Kassy had explained. "He'd learned as a young man on the trail how to whip up a decent meal out of almost anything. And when I became a Slayer he insisted I learn how to do it too, to make sure I'd never go hungry. I don't suppose he ever envisioned me being locked in a Delakite dungeon for four days without a decent meal, though."

Caleb wished that his own father had been able to cook anything at all, but dinners at the Vulcan house had been just a grade above c-rations for years now. Abigail Vulcan had been the family's cook, but dinner had been the least of the changes in the house after she died. Caleb suddenly wondered if he would ever see his father again. Over six weeks had passed since his transformation from high school senior and draftee to Cosmo-Knight, and he had to admit he wasn't yet missing his old life. He would eventually, however. Probably. And what would he do then?

"Most people at least laugh politely when I finish that story," Kassy prompted. "Are you okay?"

"Yeah," Caleb said quickly. "I was just thinking of something else. It was very funny. I have to admit though, that I find it difficult to imagine Lothar in that situation."

"You and I both, pup," Lothar grumbled. "But old stories about me isn't what I'd like to hear from you, Kassy," he continued. "You have something about Harkonnen, don't you?"

Kassy's friendly smile faded, and suddenly the playfulness in her expression was gone. Caleb reminded himself that when he first met this beautiful woman with the wicked sense of humor, she was playing Errol Flynn with a flaming sword, having just freed herself from captivity at the hands of pirates. She might appear to be Caleb's own age, but by her own admission she was an Undead Slayer, an Atlantean warrior skilled at destroying the supernatural, and as much a soldier as Caleb's father.

"Right," Kassy said. "Caleb, do you mind getting some plates out? I think you and I will be the only ones eating." She raised an eyebrow in question to the others, and both Lothar and Abbot nodded. While Caleb did as she asked, she opened the oven and pulled out the dish, eyeing it critically. Apparently it passed muster, because she set it down on a heating pad on the counter and grabbed a big spoon to ladle portions onto the plates Caleb handed to her. She handed the first plate back to Caleb, heavy with food, and then took one for herself. They both took seats at the table and Caleb began to eat while Kassy spoke.

"The Transgalactic Empire spans many worlds," she began. "In the heart of the Empire lies the Free World Council, an alliance of systems who have rebelled against the Empire and are fighting to free other enslaved worlds under the Empire's control."

She paused to take a bite, and Caleb realized that Lothar and Abbot must be aware of these sorts of things, and that Kassy was explaining them for his benefit. Slightly embarrassed at his own lack of what should have been simple knowledge, he dug into the casserole with gusto. It smelled better than it tasted, but it tasted a great deal better than what he was used to.

"It's much too big a project for them to tackle alone, so they depend on aid from outside systems, many of which are all too happy to provide it. The Kreeghor have a lot of enemies in the Three Galaxies, and the FWC is a thorn in their side that many governments like to encourage. The people of Alexandria, my world, have been sending aid since the initial rebellion of the planet Good Hope. Money, food, munitions, ships. Anything we could spare went out to the FWC. One of my cousins was a blockade runner who took the trip to Good Hope a dozen times. That twelfth trip would prove to be his last.

"The run to Good Hope was never a pleasant one; you can barely go a kilometer without bumping into a Kreeghor dreadnought. Still, many ships slipped through using cunning, magic, or cutting edge tech. The Kreeghor decided too many ships were getting through, and that the only way to stop them was to send in the Invincible Guard, the elite cadre of imperial troops, each with enough raw power to go toe to toe with a Cosmo-Knight. They put a century, a hundred troops each, on each leg of the blockade. On the border to CCW space, a centurion named Boreas was in charge. Klygestus watched for S'hree Vek vessels. And near UWW space was stationed Elias Harkonnen, a former UWW citizen himself and the only Elf in the Three Galaxies to graduate into the Invincible Guard.

"Elias is as smart as he is ruthless and overconfident. He's completely invulnerable to harm, and has enough raw strength to juggle starfighters. On top of that, he has all the extensive military training and tactical skill of a Legionnaire and an intimate understanding of the way sentients from the UWW think and work. My cousin and his allies, Zeus rest their souls, never really stood a chance.

"Running the blockade takes a series of lightspeed jumps from system to system. Short ones are best, zigging and zagging from one to another. Makes it easier to bypass the blockade and lessens the chance of accidentally encountering a dreadnought. Harkonnen knew or guessed well enough the general route the UWW ships would take to Good Hope, and he sat and waited for them to appear in system.

"When they did, he let his three dreadnoughts sit in place and lob fire at the UWW ships to keep them too busy to run, but ensured the ships wouldn't take too much damage. Then he and his century went EVA and flew toward the UWW ships. Ship sensors don't pick up human sized targets very well, and most of the Legionnaires could survive in a vacuum unaided, so they managed to cross the void between the two sides without interference. They found airlocks and used their inhuman strength to shatter their way onto the ships.

"What followed wasn't a battle in any sense of the word. Slaughter would be more appropriate. Harkonnen and his fellow Invincible Guardsmen tore the crews to pieces. The Atlanteans on board didn't do any better against them than the wizards or the warlock marines. Harkonnen killed everyone on board and then had the Guard break up the bodies and spread the offal and gore on every available surface. Then he set the controls of each ship for a timed jump back into UWW space and returned to his dreadnought.

"It would be several more years before anyone from the UWW, my people included, attempted another blockade run."

"My God," Caleb said. He didn't feel very hungry anymore, though Kassy had continued to eat throughout her tale. "That's the kind of guy we're going after?"

Lothar nodded. "Not all our jobs will be easy like the Zodoran leech," he said with a grin. "Harkonnen is as bad as they come. I've already told you how he sacrificed his crew and his base in order to escape me. Any life other than his own has little meaning to him, and he's quite capable of doing almost anything to further his goals. He no longer has a century or any dreadnoughts to back him up, but that is no reason to underestimate him."

"I hope to be able to use the resources at Xerxes to find out more," Abbot said, speaking for the first time. "With Lothar's help I may even be able to see some of the classified records the CCW keeps on Invincible Guards. At the very least, news reports should give us a clearer picture of who he is, and perhaps where he will strike next."

"I know what he is," Kassy said coldly. "He is a monster. And he needs to be stopped."

A loud beeping interrupted them, and Lothar stood up. "We're coming up on Xerxes. Caleb, why don't you give me a hand bringing her in."

"Really?" Caleb instantly brightened.

Lothar just brushed past him, growling, "Come on then."

Caleb scrambled to his feet, and almost forgot his manners. He shot a questioning glance to Kassy, and she waved him off with a laugh. "Go ahead, I'll get the dishes."

Caleb flashed her a grin in thanks and raced after Lothar.

* * *

The great spindle shaped station, twelve miles long, was once again swarming with ships. Caleb picked out the CCW ships from the Zodoran engagement easily enough; they were the eleven battle cruisers swarming with repair crews. The Zodoran machine had nearly crippled the starships, and had almost proved the end of Caleb as well. He could have died fighting that thing, virtually powerless while it hammered away at him. But he survived. Caleb grinned fiercely.

He did a pretty good job his first time out as a Knight.

"Pay attention, pup," Lothar admonished from the captain's chair. Lothar rested his hands lightly upon the controls, ready to make a correction if Caleb made a mistake.

"Right, sorry," Caleb said, refocusing on the task at hand. Piloting a spaceship was a great deal more complicated than driving a car or even a plane; with no atmosphere to work with, a spaceship didn't have or need aerial vanes to manipulate airflow. Rather, maneuvering it depended upon the careful use of strategically placed thrusters that could set the ship in motion or slow it down. The fact that the ship moved through three planes wasn't anything that concerned Caleb; he had a knack for flying. What did worry him was failing to fire the right thruster at a crucial moment, or letting one burn too long. Either mistake could send the ship on a collision course with any one of the other hundred ships buzzing around the station.

The ship shook as a starfighter buzzed too close, nearly scraping a wing along their dorsal surface. Caleb flinched and tried to correct his course, but realized in a heartbeat that he was doing okay. "Jerk," he muttered. Lothar uttered a short bark of laughter.

Somehow Caleb managed to bring the ship into range of the docking bay Xerxes had given them without any trouble. With a flick of his wrist he sent the docking claw out to latch onto the station and a dozen umbilicals snaking out to connect with power lines and air scrubbers. He sat back with a grin and looked over at Lothar.

"Nice job," Lothar said. He wagged a finger at Caleb. "But don't get cocky. If that space jockey crashed into us, it wouldn't have mattered whose fault it was. You have to keep an eye out for that sort of thing." He stood up. "Now let's go."

Abbot and Kassy were herding the prisoners out the airlock when Caleb and Lothar reached it. Paj Pandershon and his Delakite cohorts didn't look too happy, but Caleb didn't feel sorry for any of them. Pandershon tried to snarl something pithy as he was led up the corridor to the TVIA station, but a glare from Lothar had him tripping over his tongue.

Caleb decided he would have to practice that move; though it would probably be easier if he were a foot taller and had a huge wolf's head brimming with sharp teeth.

With Lothar leading the way, the four of them passed through the inspection station quickly, while the authorities carted off the prisoners for incarceration. Lothar went with them to make sure everything went smoothly, which left Abbot, Kassy and Caleb standing on the railing over the expansive central lobby of the docking level.

"Well, we've much to do," Abbot said as Lothar and the TVIA officials walked off. "Caleb, you still need to be deputized. And I need to find those records and start working on this case."

"I'll take care of Caleb," Kassy told him. "You start cracking dataspools and we'll meet up with you later."

Before Caleb could interject, Abbot was beginning to head away and a figure in a military uniform was striding toward them, calling Abbot's name. Abbot paused, leaning on his cane. Caleb glanced at Kassy, but she didn't seem to recognize the other man.

A tall, broad shouldered black man with a shaven head and a neatly trimmed goatee, he was obviously a soldier of some sort, resplendent in the white and silver uniform of the Consortium Armed Forces. He stuck out a hand and Abbot took it, shaking vigorously. "Doctor Abbot, so glad you could finally make it here. Where's Lothar and his apprentice?"

"Captain Orestes," Abbot said, his shadowy features lightening in what Caleb thought of as Abbot's smile. "I'm afraid you just missed Lothar. He's on his way to the detention level. But his apprentice is right here and very eager to meet you." Abbot gestured to Caleb. "Captain, may I present Caleb Vulcan, Knight of the Forge. And our friend, Kassiopaeia Acherean."

Captain Orestes shook Caleb's hand and then Kassy's, bright teeth flashing in his dark beard. "Good work out there, Caleb," Orestes said. "You saved a lot of lives."

"Just, ah, doing my job, sir," Caleb said, slightly self-conscious.

"And what was that exactly?" Kassy asked.

Orestes put an arm around Kassy's shoulder and steered her towards the huge windows staring out into space. "You see those ships being repaired out there? Not a single one of them would be here if not for Caleb and Lothar."

"Really?" Kassy said. She looked at Caleb in a new way, almost as if she were reevaluating him. He resisted the urge to squirm under her scrutiny.

"Indeed," Abbot agreed.

"It was really nothing," Caleb insisted. "Any one of you would have done the same, if you could have. Doing something because you can doesn't make you anything special." One of the lessons his father had taught him, again and again.

Orestes clapped him on the shoulder. "Lighten up, Caleb. C'mon, I seem to recall owing you and Lothar a drink." He grinned at them all. "All of you, actually."

Abbot demurred. "I need to get some work done, Captain, but thank you for the offer. Caleb and Kassy, on the other hand, would be honored to join you, I'm sure."

Kassy nodded automatically. "Of course, Captain. Lead the way."

Caleb hesitated for a moment, but fell in behind them as Abbot left in the other direction. He would have rather gone with Abbot or hurried after Lothar at this point, but it would probably have been rude to turn down the offer of a drink from a man whose life he saved.

But the thing of it was, Caleb didn't feel like he'd saved anyone's life. Out there at Teneb-742, with the Zodoran leech hammering him, it didn't even occur to him that by tackling the weapon themselves he and Lothar had spared the lives of the crews on those dozen ships. It really was just a job he had to do, part of being who he was now; as a Knight of the Forge it was his responsibility to put his life on the line for total strangers — the power he had made it more likely he'd survive the experience, after all — but it certainly wasn't his responsibility to feel comfortable around those strangers.

Captain Orestes' effusiveness was kind of unsettling in a way. Caleb knew Orestes was genuinely grateful, and friendly, but it still didn't sit well with him. Back home, when you did a favor for somebody, they just thanked you, and that was that. More or less; you knew they'd pay you back when the time came. None of this patting on the back and "let me buy you a drink."

Caleb smiled to himself. It had seemed like fun immediately after tackling the machine, and he had argued with Lothar about taking up Orestes' offer, but now that he was here and doing it, he found himself agreeing with the Wolfen. Oddly enough, Caleb found Lothar's gruff manner easier to deal with than Orestes' open friendliness. Caleb shook his head. He supposed that Lothar reminded him a bit of his father, and maybe that was the source of the friction between them as much as the trust.

Not that he would be telling Lothar that any time soon.

"Here we are," Orestes announced, leading them into a café packed with other men and women in Consortium uniforms. Everyone seemed to know Captain Orestes, and as soon as Caleb was identified, they all let up a big cheer and started buying him drinks. He was soon surrounded by long lost friends he'd never met, and every time he emptied a glass, someone handed him a full one. He was glad his Cosmo-Knight metabolism could handle all the alcohol; he'd only ever tried drinking once before, and the whiskey stolen from his father's liquor cabinet made him feel nearly as terrible as he did once his father discovered the theft.

Caleb lost track of Kassy in the crowd, and it was a few hours later, as the party was beginning to break up and human constitutions gradually gave in to the demands being placed upon them, that he finally found her again. She was sitting by herself at a table in the back of the café, drinking what appeared to be water. Caleb put down his drink on the nearest flat surface and made his way towards her.

She looked up as he came close. "Having fun?" she asked.

"Not really," Caleb admitted, dropping into the seat next to her. "You?"

"I think I burned out on this kind of stuff years ago. But I have to admit, soldiers know how to party. And none party heartier than the ones who risk their lives on a daily basis." She looked around at the remaining revelers. "These people lost a lot of friends out there. That Zodoran leech destroyed six Warshield cruisers before you two showed up and saved the day."

Caleb nodded, seeing in his mind's eye the floating, shattered hulks that he and Lothar had flown by and later used for cover during the battle. He had tried then to ignore the bodies floating in the vacuum, but now couldn't forget them. They reminded him of Eddie Walters, strangely enough. Eddie, star quarterback, hero of Caleb's high school, and three years his senior. He went to Vietnam and came home in a plastic bag.

"How are you holding up?" she asked.

"Okay, I guess," he said. "I was just thinking about home." He smiled ruefully. "I've been doing that a lot lately. Back home, I'm supposed to be going off to war in a place that's very far from where I live, to kill people I've never met who mean me no real harm, because they want to use a different economic system than we do in my country. I wasn't too keen on the prospect originally, and after seeing what little I have of the Three Galaxies, it all seems so pointless." Maybe the alcohol had af-

fected him after all; it certainly wasn't like him to talk this way. But he didn't stop.

"It's really strange too, because I thought I was on the other side of the universe or something, but then I met all these humans who speak English for God's sake, and I started to think maybe I'm in the future, but no one seems to know about Earth. And I'm further from home and who I was there than I could have gotten if I had just gone to Vietnam."

Kassy put her hand over his. "You want to go home," she said quietly.

"No," Caleb said. "Maybe. I don't know. There's just too much here that's familiar, and it makes everything seem more alien." He paused. "I know that doesn't make any sense, but I don't think at this point I could explain it any better."

"I understand," Kassy told him. "I do. Part of what it means to be an Atlantean is never having a real home. We're meant to wander through time and space. Even Alexandria, our base of operations in the Three Galaxies, isn't really what you'd call a home. We gave up the right to one when we destroyed Atlantis through our hubris. I've had to adjust to a lot stranger places than the Three Galaxies in my time, Caleb."

She smiled suddenly, that same smile she had shown him in the tower on Korobas, and Caleb felt his heart tumble in his chest. "Besides," she said, "you've got Lothar and Abbot and me, and you know how to do the right thing. That's more than anyone else in the entire Three Galaxies has, if I do say so myself."

"Thank you," Caleb said. He did feel better, and his head was clearing too. "I think I had a little too much to drink," he admitted. Kassy laughed, squeezing his hand.

"There you are," sounded a familiar bark. Caleb and Kassy looked up, into the emerald face of Lothar. "We've got word from Center. Elias Harkonnen just left Phase World. With Quajinn Huo's body."

Beside Caleb, Kassy suddenly stiffened and removed her hand from his. The moment had passed, and suddenly she was the Slayer again. "Huo? You don't think..." she trailed off, apparently unwilling to complete the thought.

Caleb groaned. "Who's Quajinn Huo? No, wait, don't tell me. I've had enough stories for now." He stood up. "Let's go kick some butt."

The Siege Against Tolkeen

By David Haendler

Chapter 36

There was a deep, booming sound, like thunder, and a Tolkeen fighter jet fell to the ground, black smoke blossoming from its engines. Donald Hartman smiled inside his armor, and held up his plasma revolvers. He fired again, and another one of the planes burst into flame. The remaining four began to open fire, spraying the modified Super SAMAS with a heavy coat of gunfire. Red lights and warning sirens began going off in the helmet, as the gunfire chipped away large bits of armor plating.

A flying APC threw itself to the ground, and its doors opened wide. A platoon of Tolkeen's finest crack troops began to emerge from those doors, their guns raised high, and a cry of triumph on their lips. They had their enemy outnumbered and outgunned; victory was surely theirs to savor. A platoon of soldiers backed up by a wing of fighter jets would be hard-pressed to lose against six ragtag soldiers and a power armor trooper. The Tolkeenites pressed forward, sensing a short and glorious battle ahead of them.

One of the HFA troops looked at the onrushing mass of soldiers, and suddenly turned and sprinted away. He ran behind the Mosquito, seemingly fleeing from his enemy. None of the soldiers bothered giving chase to him, concerning themselves instead with the five remaining terrorists who were firing upon them. The soldiers returned the fire, and two of the HFA men fell, in a blaze of lasers and hellfire. In the midst of battle, nobody noticed the thick, black block flung from behind the Mosquito.

There was a massive explosion, throwing the highly-trained Tolkeen soldiers around like rag dolls. Thirty men were knocked to the ground by the blast. Of those, twenty two never got up again. The survivors were badly disoriented, and many of them began to flee back to the transport. They dove behind their APC for cover, and from there began to resume the battle. A few of the soldiers never made it back to cover, and were pinned down and killed by the HFA.

Donald Hartman fired his twin revolvers, and two more of the jets plummeted to the ground. But his armor was in bad shape, his men were still badly outnumbered, and incoming fire had disabled his CD player. The situation seemed grim.

Suddenly, there was the chatter of rail gun fire, and the Tolkeen soldiers began to melt away. Hartman looked over, and saw a "Jager" power armor emerging from the depths of the Mosquito, opening fire on the enemy troops. This newcomer was too much for the surviving soldiers, who fled back into their flying carrier. The doors to the ship reluctantly slammed shut, and the thrusters began to hum into life.

"Oh no, you don't," growled Hartman, as he fired his guns again. The plasma rounds penetrated deep into the APC, and the enemy vessel exploded. The newcomer, meanwhile, busied himself by plucking the remaining jet fighters out of the sky.

In a moment all was calm, as the survivors of the battle surveyed the wreckage and devastation. "Nice shooting," Hartman remarked, finally breaking the silence.

"I do my best," said the Jager pilot. "I'm Mr. Reiser. Let's get these weapons away from here before reinforcements arrive, shall we?"

* * *

Lucius Mallen breathed a sigh of relief as he saw the doctor step out of the emergency room. "How is he, Doctor?" he asked anxiously, grabbing the man by the arm.

"Well," the doctor replied, his voice somewhat muffled by the surgical mask still on his face. "He's stable. We've managed to stop the bleeding and bandage the wound, and we'll get a magical healer as soon as possible to finish up the job."

"Were you able to save his arm?"

The doctor shook his head. "Sorry. There was too much nerve and muscle damage. If he had gotten in here twenty minutes earlier we might have been able to reattach the limb, but by the time we got him it was too late."

"Can you give him a transplant arm? You know, bio-systems?"

"No. Same principle. There's too much damage. We can give him a bionic arm, but that..."

"That would destroy his magic."

The doctor nodded. "We're going to leave the decision up to him, when he wakes up. We've got him on some heavy anesthetics right now, but he should be conscious by tomorrow morning. You can go in to see him if you want."

"Thanks, Doctor," the Wolfen detective said, as he walked into the room. Pete Fransisco lay unconscious on a bed in the small, stark room. A bloodstained mass of bandages and wires adorned the shoulder where his arm had once been.

IV tubes were jammed up his nose and into his remaining arm, and his breathing was labored.

"Hi, Pete," said Mallen softly. "I hate to see you like this, buddy."

The unconscious detective provided no reply.

"We shut down that arms dealer real good. The robot that did this to you is sitting in a scrap heap right now. The place's computer records were encrypted, but we've got a Techno-Wizard working on breaking their code. We should have it by the end of the week."

The Wolfen looked at his silent, sleeping partner once again. "Sure hope you can make Uzieth's funeral. Well, anyway, I'll

see you in a while." The Wolfen gently patted his friend on the head, and then walked away.

The doctor, looking in on this scene, wished that he could feel more sympathy. He'd seen so many one-sided conversations like this over the years that he felt numb to them. With the war going on, he had seen more and more such occurrences lately. The doctor sighed, and walked back to his office.

He opened up the door, and reached for the light switch.

"Turn on that light and I'll blow you in half," said a female voice. The doctor looked into his dark room, and could make out the impression of a woman crouching on his desk, holding a pistol. The surgeon put his hands up in the air.

"Wh- what is this all about?" he demanded.

"Shut the door, Doc," she said. The surgeon grudgingly complied, plunging the room into total, inky darkness.

"If it's money you want, I'll give you my wallet."

"Keep your money in your pocket, Doc. What I need is a prescription. I've got a friend who's been magically tortured by the pigs who run this city. He's in a near-coma. What would you recommend for him?"

"Uh," said the doctor. "It's hard to say without examining him. But we sometimes get escaped POWs here who were tortured by the Coalition. I give them Verflex. It's a lot like Prozac, but it also gives them extra pep."

"Give me a prescription," said the woman, thrusting a pen and his prescription notepad into the doctor's hand. He filled the sheet out as best he could, and handed it to the woman.

"Thanks, Doc," she said, climbing up into a ventilation shaft. "And remember, don't tell anyone about our little conversation." With that, she left the room, leaving the doctor in darkness.

A few minutes later, Sonja, dressed in street clothes and accompanied by Jack Perrin, used the prescription to buy a vial of Verflex from the hospital pharmacy. With the precious drugs in Jack's pocket, the two walked out of the hospital.

"We've got to do something nice for that doctor," said Perrin. "We owe the poor guy one."

"Provided that this stuff works," replied Sonja, mildly confused by her companion's attitude. "If he gave us poison pills, then I'm going to be paying him another visit."

* * *

"Not again," snarled Donald Hartman, glancing at his suit's radar screen as he hauled a crate of rail gun ammunition down towards a hole in the ground, where a few dozen hover-dollies waited to carry the precious cargo away. Other HFA troops had been showing up to help carry the NGR power armor away, but it was still going too slowly. "Hans!" the CS pilot yelled. "We've got more company coming!"

"No. We do not," replied the spy, grinning broadly. He had been fiddling around with a machine that had been in the plane, a machine which looked like an old-fashioned mortar with an ammunition drum. Reiser began to fire the thing up into the air, launching out six small mini-missiles which shot out towards Tolkeen at an incredible speed.

"Six mini-missiles won't bring down those planes!" yelled Hartman. "There's like twenty jets headed at us!"

"Just watch your radar screen," said Hans.

"H-hey! They're turning back. The jets are turning back! What did those mini-missiles do, buddy? Did you just fire miniature nukes at Tolkeen or something?!"

The spy shook his head. "Their sensors are going crazy right about now. According to their technological sensors, a massive air strike is headed towards Tolkeen. Their magical sensors won't read a thing, but that'll only scare them more."

"Cool!" said Hartman, as he got back to work. "Got anything else like that, or is it just armor and ammo?"

"It was supposed to be secret," said Hans reluctantly. "The NGR just finished up a major trade with the Coalition States. They gave us about five billion credits worth of top-quality composite steel, and we agreed to give them some of our nicer technological secrets in return."

"Like what?"

"Well, ever since the Gargoyles learned about technology, we've been trying to use their own weapons against them. Gargoyles tend to overreact to danger, so we create false dangers, then outmaneuver the monsters and hit them with a lethal surprise. We use the Radar Missiles that I just showed you for that particular purpose. We've got code-breaking machines and fake voice modulators that we use to issue false orders onto their radio frequencies, and jammers that we use to prevent them from using their radios. My personal favorite has got to be the Mega-Hologram. It's a hologram projector that creates an enormous image we use to frighten or misdirect the Gargoyles. Generally, we make holographic Devastator robots for the Gargoyles to attack, so that they ignore the real troops. But we can reconfigure the thing to make holograms of evil gods, Alien Intelligences, or even massive explosions. Fun stuff."

"Oh, I think Perrin is going to like you a lot," said Hartman. Off in the distance, the anti-aircraft guns of Tolkeen could be heard firing away at a threat that wasn't there.

Chapter 37

"Sir, we've found something," said the red-suited forensic scientist, as he sifted through the assorted machine parts at the Naruni garage. He held up an ancient CD, and looked at it in the dim light of the garage. "Prints," the scientist said, smiling blandly. "Human fingerprints."

Lucius Mallen walked over, rubbing his eyes blearily. He hadn't slept in a couple of days, and had only talked to his wife once or twice in the past week. This case was putting an awful strain on their marriage. But it couldn't be helped, really. The paperwork for this situation was incredible, and he had had Uzieth's funeral to attend. The Wolfen detective gulped down the remnants of his rapidly cooling coffee as he peered at the disc.

"Can you put those fingerprints into the criminal database?"

"Sure thing, sir," the scientist said, tucking the CD away into a sterile plastic baggie. "If I go back to headquarters right now, I can have the results for you in fifteen minutes."

"Go," said Lucius, his weariness creeping into his voice.

"With all due respect, sir, you don't sound so good," said the scientist, as he began to leave the room. "You can't solve a case when you're so tired. Sleepy people make mistakes."

"I must have been pretty sleepy when I joined the force, then," growled the Wolfen, under his breath.

* * *

"Errgh," groaned Hubert Possman, as he slowly rolled out bed. "What a vicious headache I've got. Isn't that just typical? I get crazy nightmares about being trapped in Tolkeen and I wake up feeling like garbage." He laboriously got onto his feet, and walked out of the small, dark room he was in.

Suddenly, he found himself in the HFA beer hall, surrounded by city rats and terrorists who were fiddling around with crazy gadgets. "Just typical," he groaned. "It wasn't a dream."

"How are you doing?" asked Perrin, walking over to the dazed ranger. "You've been asleep for quite a while, buddy!"

"Just a few hours more, please."

"It's okay if you're still tired. We've still got a couple of weeks left before the solstice. As long as you're up and on your feet by then. We'll really need your help on that one. You're the only one who's seen the inside of that pyramid, so you'll have to be the one who guides us through."

"Great. Going back into that den of evil was the first thing I thought about doing when I woke up. I'm really excited about letting them shoot at me again."

"Just think of it as payback."

"Too mild. I don't like to just do payback. I like to do vengeance on a cosmic scale. Call back when we've got some nukes."

"We've got the next best things! Courtesy of the NGR." Perrin gestured around, displaying the variety of complex gadgets and devices which lay about the place.

"Yeah, what is all this stuff? I was wondering about that."

"Some German flyboys got shot down by Tolkeen. But we managed to save one of them, and he let us have all of the power armor, ammunition, and electronic countermeasures onboard."

"Decent of him. Where is the guy? I speak a little Euro."

"Went shopping. The fellow didn't have much in the way of street clothing, and didn't feel like walking around Tolkeen in his uniform."

Suddenly, there was a little cry of joy from the rear of the room. Sonja rushed over to Possman, and gave him a little peck on the cheek. "Glad to see you're awake!" she said happily.

"Glad to be awake," he said, looking appreciatively at the Juicer. "There any coffee around here? I'm never any good in the morning without my pot of coffee."

"Thought you said you were going back to sleep," said Perrin, fetching a chipped mug from a cabinet. "Changed your mind?"

"To heck with more sleep," said Possman triumphantly, casting a sideways glance at Sonja. "There's work to be done."

* * *

Shaard, the ancient ice dragon, knelt in the center of a circle of black flame in a place of darkness. A grimoire with an unpronounceable name, bound in the flesh of demons and inked in the blood of a god, lay before him. The ritual components of his spell were neatly laid out. This spell could be catastrophic if cast poorly.

The dragon chanted a brief prayer in a tongue that predated man, and a small Rift between dimensions tore open before him.

He grabbed up a massive handful of soil, and then carefully opened up an old wound in one of his claws with a ritual knife. Drops of freezing cold blood dripped down and mingled into the dirt. Shaard reached into a small bowl to his right, and carefully scooped out a little bit of thick blood from an extinct species. He mixed it into the dirt, and then did the same thing with a bowl to his left. The dragon steeled himself against the pain, and shoved the handful of soil into the Rift.

Searing magical energies shot up his arms, but he ignored the agony and skillfully shaped the dirt. Massive amounts of mystical energy flowed into his creation as he formed it, endowing it with some sort of life. When Shaard felt content that the thing in his hands contained enough power, he pulled his burnt arms out of the Rift. The tear in dimensions sealed itself off a moment later.

The dragon then looked down at what was in his hands, and smiled. A nude human woman, burning with the energies of life, lay before him, recuperating from its creation. The workmanship had been perfect. The spell had gone exactly as planned.

"Who's your lady friend, my liege?" asked a deep, fiery voice from the shadows. The dragon turned, and saw his personal Sunaj assassin standing outside of the circle, in full body armor. The assassin's gauntlets were stained with blood.

The dragon thought about telling the Sunaj to stay away during rituals, but then thought better of it. The assassin knew the risks involved in disrupting a ceremony, and had far too much self-interest to ever take those risks. "I would like you to meet Elizabeth Perrin," said the dragon, with a little flourish. "I have greatly improved her from her days as a creature of flesh."

The woman looked at the assassin, and suddenly her eyes glowed red, and her teeth elongated into savage fangs. But a mere moment later, she was back to her normal beauteous self, as if the horror had been only a mirage.

"Very nice," the assassin said, visibly impressed. "My liege, I have just returned from the front. The defecting officer that you told me about has met the fate that he richly deserved."

"I shouldn't have wasted your precious time with that fool," said Shaard. "The war with the Coalition doesn't even matter any more. The only one with the power to stop me is Perrin, and the steps that I have just taken have assured his doom. Tolkeen — my legacy — is secure."

Chapter 38

In a place of darkness, where time meant little and space could be molded like putty, there was a castle of glass and obsidian. The castle sat on a mountaintop, its twisted spires reaching up towards the heavens and very nearly pricking the fluffy, black clouds. At the foot of the mountain, mindless gibbering things with many eyes and power beyond that of any mortal man danced an endless dance, praising the sole inhabitant of the black castle in a tongue that even they did not understand. They understood very little of the world. Their purpose was to dance and to sing in honor of their lord, and they intended to do it until the stars burned out.

The lord of the castle sat on a throne of dragon skulls, brooding and thinking dark thoughts. Although he had been a servant (some would say lap-dog) of the Old Ones and was therefore an unbelievably ancient being, the lord of the castle was stuck in

"Hhhheelllppp..." growled the darkness, its voice badly distorted. "I-immprisssoned... b-b-by Shhhaaarhd. Ggoiinnng to... bbbeeee... slaaaainnn."

"What?" asked the lord of the castle, badly shocked by what he heard. He invested some of his own energy to widen the portal, only to find his efforts blocked by some invisible force. Something was terribly wrong. He hadn't seen any mortal magic of this caliber since that silly conflict between the Elves and the Dwarves. "How are they doing this?"

"Shhhaaaard iss... the key," said the darkness. Suddenly, there was a crackling noise, and the mystical portal slammed shut before either of the two entities could react.

For the first time in several hundred years, the lord of the castle rose from his throne. This was disturbing. If the mortals had sufficient magic to imprison one of his brothers, then they could set back his plans to wake the Old Ones. This could not be stood for. Shaard was one of the most powerful dragons in existence, but even he could be swept aside if the situation and desperation demanded it. A trip to Earth was dangerous, but he saw no other options. If the mortals succeeded in this endeavor, then they would doubtless try it again. That could not be tolerated.

The lord of the castle strode over to his closet, opening it with a thought. Inside was his armor, a full suit of gleaming, jet-black metal forged in the heart of a sun. He put the enchanted armor on, and then shut the closet with another thought. Then, he walked to the center of the room, where his sword hovered in the air, just inches above the ground. It was a black blade, of the same star-metal as his armor, with a serrated edge that could slice the electrons off of an atom. As he picked it up, the lord of the castle relished how good the thing felt in his hands. After fashioning a crimson cape for himself with a muttered spell, he felt ready for battle. There was a flash of lightning, and the lord of the castle, servant to the Old Ones, thinker of dark thoughts, departed for Earth.

* * *

Shaard suddenly shuddered, as images of apocalypse and fire filled his mind. Screams, gunfire, and a terrible explosion overwhelmed him for a brief second.

"What's wrong?" asked the Godling, suddenly concerned.

"Nothing," snapped Shaard, suddenly regaining his calm composure. "Just got a little jolt. The ley line energy will do that to you sometimes."

"No," said the Godling. "One of the lesser races might get those once in a while, but not you. An ancient ice dragon should not be getting jolts from the ley lines. So tell me, what's wrong?"

"Nothing's wrong!" said Shaard, more than a little defensively.

"It's the flashes, isn't it?" said the Godling. "You've been seeing flashes of the final conflict. I've been getting them, too, along with pretty much every other psychic sensitive in Tolkeen. The solstice, which seems to be shaping up as the final battle between us and the Coalition, is just about a week away. And if what you saw in that clairvoyant moment is enough to make even you flinch, then you know how unsavory that final clash is going to be. Shaard, I'm afraid we're going to have a

the frame of a lesser being. During the fall of his masters, a spell had shattered his physical body, reducing him to a powerless spirit. After several millenia of wandering the astral planes and other realms for a suitable host, he had finally come upon one. Unfortunately, the only being whose soul resonated properly to subsume had been a peasant. A stinking, sweaty, Elf peasant. For countless years, a being of great power had been forced to inhabit the weak and fleshy body of a pointy-eared dandelion eater. Although the lord of the castle was not terribly conscious of his looks, this seemed to be a cosmic insult of some sort.

The only beings who could give him back his former glory were the Old Ones, his masters, and they were sleeping. The lord of the castle wanted to wake them for the purpose, but could think of no way to do so. Every so often he would enter their dreams for clues, but gained little insight and much distress from that. The nightmares of the Old Ones would madden any other being, and badly disturbed the lord of the castle. He spent much of his time thinking about how to save his masters from their slumber. It took him eons to make even the simplest insights into how to resurrect them, but time was meaningless to one such as him. In a few billion years, perhaps he would have the answer, and then everything would be as it had been before.

Suddenly, there was a disturbance, and the lord of the castle sat up in his chair of dragon bone. A mystic portal opened up before him, sparkling with chains of vibrant green and blue energy. A shifting, sentient blackness could be seen on the other end of the mini-Rift, tiny tendrils reaching out from its world to his.

"How are you, my friend?" asked the lord of the castle, in a forgotten tongue. "Have the ages been treating you well?"

pyrrhic victory here. Whether or not we wipe out the Coalition States with this pyramid, it looks like the Dead Boys are going to stomp all over us."

"That doesn't matter. Without supplies and reinforcements, the army will fade away before they can wipe Tolkeen off the map. We can rebuild very easily."

The Godling pondered this for a moment. "You know," he finally said, "Some of the other Council members have been talking about evacuating citizens, getting them to other dimensions so that they'll survive no matter who wins. To tell you the truth, I like that idea a lot."

"No good," said the dragon, shaking his massive head. "We can't afford the energy that opening those Rifts would require. Everything has to go into the ritual if the spell is going to work properly."

"Shaard, these are our own people that we're talking about! You are willing to let the civilians of your own nation be massacred? That's inhuman!"

"Inhuman? My friend, you've been living amongst these 'squishies' too long. Mortal things come and go. They achieve nothing, they consume resources, and they die. Tolkeen is more than its citizens. It's more important than you, it's more important than me. If we take care of this city, it'll last forever, an eternal testament to our greatness."

"If you keep on like this, Tolkeen's going to be a cinder, an eternal monument to our stupidity! Shaard, do you honestly think that the Coalition States are the only enemies we have? That flash you just had, I know that it takes more than visions of war to make you shudder. If a flash of the future made someone like you quake, then our future has got to be something horrible." The Godling stood up, and began to walk out of the room.

"Don't do anything stupid," said Shaard. "Just remember, the ritual can proceed without you."

With that, the Godling walked out of the room, leaving the great dragon alone with his thoughts. And although Shaard was never fazed by even the most frigid of temperatures, the dragon felt cold somehow.

Chapter 39

"Behold... your destinies," said Shaard in an uncharacteristically amused tone of voice. He gestured to a little table, on top of which lay nine golden rings. Each of the rings was plain and unadorned, but they all glowed softly, with an inner brightness. One by one, the Council members picked up the gold bands, and slipped them over their fingers.

"When the solstice comes," said the dragon. "These rings shall help you channel your energies through the pyramid to complete the ritual. Isn't it odd to think that these little bands of metal shall earn each of you a place in the annals of this nation's history?"

"I must admit to not liking this, Shaard," said one of the human members, gazing at the shining gold. "In my experience, relying on magical trinkets like this has always led to trouble. True power comes from inside, and you know it."

"I sssuppose that the Dead Boysss do not feel the sssame way," snickered one of the two Lizard Mages. "They have no choice but to rely on their lasssser gunsss, and we have no choice but to rely on thesse rings."

"I couldn't have put it better myself," said Shaard, reclining in his throne.

"Hmph," muttered another one of the sorcerers. "You're seeming far more mellow than usual, Shaard. I would've thought that the upcoming Armageddon would have made you tenser than a constipated goblin."

"What can I say?" laughed Shaard, although this laugh was harsh and humorless. He looked around him, at the inner walls of the great pyramid, at the glittering bands on the fingers of the Council members, and at the skulking devil-woman in the likeness of Elizabeth Perrin, and laughed again. "I've got some insurance."

* * *

Lucius Mallen, the Wolfen detective, glumly sat at his desk playing computer solitaire. He had gotten stymied in the past few games, and it looked like it was about to happen again. In the back of his heart the D-Bee just wanted to put his meaty fist through the screen of the computer, but knew that it would accomplish nothing. He just felt so helpless, sitting around on his butt killing time while the lab boys tried to pull a fingerprint off of the CD he had found.

Things had been going pretty badly ever since the psycho he was tracking had made his first kill. Both of Lucius's partners were incapacitated, one dead and one recovering from bionics implantation, the war was going real badly, and he had been running into more and more problems with his wife. Just the last night they had gotten into a big fight when he had suggested that she take a two week vacation to some other dimension while the war reached its conclusion. The thought of her being in Tolkeen

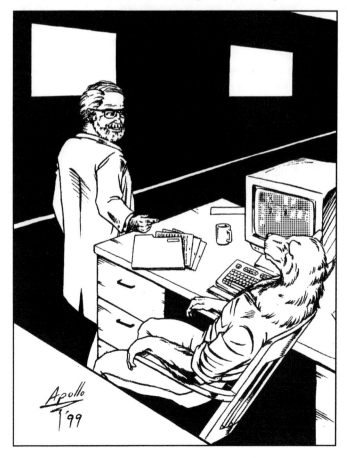

when the CS panzers rolled into town sent a cold shiver down the Wolfen's spine. But no, she had to stay here, to see things through to the end. All in all, these were taxing times to be living in.

Suddenly, one of the lab boys ran in, breathless and carrying a sheet of paper. "Hot off the press, sir!" cried the cheerful technician, slapping the printout down on his desk. "We finally got an ID out of those fingerprints. It turns out that our music lover is a Coalition power armor jockey named Donald Hartman. He was one of the men who led that big air attack a while ago."

"So he survived the attack, but was stranded in Tolkeen?"

"Sure looks that way."

"Hmm... our psycho may be involved with a Coalition operative? I don't like the looks of this."

"Hmm. Anyway, anything I can do for you on the way back to the lab? I'd hate to disturb you from your police work." With that, the technician cast a sideways glance at the computer solitaire game in progress.

"Yeah. Could you put out an APB on this Hartman guy? If any beat police or cameras in the city spot him, I want to be told. If we can track this fellow, he might lead us to our killer."

"Can do," said the technician, as he began to walk out of the door. "Oh, and by the way, put the eight of diamonds on the nine of clubs."

* * *

There was a flash of blue light and the thick stench of cordite, and suddenly the servant of the Old Ones found himself standing in a dusty field. The Alien Intelligence was disoriented for a moment, as this journey through space and time had been especially chaotic and bewildering. The Intelligence looked around, and realized that this was definitely not Tolkeen. There was nothing but never ending plains as far as he could see, with dry scrub and a few curious rabbits. *Interesting*, the monster thought, rubbing its angular chin.

It appears that the Tolkeenites have set up a mystic shield to prevent beings of my power from rifting into their land. I was lucky not to wind up in Olympus, or the pits of Hades. Now, to find out where I am.

The Intelligence sniffed the air, and smiled. There were humans, and plenty of them, just beyond the horizon. Hopefully, one of them would know the path to Tolkeen. And if they refused to cooperate, well, the Intelligence had ways of extorting information out of lesser life forms. The monster pulled out its star-blade sword, and casually bisected a bunny which had dared to venture too close. The Intelligence laughed, rose up a few feet in the air, and then sped off to this settlement, to try and procure a map.

* * *

"First," said Perrin, pointing at a map of the area around the pyramid. "We send the vans containing our men into their positions. We'll have to do it all at once, to minimize the chances that they'll check them out. When all of the vans pull up, the guards will know that something is up, and they will most likely

attack. But that's okay, because we'll be attacking as well. We use the NGR electronics to jam all of their communications and sensory technology just as our men are getting out of the vans. Plus, we use high-pitched squealers to take their devil dogs out of the equation. Those distractions ought to occupy the guards long enough for our boys to get to cover."

"Have we told the men where each of them is to hide?" asked one of the HFA mercenaries.

"We're going to," replied Perrin. "It's not all finalized yet, but they're definitely going to know where they're all going before we make the attack. Anyway, they get to cover, and begin trading shots with the guards. At this point, we're just trying to force the guards into keeping their heads down, so that our pre-positioned snipers can take out the anti-air batteries from a distance. At this point, the fun really begins."

"You have a strange definition of fun," remarked one of the terrorists.

"With all of the stuff that I've been through in the past few months, taking out these demons sounds very fun. That's when our flying forces take over. We jet overhead, and drop grenade satchels onto anything that looks angry or explosive. Once we're all out of satchels, we hit them with energy blasts until they're dead. Our boys on the perimeter come in and take over the walls, and Alpha team assembles to break into the pyramid itself. That's as far as I've gotten."

"When can we expect a finalized plan?" asked the mercenary.

"By tomorrow afternoon. I'm going to assemble Alpha team, and get Possman to give me a rundown on what the inside of the pyramid looks like. Any more questions?" Looking around the room, he saw that there were none.

"All right then, men," Perrin said, saluting his officers. "Let's get ready to rumble."

Chapter 40

There was a sick, wrenching crack, and a deputy's head twisted in a way that human heads were never meant to twist. The man made a little gurgling noise in the back of his throat as his lifeless corpse slumped to the ground. The servant of the Old Ones looked down at the dead body, and at the bodies of the sheriff and the other deputies. This was not going very well. Mortals were never very cooperative.

A laser shot rang out, and a beam of energy crashed into the back of the alien's head. The being felt a swift sensation of pain, not unlike that which a mortal receives when being singed by a candle. This Elven frame was far too fragile, and the star-tempered armor left the head regrettably exposed. The alien turned, and saw half a dozen more mortals standing in the road. Apparently this town still had some living beings in it after all.

"All that I want are directions to Tolkeen," said the alien, beginning to lose its patience. "Give me a map, and I will leave you alone."

"Shut up, freak!" growled some odd D-Bee that looked like a living cactus. "We got armed men all over town gunning for you! You ain't walking out of here alive, never mind goin' to this Tolkeen place of yers. Open up, boys!"

Concealed settlers emerged from hiding places, rooftops, and doorways all over the place, their guns blazing. Most of the shots bounced harmlessly off of the armor, but a few painfully struck the head. A little cut opened up on the monster's forehead, and for the first time, it saw its Elven blood. The alien growled in anger at the wound.

"Very well!" it cried, focusing its mental energies. "If you are unable to listen to reason, then I will find others who will!" The ground began to shake, and little pebbles and chunks of dirt began to float up into the air. Every glass window in town explosively shattered.

"Kill it!" cried the terrified cactus-man, unloading his E-Clip at the murderer.

"Kill me?" chuckled the alien, as waves of mystical energy began to envelop the town and every wooden building burst into flames. "I don't think so." The entire town was surrounded by a pillar of blue energy, baking the flesh of the surviving inhabitants. That pillar then exploded, and the agonies of the mortals were cut short as their bodies were blown into vapor. The smoke cleared, and the Alien Intelligence was the only being left, hovering a few inches above the glass circle which would serve as an eternal memorial to the town of Hopefield.

Suddenly, the monster saw something that it was intrigued by. In the ruins of the old general store lay a tattered, blackened pamphlet labeled, "Erin Tarn's Maps of North America." The intelligence hovered over it, and picked it up. Tolkeen was conveniently marked. The Alien Intelligence flipped through the pages, quickly memorizing the information contained within, and then flew off at the speed of sound.

* * *

Perrin slowly walked towards the Tolkeen library, sadly watching a convoy of troop carriers pass through the streets. For the past couple of weeks, he'd been spending more and more of his free time at the library. Since in just a little bit of time the mighty Coalition States would be occupying the area, and the library would be either sealed away in the Emperor's vaults or bombed into a memory, he figured that he might as well get some use out of the place while he could. The books on philosophy, politics, and magic were all tepid, demon-influenced garbage, of course, but there were a few gems mingled amongst the stones. Some of the novels he had read were pretty good. And there was a fascinating xenology section, containing books about everything from cute (yet deadly and hateful) little Faeries to city-busting monstrosities hundreds of feet tall. Perrin wasn't a great reader, but he knew his letters.

Suddenly, the pilot's meditations were interrupted by a very loud beeping noise. Perrin turned, to see a spider-legged APC headed right at him! He hurled himself out of the street, very nearly landing in the path of a civilian car, and landed in a heap on the sidewalk. The APC continued by, not even slowing down.

"Hey, you crazy moron!" Perrin scramed at the troop carrier. "You've got brakes, you know!"

"Ah, those military drivers are a bunch of lunatics," said some bizarre creature with a pair of goat-like horns emerging from its forehead and four spindly arms. The fact that the D-Bee was wearing a tweed suit and a pair of gold-rimmed spectacles only added to the weirdness. It offered one of its hands down to

Perrin. The pilot, not wanting to arouse suspicion, resisted the urge to pull away, and allowed the monster to help him up.

"It's really a shame what the city's doing," said the D-Bee. "Not only do they close off access to the D-Gates in order to Rift in soldiers from dozens of worlds, they give car keys to aliens who've never seen any vehicle that they didn't have to feed. One of those barbarians smashed into my flying carpet yesterday, and just sauntered away."

"They closed off the D-Gates?" asked Perrin, suddenly concerned. HFA spies working in that area should have told him about it by now. "But what about people who want to get out of Tolkeen before the solstice?"

"Oh, they're free to go," said the D-Bee. "As long as they don't mind traveling through CS blockades, forests full of snipers, and miles of minefields."

"Jeez. That's a lousy thing to do," said Perrin, as he continued on his way towards the library. Only when the goat-horned man with the four arms and the tweed suit was out of sight did the pilot realize that he had meant it. He had felt sympathy for the demons! How did that happen? The pilot still wanted to go through with the mission and devastate Tolkeen. He wanted that with all of his heart and soul! So how could he feel pity for these baby eating D-Bees?

The pilot looked out at the street, and saw another one of the armored personnel carriers. His heart suddenly burned with hatred. Then, he looked over at a tentacled D-Bee who was waiting at the crosswalk. Surprisingly, he couldn't find any loathing for this being. This was disturbing.

The pilot turned to his left, and he saw a red-suited city guardsmen walking by. Perrin was consumed by hate. He turned to his right, and felt no scorn for the bizarrely dressed mage whom he saw there. This was a problem for the savior of the Coalition States. He looked up at the pyramid, and at its orbiting crystals full of malevolence, and felt a profound doubt.

* * *

"Take that, you blood-sucking, baby-eating monsters!" cried out Donald Hartman, as the Mechanoid invasion forces gathered before him prepared for their charge. He began to unload his firearm at them, bringing down or crippling one of the machine-men every time he pulled the trigger. "Dan, you take out the base's weapons system while I hold these guys off!"

His companion began to fire at the distant base. However, Dan's aim had never been sharpened by any SAMAS training. Most of his shots harmlessly thudded into the thick armored walls of the fortress, and those that hit did not destroy the powerful energy cannons of the Mechanoid invaders. "Gimme some help here!" Dan yelled, as the massive beam guns began to turn in their direction.

"I'm trying!" said Donald, bringing his gun to bear against the base. However, it was too little, too late. The Mechanoids fired their cannons, easily tearing through the armor of Earth's defenders and reducing their best weapons to piles of useless slag. The charge of the remaining robots ended all hope of saving the planet.

"Game over," the arcade machine said, in an infuriating feminine voice. Donald threw down his light gun in frustration.

"We're dead, Dan! We were on the last level, too!"

"Sorry, man. Those guns are hard to hit, though! And you'd been getting the best weapon power-ups throughout the game. You had a long range plasma cannon, with the energy crystal! All I had was a wimpy little variable frequency rifle."

"And a grenade launcher! You could've used that on the turrets."

"They were anti-personnel grenades. Those don't make a dent in any of the bosses. I should've held the line, while you took out the turrets."

"It's a moot point now that I've lost my credits. You want to go get a pizza or something?"

"I dunno. I'm kinda tired of pizza by now. How about Mos Mell instead?"

"Never heard of it."

"Oh, it's great, man! It's seafood from some other dimension. See, there's an outer layer of skin, and that tastes a little like chicken. And inside the skin, there's this sauce... it's wicked good. Real spicy and filling. You should try it!"

"I guess so," said Hartman, as the two men left the dark, smoky arcade. "But you know, the last time I ate food from another dimension, I was sitting on the toilet for three hours! You'd better not be trying to poison me with this stuff."

As they walked off, a slim, unhealthy looking man in nondescript clothing looked on. A quick scan with the cybernetic identifying systems in his eye recognized the dark skinned man as being Donald Hartman, wanted fugitive, terrorist, and war criminal. The policeman had been right after all. The slim man began to follow Hartman, knowing that there was a promotion in this for him if he played his cards right.

Chapter 41

Rick Freedom looked down at his hand, and tried to hold it steady. His brain, enhanced by M.O.M. implants, should have been easily able to keep the limb as still as stone. But he could not. His hands were shaking to the point where he could hardly pick up a glass of water, never mind a weapon. He felt sweaty and feverish, yet was wracked with chills. An ordinary man would have interpreted these signs as being the onset of a cold. But Freedom knew differently. He knew that his mind was breaking down again.

The Crazy picked up a bottle of medication that lay on his night stand and swallowed half a dozen pills in one swift gulp. Almost immediately, he could feel the sweet chemicals going to work, easing his nervous system and his shattered composure. His trembling began to stop, and the spinning, undulating bionic implants on his scalp stopped their mad dance. Freedom's sanity, or what little remained of it, was intact for the moment. But the pills were only a stopgap measure. They would not keep him sane forever. And he was starting to run out.

The Crazy got out of his lice-ridden bed in his tiny, dirty apartment. His legs felt like rubber, but he could still walk. He staggered over to his chest of drawers, trying to pick out some clothes. He had to get up, had to help Perrin prepare for the final attack against the pyramid. He opened up the top drawer, only to see a row of bloody skulls neatly arranged there. Other than their eyes, the decapitated heads had been totally shorn of flesh. But their eyes were still perfectly intact, still bright and blue and alive. Those terrible eyes looked up at Freedom, and the skulls said, "It is your duty to slaughter the wicked," in an eerie unison. Then they began to laugh, and their laughter was enough to drive any man to madness.

Freedom screamed, shut his eyes, and held his hands over his ears. When he opened up his eyes again, the skulls were gone. The drawer contained only his clean and folded underwear, with no signs of the apparitions which had threatened him a moment before. Rick Freedom, who had fought in dozens of battles and performed many an atrocity in his lifetime, thought of the skulls again, and began to cry.

* * *

"You're sure that this is their headquarters?" Lucius Mallen asked, holding the telephone so tightly that his paw marks were left on the plastic casing afterwards. "Okay, about how many of the terrorists do you think are in there? That many? Jeez. We're going to have a real bloodbath on our hands. I'll see what I can do about getting some demons for when we raid them, but with or without demons we're going to be soaking up casualties." The Wolfen thought things over while he used his computer to pull up a map of the area.

"All right," he finally said, gazing at the screen. "Call for some backup, but DO NOT make your presence known. I want a couple of men watching every entrance and exit. If they start moving out or bringing in weapons or mobilizing for an attack, call back. Tomorrow morning, we'll hit them with the raid. If we're lucky, the psycho-killer associated with these guys will be there and we'll get the personal pleasure of watching our demons hack the monster into fish bait. If he doesn't show, a nest of terrorists goes down nevertheless. I'll call you back in a few hours."

The detective hit the END button on his phone, and heard the beeping of a dial tone. After a moment of musing to himself, he dialed another number.

"Department of Summonings?" he asked. "This is Lucius Mallen, badge number 617-478-3C. I'm going to need the nastiest batch of devils you can conjure as back-up."

"I understand that, detective," said the bland voice of a bureaucrat from the other end of the line. "But we just got a new set of orders from the High Council, restricting our summoning privileges until after the solstice. We're not allowed to summon anything over a Class II entity."

"What's a Class II entity? Shedim? Night Owls?"

"Gremlins. If you want, I can have a strike force of about 16 gremlins ready and waiting for orders by tomorrow morning, but that's the most that I could possibly procure."

"Forget it," growled Mallen, as he hung up the phone. *This is trouble*, he thought. *The bean-counters would have me and the tactical team walk into a terrorist lair with no demon backup. The military can't help me, because they'll be too busy holding the Dead Boys at the gates. Looks like my only option for victory is to circumvent the rules.* The Wolfen detective picked up the phone again, and dialed another number.

"Hello, evidence warehouse?" he asked. "Remember a large shipment of Naruni Enterprises weaponry and military equipment that came in a while ago? The arms dealer is going on trial, and we need to present the weapons at court. I'll be down in a few minutes with my ID card to pick 'em up." Mallen hung up the phone, and then put his head in his hands. He was tired of all this, and the hardest part was still ahead of him. The detective picked up the phone one last time, and dialed another number.

"Hi baby," he said gently. "I want to take another stab at convincing you to leave..."

* * *

Hans Reiser wandered through the city streets, gazing at the great pyramid and the buildings which surrounded it as he planned his assault. The NGR agent was out of his league here, and he knew it. He was used to wiping out grubby little groups of Unmutuals or finding out the locations of Gargoyle bases. Nobody had ever trained him for life as a secret agent in the midst of a city of magic. But here he was, and there was nothing that could be done about it.

It certainly is a fascinating place, he thought, seeing a flying carpet pass over his head while a group of centaurs passed by. *Pity that I'm going to have to help our American allies blow it all up.*

Suddenly, Reiser tensed. He could see one of the Brodkil guarding the pyramid look over at him. The demon had M.O.M. implants sticking out of its lumpy skull, which was often a sign of psionic powers. Was the monster mind-scanning him? Reiser had been taught how to deal with that, at least. There was a little hunk of metal in the back of his skull which sent out mental static to deal with telepaths. Furthermore, Reiser relaxed his mind, focusing on the image of a clean white slate.

The Brodkil grunted, and began rubbing its eyes. The mental defenses had worked. Even so, now the demon would definitely know that something was up. This place was not safe. Reiser turned, and began to walk away. He had already figured out the best places to put the white noise generators, the holographic projectors, and the EMP generators. There wouldn't be time to set up any anti-targeting devices, but the Tolkeenites doubtless had countermeasures against the things anyway. All was in readiness.

The spy decided that he would spend the rest of the day walking through this city of wonders. Back home in Germany, they simply didn't have any spectacles of this magnitude. It was a pity, but Reiser didn't want to live his entire life surrounded by filthy D-Bee scum. Tolkeen was a nice enough place to visit, but he sure wouldn't want to live here. Especially after the Coalition started obliterating everything.

* * *

As the Alien Intelligence shot over the landscape at tremendous speeds, he felt a soft buzzing at the base of his skull. Looking off into the distance, he could see the burning, blighted forests surrounding Tolkeen, and the massed armies of the pathetic humans. Even further off, he could see the spires of Tolkeen itself as they really were, without the feeble masking which the mortals had applied. It was there that his brother was imprisoned.

The Alien Intelligence slowed his flight, and then came down for a gentle landing. It would do no good for the humans to spot him and force the battle early. He would slip in unnoticed, and bring havoc to those who thought they could control gods. *By the time that I am done*, the monster thought, *the mortals will never dare to insult us again.*

THE TERRITORY OF ARZNO PART ONE

Optional Material for Rifts®
By Jason Richards and Nathan Taylor

In what was once Northwestern Arizona, a new territory has arisen out of the chaos of the New West. This territory revolves around the city of **Arzno**. Unlike many communities in post-cataclysmic Earth and especially in the New West, Arzno was built from scratch, not on the broken bones of some pre-Rifts city. Other than that, its history is somewhat of a mystery. Due to the uncommonly high percentage of magic practitioners, especially Techno-Wizards, it is commonly believed that the city was founded by refugees from the Federation of Magic, possibly a group of Techno-Wizards seeking something besides the wars, feuds and general violence of the Magic Zone. Others think that a group of mages came North to escape the ever-advancing vampire threat, a theory that is backed up by the large percentage of the people who speak Spanish, most out of pride in their heritage. Whatever the situation, the outcome was a small town predominantly peopled with magic users, human and D-Bee alike. The year that the town was founded is another lost historical tidbit, but it's estimated to be around 50 P.A. What's known is that the population of the city hit a boom with the instating of Arzno Weapons Manufacturing and the Arzno Mercenary Corps in 92 P.A.

Arzno is located about a mile (1.6 km) north of the Grand Canyon in the cooler regions of the desert. If it's true that a group of mages founded the city, they chose a good place for it since Arzno is located amongst the vast network of small ley lines that crisscross the canyon region. In most of the city and surrounding territory, P.P.E. levels available to mages are high, doubling spell duration, damage and range, and giving them an additional 10 P.P.E. per level every twelve hours. There are two small nexus points within the city walls, one at the Arzno Mercenary Corps compound and another on the other side of town at Arzno Weapons Manufacturing. Both are carefully controlled and used by Techno-Wizards in the creation processes of their unique devices.

The territory claimed by Arzno extends roughly 30 miles (48 km) in every direction except southward, where the border stops at the canyon. There are about a dozen small towns within the territory and various groups of nomadic trappers, wilderness scouts, and cowboys who are all considered to be under the protection and authority of Arzno. The Indian tribes that travel the land are allowed to move about as they please and are generally left alone unless they cause some harm to or otherwise interfere with any of the citizens of the territory. This is a rarity, as the canyon protects the territory from most outside dangers such as violent Indian tribes, Worm Wraiths, and roving bandits.

Tech level in the city of Arzno is about that of the 1920's, but many of the comforts citizens enjoy are not technnological wonders, but magical marvels accomplished by the many Techno-Wizards in the city. Most of the city's power, water, and protection comes from, or is at least partially reliant on, Techno-Wizardry. The surrounding territory includes several small villages whose tech level is significantly lower, about the late 1700's or early 1800's.

The Arzno Territory

Population: Difficult for an accurate census due to nomads, trappers, and small villages that come and go. Estimated to be around 15,000, give or take a few hundred.

Racial Breakdown: The Arzno territory is well-protected by the Grand Canyon and is thus well-suited for Fennodi, Cactus People, and others who just want to live their lives in peace.

59% Human

10% Fennodi

8% Cactus People

5% Psi-Stalkers

3% Mutant Animals

15% Other D-Bees

Transients: 4D6x100 transients can be found throughout the territory at any given time, though 3/4 of these are in, en route to, or leaving the city of Arzno. This number fluctuates during the different times of the year since it includes the various nomadic tribes of D-Bees and Indians in the area, as well as the Lyn-Srial who pass through during the Festival of Light.

Surrounding Communities: Northern Arizona is largely uninhabited. The Lyn-Srial live in the Grand Canyon, and have trade relations and a peace treaty with Arzno. Through this alliance Arzno has learned of the Gargoyles living in the canyon as well, and is performing intelligence-gathering missions on this possible threat. The Navajo and Hopi are to the East, but have no real contact with the territory other than the occasional commercial transaction. The farms, ranches, and villages that surround the city of Arzno account for easily half of its commerce. There are dozens of ranches and farms surrounding the city, not to mention the shops that lie outside the city limits, which are just outside the walls and virtually part of the city. There has been talk of extending the official city limits to include this area, and it will be on the ballot come the next territory election. Nearby there are also several smaller towns that act as suburbs to Arzno, including Magebrush (pop. 1250), Stony Ridge (pop. 900) and Terrell (pop. 175).

Level of Education: Fair to good. In the territory, most are fluent in American (50% of the population), Spanish (20%), or both (20%). The remaining 10% speak a variety of different D-Bee and foreign languages. About 45% are literate in at least one language. As far as non-traditional education goes, 90% of the population over the age of 12 has one modern W.P. (usually some sort of pistol or bolt-action rifle), two Wilderness skills, and at least one Cowboy skill. This is due to various "help others help themselves" programs offered by the city and funded by the AMC and AWM.

The City of Arzno

Population: 12,500
Racial Breakdown:
68% Human
5% Fennodi
4% Psi-Stalkers (most employed by the AMC or the Civilian Patrollers)
4% Cactus People
2% Mutant Animals
1% Golden Ones/Lyn-Srial

1% True Atlanteans (the names of Lanis and Onra of the clan of Libson have drawn some attention)
15% Other D-Bees (including a few dragons, Sphinx, and other supernatural beings)

Transients: 3D6x100 transients can be found in the city at any given time. Among these are several Justice Rangers, about twenty or thirty Cyber-Knights, and many mercenaries, bounty hunters, Techno-Wizards, and Gunslingers who make regular visits. Most come to catch the latest TW item, visit with old friends (many are former AMC soldiers), or have a night that they know will be peaceful and not require them to be on their guard.

O.C.C. Breakdown of the Population:

*Note: Of the total population, only about 32% are in the work force.

31% Techno-Wizards; most are employed with either the AMC (8%) or AWM (69%). The rest work as Civilian Patrollers, private shop owners, mechanics, or in any number of other occupations. Several veterans of the AMC have opened a private investigating business and two others have become healers. Several local Techno-Wizards have opened a large farm just outside of the city walls that grows the most impressive crops every year, including those not native to the land (i.e. oranges, bananas, coconuts, coffee, etc.), using magic to change the environment. They have a large grocery near the center of town.

12% Operators

11% Line Walkers

11% Mystics

8% Other Professionals (doctors, lawyers, etc.)

3% Mind Melters, Bursters, and other powerful psychics

14% have some other O.C.C. that allows them to be employed as a mercenary (Gunfighter, Gunslinger, Crazy, Juicer, Headhunter, Bounty Hunter, etc.)

10% Others, including cowboys, laborers, gamblers, etc. The low number of "other O.C.C.s" is due to the fact that Arzno is basically a Techno-Wizard and mercenary town. Former mercs and mages are responsible for most of the commerce and local industry.

Level of Education: Good to excellent. 95% of the population is fluent in either English or Spanish, with many fluent in both. Literacy rate is an impressive 75%, with a third of the population literate in an additional language. Virtually every citizen over the age of 12 has one modern W.P., Land Navigation, and a Pilot skill (usually Horsemanship). Classes in various skills are available for a low price (sometimes for free) at Civilian Patroller precincts, AWM, and the AMC compound.

Government

An elected council known as the Council of Elders governs the city and territory of Arzno. The Council is a senate of 11 elected citizens, with one of them serving as the Chief Elder, who has no special governing power other than setting the agenda and running the meetings. Major issues are sent to the public to be voted on, and anyone over the age of 16 may vote. There are no political parties or sophisticated politics in the Council. In fact, there are not even campaigns. An open-ballot vote is held every three years and the person with the most votes is Chief Elder. Two alternates for Council members are placed on reserve and attend all Council functions and meetings to serve as secretaries and perform various administrative duties. Membership to the Council can be declined, but that has not occurred to date. Membership doesn't garner any wages, and all members must support themselves in some other way, most often by owning a business in town. The Council has managed to evade corruption and the basic dishonesty of most politics because of the lack of pay and relative lack of power. All of this is possible because the territory is small and lacks many problems of larger communities. Council members are the most highly regarded citizens in the territory and it's common law to tip one's hat when passing a current or former member of the Council.

The Council is directly responsible for electing the leadership of the peacekeeping body of the city, the Civilian Patrollers. The Council nominates and elects the chief officer of the Patrollers (who holds the rank of Lieutenant) and must approve his choices for Sergeants. The only qualifications for either position are: the candidate must be a citizen of the city of Arzno, must accept the job and its duties full-time and therefore cannot be a member of the Arzno Mercenary Corps (though most are veterans of the AMC), must be 30 years of age, and must not be on the Council of Elders.

Current Council members of note include:

Sinsonue Wisp (Sin-son-ew-way), Chief Elder, lady-killer, and 12th level Elven Mystic (Unprincipled alignment; I.Q. 15, M.E. 10, M.A. 18, P.E. 11, P.B. 20). The people (particularly the ladies) adore Sinsonue, and their affections are returned. He's less than modest, a fact that wasn't helped by being named Chief Elder. He's just completing his first term and might not be renamed Chief Elder, which would be a major blow to his ego. He'll undoubtedly be re-elected to the council, but may retire if he gets wind that he might not retain his Chief seat. As an Elf, he looks much younger than he is and is constantly flirting with the women of the town. He is an honorable character, and doesn't do anything to disgrace his position as Elder or embarrass himself. He just enjoys attention in the form of whispers and giggles. He owns two of the larger hotels in town.

Lanis Nemesio (Lah-niss Ne-mess-ee-oo), a distinguished 8th level Techno-Wizard, founder and owner of Arzno Weapons Manufacturing, and co-sponsor of the Arzno Mercenary Corps (Scrupulous alignment, I.Q. 17, M.E. 14, M.A. 19, P.E. 13). Lanis is responsible for making Arzno what it is today. With Mage Onra Misvina III (his fellow clan member) he is involved in a quest to rid the Earth of the vampire threat and it was he who has developed the "help others help themselves" attitude held by his company as well as the Arzno Mercenary Corps. See the description of Arzno Weapons Manufacturing for more information. Lanis is sincere in his quest to exterminate the vampires, though some just view him as a salesman. The truth is evident in the way he runs AWM, selling items for fractions of what they're worth on the mass market, just for the sake of helping others. Lanis isn't rich, but could be. AWM is worth millions, possibly a billion credits.

Lanis' name comes up for Chief Elder every time an election comes around, but he has not been elected due to his heavy involvement in the AMC and AWM, the two primary businesses of the city. Some fear that may be too much power for anyone, even the highly honorable Lanis.

Lanis has a daughter, Patria, who is, much to his dismay, an Undead Slayer and Sergeant in the AMC. His history with his daughter is rocky and they're constantly on the outs. Lanis has always been a leader of people first and father second, a choice which he is beginning to deeply regret.

Braythia Stayma (Bray-thee-ah Stay-ma), commonly known simply as "Bray," is a 5th level True Atlantean Undead Slayer (Aberrant alignment, P.S. 25, P.P. 20, P.E. 22) and one of the two reserve Elders. He's a bright young man (97 years old but looks 24, practically a kid) with big plans and little time, so he says. He sees the city as one not being used to its potential in the fight against the undead, and is anxious to change things. If he gets an audience, most will reject his ideas of violent glory and only frustrate him greatly. The minority that follows him will easily be led into fanatics and could possibly spell big trouble for the city and territory. He greatly respects (almost reveres) Onra and assumes that they have the same outlook on how things should be done. Bray is currently working his way up the ranks in the Civilian Patrollers and has gotten as far as Patroller 1st Class. If the vampire conflict erupts soon, he'll undoubtedly leave the Council and the Patrollers to join the AMC and follow his idol into glory.

The Law

The Civilian Patrollers, a militia-style police force made up largely of ex-mercenaries, keep the law in the city of Arzno. They are a totally civilian militia, but can be called to active military duty should a crisis arise. In this case, they basically become extra troops under the control of the Arzno Mercenary Corps. The head of the Patrollers holds the title of Lieutenant and is appointed by the Council of Elders. The Lieutenant selects (with the approval of the Council) four Sergeants: one at the city court precinct in the center of town (Precinct 1), one in the Northwest (Precinct 2), another in the Southwest (Precinct 3), and one in the East (Precinct 4). Officers in the AMC (lieutenant on up) also have police officer authority in the absence of a Patroller presence. For each Sergeant, there are three Deputy Sergeants who help their superiors in the administration of justice and keeping of the peace. All officers carry a sidearm (standard issue is a Wilk's-Remi 130 "Six Shooter" or AWM equivalent to the TW-45 Revolver, but officers generally have their pick of weapons) and either a second sidearm or a rifle (standard issue is Wilk's-Remi 157 "Judgement Day", Wilk's 567 "Long Gun", or TW Hellfire Shotgun). They may wear a variety of armors, but it's usually something light. Most common are Bushman, Branaghan, Dead Boy, or Bandito armor, often with some TW enhancement.

There are three classes of patrollers. Patroller 3rd Class, called a P3, is your basic beat-cop. They walk the streets in pairs doing the routine, everyday police stuff, mainly breaking up fights or settling disputes between citizens. They will carry a sidearm (standard issue is a Wilk's-Remi 130 "Six Shooter") and may use their own equipment with their Sergeant's approval. Most wear light armor, standard issue is Bushman. The average P3 will be a level 1-3 Cowboy, Deputy, Mercenary, or the occasional Techno-Wizard with at least two W.P.s, an average I.Q. and physical attributes of about 12. There are 20 P3s per precinct, about half of whom are on duty at any given time.

Patroller 2nd Class (P2) is the typical patrol-cop, generally working in pairs patrolling the streets in patrol cars, on motorcycles or hovercycles, or occasionally on horseback. They are responsible for being quick to the scene of a reported crime and chasing down escaping criminals. Each carries a standard issue sidearm and one of the pair will have a standard issue rifle. Bushman or Bandito armor is standard issue for P2s. The average P2 will be a level 3-6 Deputy, Mercenary, sometimes a practitioner of magic, or an Operator with Read Sensory Equipment, a Pilot skill, a modern W.P., an average I.Q. and physical attributes of about 12. There are 20 P2s per precinct, about half of whom are on duty at any given time.

Those with the rank of Patroller 1st Class (P1) hold the positions of either modern-day detectives or other specialized field. The mechanics and Operators who maintain the armor and fleet vehicles at each precinct are all P1, as are the criminal investigators. So are many of the desk jockeys who work on the meager computer systems, act as personal aids to the officers, or other secretarial work. Most field P1s such as detectives will be a level 4-8 Bounty Hunters, Super-Spies, Military Specialists, or other men-at-arms with skills in police investigation. Desk jockeys will be of O.C.C.s such as Technical Officer, Traditional Hacker, Cyber Detective, or Operator. Mechanics will be Techno-Wizards (often Gun Bunnies or Aviators), Operators, Technical Officers, or other O.C.C.s with mechanical skills. Armor and weapons vary per assignment, but the Branaghan armor is extremely popular with field P1s.

The uniforms of all members of the Civilian Patrollers are basically the same. Dress uniforms have black trousers (men and women) with a double-breasted dark red shirt with silver buttons and black accents. The CP's silver badge is worn over the left breast and a pin showing rank is worn on both collars. No hats are worn on formal occasions. Working uniforms are black jumpsuits with red stripes down the legs and arms with a red "CP" emblem on the right breast and a larger one on the back. A black ball-cap with the red emblem is worn as well. A silver badge indicating the rank of the Patroller is worn over the left breast, as well as an emblem on the right collar. Officers and P1 detectives aren't required to wear a uniform while on duty, and technical occupations such as Operator or Techno-Wizard are issued an alternative uniform for work, usually just a plain black or red jumpsuit with their name and rank over the right breast. Armor is painted red and black with the CP logo on the back and the rank on the upper-right torso.

Other Defenses

In addition to relying on the Civilian Patrollers and Arzno Mercenary Corps for protection, the main city is surrounded by walls on every side. The walls are 20 feet (6.1 m) tall and 10 feet (3 m) thick. Gates on every side are open all day, but are closed at night except for the main northern entrance, right by the AMC compound. The AMC and CPs share the duties of guarding the gate at night. The gate may be closed in the event of an attack, high winds, or some other emergency. The walls have 35 M.D.C. for every 25 square feet (2.25 sq. m). Not enough to repel an invasion, but enough to give the city and its protectors time to rally a defense.

The Arzno Mercenary Corps

The young soldier, Emory Reins, awoke with the scent of the desert in his nostrils, and momentary confusion raced through his mind before he remembered where he was. He groped in the darkness for his lamp and toggled its switch, illuminating his small, one-man tent so quickly that it stung his sleep-filled eyes. As he adjusted his eyes to the new light, he found the tent's control box and flipped a switch down. A brief crackle was heard as the one-man shelter dissipated into the air and left the private sitting on his bedroll in the middle of the advance camp. The warm desert sun could just be seen in a marvelous sunset as its waning rays sifted through the remnants of a small dust storm to the west. Emory hurriedly laced up his boots and began to slip on his armor.

Taking a moment to look around, Emory's eyes rested on his commanding officer sitting at the top of a small hill and gazing toward the sunset. He stopped in his preparations long enough to ponder one more time the mysteries of his Atlantean commander. Before every battle the mysterious mage, Onra, found some place to himself where he could sit with his magic blade and a whetstone, sharpening away. What was unusual was that everyone knew that Onra's blade would never dull and only ate away at the stone. Whenever the stone was worn to dust, it was time to move out.

As if on cue the somber Atlantean stood, shook the powder from his hands, and walked toward the transport. A slap on the shoulder awakened the private from his daze. Emory looked up to see the pale-skinned face of his hero, Psythe. "Let's book it, Rookie."

Emory grabbed his water rifle and paced the seasoned Psi-Stalker to the transport.

A. Sponsorship: Government and Company (Arzno and AWM) 0 Points
B. Outfits: Specialty Clothing 20 points
C. Equipment: Magic Technology 40 Points, Electronic and Good Gear 5 Points
D. Vehicles: Combat Cars 20 Points
E. Weapons, Power Armor, and Bots: Basic Weaponry 10 Points
F. Communications: Basic Services 2 Points
G. Internal Security: Tight 10 Points
H. Permanent Bases: Fortified Headquarters 20 Points
I. Intelligence: Scout Detachment 5 Points
J. Special Budget: Small Potatoes 15 Points
K. General Alignment: Unprincipled and Scrupulous 7 Points
L. Criminal Activity: None 0 Points
M. Reputation: Known 10 Points
N. Salary: Good 10 Points
   Total Points Spent: 174 Points
   Size & Orientation: Free Company

History

Onra Misvina III, a True Atlantean Weapon Mage, founded the Arzno Mercenary Corps about the time of the Arzno population boom in 92 P.A. Land was granted by the city with funds and equipment given by the company's fledgling sponsor, Arzno Weapons Manufacturing. The company is actually the private army of the city of Arzno as well as a mercenary corps of soldiers of fortune. The group specializes in destroying the many supernatural menaces that plague the Southwest, especially vampires. In the past couple of years, the nemesis of the Corps has been a new vampire kingdom that has sprung up it Southern Arizona and New Mexico led by the master vampire, Xavier Stuart (see **Rifter #8**). This militant faction of vampires has presented a whole new challenge to Onra and his team of elite demon hunters. Officially, Arzno is at war with the various vampire kingdoms and engages all vampires on sight. Other contracted jobs for the mercenary army include the extermination of demonic raiders for towns and businesses, protecting towns from raiders and bandits, or any other job suitable for a scrupulous merc organization. These jobs can include the occasional stealing of an item or information, assassination, or bounty hunting provided the party in question is an evil one. Such jobs are always well researched to ensure that the wool isn't pulled over the AMC's eyes.

The fees charged by the company are reasonable and consistent with the market. The Corps frequently takes jobs for a bare minimum cost (if any at all) for underprivileged towns and villages, especially when it comes to eliminating vampires.

Tactics

The Arzno Mercenary Corps never takes anything for granted. While most vampire hunters stroll into a town during the daylight hours and start staking their "easy" prey, they frequently don't get the entire hoard, leaving a few to spread the vampire curse and continue on in their marauding. The basic mode of operations for the AMC is a late-night recon mission where caskets are counted and the vampires returning from their hunting are watched to be sure that none are missed. In addition, the twilight reconnaissance allows the squads to locate feeding and slave pits, allowing them to set more civilian hostages free. Another common problem is that vampires usually have some sort of minions guarding them during the day and it's a little easier to tell what you're up against if you sit back and observe a little. A second team usually arrives at sunup to relieve or strengthen the first team and aid in destroying the vampires.

Occasionally, when deemed appropriate, a surprise attack first thing in the evening is the best strategy for dealing with the undead. Especially since the introduction of Xavier Stuart's new kingdom, vampires tend to find avenues of escape or alternative means of protection during the day that one might not expect. A well-placed ward or explosive device can make a vampire hunter very sorry that he opened a casket.

In a nutshell, Arzno tactics are honorable, but sensible. The formula has accounted for Onra's success as a vampire hunter as well as the success of his team. The style is starting to spread throughout the New West as more and more AMC veterans start their own small-time operations.

The Arzno Mercenary Corps' Colors and Banners

The official colors of the AMC are, like the city, red and black, although accents of blue and silver are used often. The emblem of the Arzno Mercenary Corps is a wooden crucifix crossed with a silver sword, with an overlay of a flaming "AMC" against a solid background (color varies, usually black or blue). Beneath the symbol is the text:

The Arzno Mercenary Corps
"Stake 'em, 'Cap 'em, Light 'em"

The slogan is derived from the first rule of fighting the undead — how to kill them: stake through the heart, decapitation, and burning the body. Uniforms and armor vary in color, but are frequently black or dark blue and bear a simple crimson "AMC" with "Arzno Mercenary Corps" written under it. The emblem is worn on the right breast and a larger emblem is on the back. Rank is painted on the left breast, the back directly under the neck, and the front of the helmet on armor, or just on the right shoulder and left breast of a uniform.

Rank

Rank in the AMC is loosely based on pre-Rifts military, though they have been altered to suit the smaller mercenary unit. There is a rough timetable for advancement, but it can be greatly hurried by a hard-working and disciplined soldier, especially if proven in combat. Pay is actually less dependant on rank than it is on skill and worth. As a mercenary army, the soldiers can leave as it pleases them, though most sign a contract for 1, 2, 4, or as many as 10 years. Pay fluctuates with what the AMC makes on contracts and the sometimes high expenses of the mercenary organization.

Until basic training is completed, the soldier is referred to as "Cadet" and holds no rank, calling even privates "Sir". Training lasts for at least eight weeks, possibly more if the recruits aren't up to par after the allotted time.

Entering rank is private, symbolized by one horizontal bar. Privates are the workhorses of the AMC, doing jobs from basic maintenance to ground-pounding infantry. Typical time as a private is between one and two years, depending on the skills of the soldier and the incoming flow of recruits.

Corporal is the rank of most skilled enlisted men, from radio operators to pilots to medics. Most corporals have some additional job to their usual combat duties, setting them apart from and above the lower grunts. A corporal wears two horizontal bars. Typical turnover is two years, but is often sped along by exceptional work or the loss of those higher on the chain of command.

Sergeants are the low-level leadership of the Corps and oversee most of its basic operations. Sergeants can command small squads of soldiers, but never much more than that, and must always be supervised by a superior officer. The insignia of a sergeant consists of one chevron. Sergeants generally maintain that rank for three to five years. Sergeants are also eligible for other jobs, the most prized of which is instructor, those who train the incoming soldiers. This special job is usually only performed through one or two recruit classes and is a high honor.

Chief Sergeants carry on the same duties as a sergeant, but on a larger scale and less-involved position. They tend to oversee the sergeants in their jobs and can actually command a unit under some circumstances, though they are usually the second gun to a Lieutenant. The C-Serge, as they are often called, wears a chevron over a small triangle. Lucky chief sergeants who have formerly served as instructors can hold the position of chief instructor, the overseer of training for one specific recruit class. Holding this position for more than one session of training is a rarity. Turnover for the average c-serge is about four years.

The Lieutenant is the primary commander of the Corps, running squads, overseeing major areas of technical and logistical work, and generally overseeing as many as a dozen c-serges in their jobs. They wear one chevron over one bar. Before becoming a lieutenant the soldier must pass a short, three-month evaluation of command, all the while wearing the c-serge rank. The advancement past lieutenant basically depends on position availability, since the number of captains is set and it is a rare thing when a spot opens up.

Captain is about as elite as one can get in the AMC, overseeing a major area of operation. For example, there is a captain of infantry, mechanics, mechanized infantry, training, and every other major area of operation in the Corps. The job is not unlike one of a department head in a major corporation. For all intents and purposes, their word is law. The captain's insignia is one chevron over two bars. There is one captain who outranks all others and is second in command of the AMC. Currently this is Psythe Komodo, one of the Corps' founding members. A small, four-pointed star overlaying the bars on his rank distinguishes him from his peers.

The head of the AMC holds the rank of Commander, and wears a large, four-pointed star for his rank. This is currently Onra, founder of the AMC. This position will only be available upon the death or resignation of Onra.

AMC Players of Note

Mage Onra III

Commander, Arzno Mercenary Corps

Clothed in his finest red robes and carrying his trusty Pyrus Blade by his side, the Weapon Mage Onra climbed the marble steps of the ancient Temple of Libson, the temple of his clan and forefathers. At the top of the seemingly endless staircase, Onra found himself far above the clouds and before an altar made of pearl and trimmed in silver. As he knelt before the altar, he heard the voice of his father say to him from the clouds, "Son, you have a great task set before you. Our enemies threaten your brethren, your cousins, your people, who are now your charge. A threat has come to the Earth that you must quell. The demons must be rid of and humanity saved. Gather together an army of the purest warriors, one hundred and forty-four strong. Train them as best you know how and pit them against this new threat." A bright light shone from the altar and on it appeared a wooden cross, trimmed in silver and held on a silver chain. "Take this. Remember this always, my son: This cross will save you. This cross will save us all. Now seek your clansman Lanis. There will answers begin to come clear and your methods be made known."

Onra awoke on his bedroll in the middle of the desert with his sword by his side, his clothes soaked with sweat, and a large cross medallion around his neck. His fire dead and the clouds blocking out the night's heavenly lights, he could just make out the lights of a small town across the huge ravine. He quickly gathered his few belongings and began to trek across the bleak wasteland to what he hoped might be a clue to his new task.

Mage Onra was given a task through a visitation by his father, long dead. To a True Atlantean there is no greater mission than one given in so dramatic a fashion. Onra went to what was then the small town known as Arzno, just to the north of the Grand Canyon in what was formerly known as Arizona. There he found a community rich with mages, particularly Techno-Wizards, a form of magic with which he was only mildly familiar. After entreating on the hospitality of some local townsfolk for several days, word reached him that another Atlantean had stumbled onto the town. As it turned out, it was Onra's clansman, Lanis, of whom the vision had spoken. Lanis, too, had been guided to the city by strange happenings and with the desire to help his human brethren help themselves. That was the day that the concepts of the Arzno Mercenary Corps and Arzno Weapons Manufacturing were born. The joint venture was to help humans fight against the hordes of vampires who were starting to head north, as well as other demonic threats.

Little did Onra know how serious the battle against the undead was to become. There was, in fact, a specific faction of the legions of the damned that was to arise later and prove to become Onra's primary enemy and the most significant danger to humankind. The days of random and scattered vampire tribes

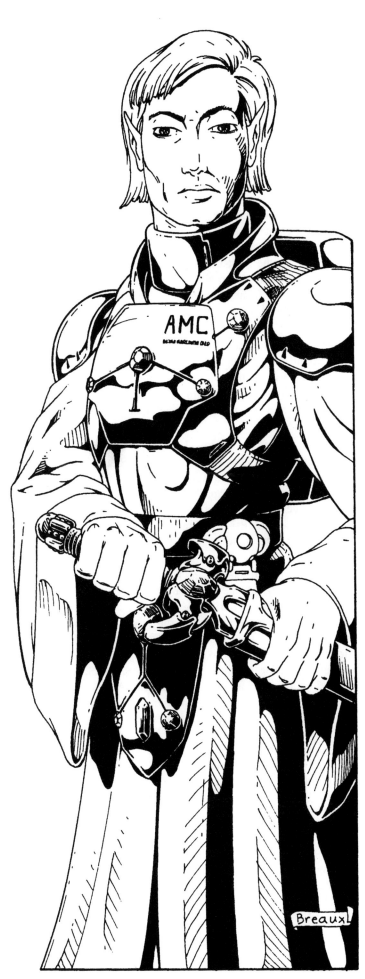

bickering and fighting amongst themselves were about to be a luxury no longer available. A new Intelligence was about to introduce a new type of warfare: the vampire army. Not just a legion of the undead, but an organized unit of soldiers with a competent military strategist at the head of the movement. This leader was a turned CS Military Specialist named Xavier Stuart.

Xavier's story, in short, is this: The Coalition States mistreated him. He became angry and wanted a chance to lead, as he felt he should have been allowed to. He was given this chance by a supernatural power. He took it.

After Lanis and Onra had been operating for about twenty-five years, Lanis building a large and successful TW company and Onra building a relatively small but positively dedicated and potent mercenary corps, Xavier started his operations in New Mexico and Arizona. Surgical military strikes on towns were used to gather slave stock, blood and supplies, and train the army of vampires as well as test what methods were most effective. As Onra and his elite team of vampire hunters (including Samantha the Werejaguar, Psythe Komodo the Psi-Stalker, Rumble the Borg, and Fidel the Dog Boy among others) started to get contracts to stop these attacks, the two chosen heroes of their respective causes began to clash. Xavier and Onra have a mutual respect for one another, which is probably why they're both still alive. The two know each other well and trust the other not to make stupid mistakes. Xavier is constantly adding to his forces and Onra to his. Onra knows his final number: one hundred and forty-four. Right now (105 P.A.) he's at one hundred or so, though many of them aren't the purest warriors. In roughly three years, Onra figures he'll have the strength, power, and purity to attack his nemesis in the final battle. Nobody knows how it will end, but Onra has faith in his cause. You can't ask for more than that.

The dream has revealed most of its mystery except that of the cross. Onra has no idea what his father meant when he said, "This cross will save us all." He suspects that this means there will be a climactic battle between he and the master vampire and the cross will play some part in the outcome. He carries it with him at all times for luck, and as a reminder of his mission.

Real Name: Mage Onra Misvina III of the clan of Libson
Rank: Commander
Alignment: Scrupulous
Hit Points: 48
S.D.C.: 142
P.P.E.: 156
I.S.P.: N/A
Attributes: I.Q. 18, M.E. 22, M.A. 18, P.S. 26, P.P. 18, P.E. 23, P.B. 19, Spd: 36
Experience: 10th level True Atlantean Weapon Mage
Weight: 260 lbs (117 kg)
Height: 6 feet, 5 inches (2 m)
Sex: Male
Age: 126
Disposition: Chivalrous and fair, but brutal to those who would oppress or harm. Especially hates the vampires and Splugorth.
Natural Abilities: All the normal abilities of a True Atlantean.
Psionics: None
Magic Tattoos: Marks of heritage, eye of knowledge, flaming shield, knight in armor, and crossed swords.

Magic Spell Knowledge: Ignite Fire, Fuel Flame, Blinding Flash, Globe of Daylight, Chameleon, Magic Net, Carpet of Adhesion, Energy Field, Invulnerability, Impervious to Fire/Heat, Fire Ball, Fly as the Eagle, Fear, Paralysis: Lesser, Thunderclap, Sense Evil, Sense Magic, and Telekinesis.

Skills: Literacy: American 98%, Language: American and Spanish 98%, Magic Lore 89%, Demon Lore 79%, Land Navigation 86%, Horsemanship: General 95%, Wilderness Survival 89%, Pilot: Hovercraft 95%, Pilot: Automobile 82%, Demolitions 91%, Intelligence 77%, Tracking 79%, Basic Math 94%, Detect Ambush 84%, Acrobatics and Gymnastics, Prowl 89%, Boxing, Running, Athletics, and Body Building.

Weapon Proficiencies: Sword, Knife, Chain, Automatic Pistol, Energy Rifle, Heavy Energy.

Combat: Hand to Hand: Martial Arts, Boxing, and Fencing.

Bonuses when using his magic blade:

Attacks per melee: 8

+10 strike

+14 parry

+8 dodge

+11 roll

Critical Strike on unmodified 18-20, Paired Weapons, Body Flip, Karate Kick, Jump Kick, Entangle, Leap Attack.

Allies: The members of his Arzno Mercenary Corps, the citizens of Arzno, other Atlanteans, and warriors of light.

Enemies: All evil, especially the vampires of Xavier Stuart and the Splugorth.

Equipment:

The Pyrus Blade — a magic blade created for Onra by his master that, when activated, is covered in red-hot flame that will only hurt its intended target. The blade inflicts full damage to vampires.

Damage: Blade inflicts 1D4x10 (Mega-Damage to M.D.C. targets, S.D.C. to S.D.C. targets) and the magic flame inflicts an additional 1D4x10.

Other abilities: Fire Ball (100 feet/30.5 m, 1D4x10 damage, once per round), creates a fiery protective aura of 60 M.D.C. around the user (double at ley lines), and makes the user impervious to fire and heat.

TWA-1600 Exterminator Armor, a TWW-3550 Water Rifle, a TWW-1150 Light Dagger, a silver-trimmed wooden cross medallion (magically indestructible), and virtually any TW or survival gear needed. Has all of the resources of AWM and the AMC at his disposal.

Money: Onra has about twenty or thirty thousand credits in savings from his work with the AMC, but doesn't really keep track of it. He has everything he needs already provided for him.

Psythe Komodo

Second in command of the Arzno Mercenary Corps

Psythe released another burst from his rail gun into the throngs of pale undead that surrounded him. He didn't intend to kill any of the inhuman beasts, there were too many of them and they were regenerating far too quickly for him to be able to destroy any, even with wooden rounds loaded in his USA-M31 rail gun. No, Psythe's intention was simply to keep them off-balance, to hurt them and prevent them from getting too close; it was barely working. Two men lay dead on the ground, their armor torn to shreds by the vampires' claws. Another lay on the ground seriously wounded and unable to move. The vampires plodded on through the shower of wooden shards towards the fallen man. The situation was desperate but not hopeless, thanks in part to Psythe's sixth sense and quick thinking.

Even so, they were not out of the woods yet.

Psythe focused on the vampire closest to him, the red circle imposed on the vampire by the U.S.A. SAMAS's combat computer filling his eyes in the confines of the power armor's helmet. Psythe raised his left arm and levelled it squarely upon the vampire's chest until the circle changed to green. "Take this, you monsters." Psythe mumbled. A pair of flaming tails jumped forth from Psythe's outstretched arm. The two missiles flew like comets into the lead vampire's chest and erupted into two brilliant globes of flame, illuminating the dark midnight ground with red light. A dozen of the vampires were flung back onto their backs by the force of the explosion, unhurt but stunned.

Psythe took advantage of their position and swooped down to the ground to pick up one of his fallen comrades. Turning around, his back to the vampires, Psythe hit the armor's rockets and flew like a bullet off into the night, delivering his fellow mercenary from certain death. He could only hope the others got his message in time.

Psythe is one of the original professional vampire hunters in the deserts of the old southwestern United States, and one of the founding members of the Arzno Mercenary Corps. Psythe was born and raised at Fort Apache and his true Indian name is Eric Serpent Eye, though he prefers to go by his long-time nickname Psythe Komodo. A Psi-Stalker and a natural warrior, Psythe was quickly given the honor of a post with the Apache's warriors. He served extensively as a scout due to his psionic abilities and the fact that his presence at the fort tended to make many there nervous — Psi-Stalkers were not looked well upon by most of its inhabitants. It was during these scouting missions that Psythe discovered and came to despise the wandering tribes of vampires that plagued the land. Psythe had that hatred in mind when he requested permission to enter the Apache's robot and power armor unit using the recovered U.S.A. SAMAS, after seeing them in action against a Plumed Serpent. After a great deal of debate, Psythe was granted permission to join the elite unit and began training in earnest. Shortly after completing his training, Psythe and his squad came across a D-Bee village decimated by vampires. Psythe was deeply disturbed, but his superiors refused to wage a war against the vampire tribes, especially when they were not specifically threatened. Enraged, Psythe left, taking a U.S.A. SAMAS with him. It was about this same time that Lanis and Onra were forging the beginnings of the Arzno Mercenary Corps, and Psythe upon finding them gladly joined. He has been there ever since.

Psythe gets along well with the rest of the AMC and is greatly admired by many of the younger members, who see him as a brave warrior who listens to his heart and won't back down from a fight. Psythe is somewhat uncomfortable with his status as an idol to many of the younger men, but thanks to urging from Lanis, he accepts his image as the AMC's perfect warrior, if only to inspire greatness in the men under his and Onra's

command. Psythe would simply prefer the excitement and intensity of the battlefield to the hounding of admiring fans.

Real Name: Psythe Komodo

Rank: Captain

Alignment: Unprincipled

Hit Points: 53

S.D.C.: 62

P.P.E.: 8

I.S.P.: 107

Attributes: I.Q. 10, M.E. 17, M.A. 10, P.S. 17, P.P. 20, P.E. 14, P.B. 9, Spd 23

Experience: 4th level Psi-Stalker, 4th level RPA Elite

Weight: 169 lbs (76 kg)

Height: 6 feet, 1 inch (1.85 m)

Sex: Male

Age: 32

Disposition: Psythe has a tough, no nonsense attitude and rarely gives up his alert and serious warrior's pose. He is observant and a quick thinker, able to summarize a situation quickly in the thick of combat. What he lacks in tact he makes up for in ferocity.

Natural Abilities: As per standard Psi-Stalker; see **Rifts®** or **Lone Star** for details.

Magic: None

Psionics: Sixth Sense, See Aura, Mind Block, Sense Evil, Telepathy and See the Invisible in addition to the natural abilities above. Considered a major psionic.

Bionics/Cybernetics: None

Combat: Hand to Hand: Expert: 4 attacks per melee. +6 to parry and dodge, +5 to strike, +1 to damage and +4 to pull/roll with punch, fall or impact. Robot Combat Elite: U.S.A. SAMAS: 6 attacks per melee, +8 to parry, +8 to dodge on the ground, +11 flying, +7 to pull/roll with punch, fall or impact.

Bonuses: +4 vs psionics, +2 vs magic, +6 vs Horror Factor, +6 vs mind altering drugs.

Vulnerabilities/Penalties: Requires regular nourishment of P.P.E. to stay healthy. Psythe also tends to get himself in over his head in combat, particularly with vampires, though so far he's been lucky enough to have always escaped with minimal injuries.

Skills of Note: Language: American and Spanish 75%, Radio: Basic 70%, Pilot Hovercraft 80%, Pilot Tanks & APCs 63%, Robot Combat: Basic, Robot Combat Elite: U.S.A. SAMAS, Read Sensory Equipment 55%, Weapon Systems 65%, Climbing 60%/50%, Prowl 50%, W.P. Energy Pistol, W.P. Energy Rifle, W.P. Heavy Energy, W.P. Knife, Hand to Hand: Expert.

Allies of Note: Outside of Arzno, Psythe has a few small bandit clans who respect him or are in his debt.

Enemies: Apart from vampires, Psythe gained the enmity of several Indian tribes and gangs during his years as a scout and fighter for the Apache.

Appearance: A tall, pale-skinned man with the bald head and war paint typical of a Psi-Stalker. Psythe would be an attractive man if it weren't for his weather beaten and scar covered face, or if he smiled on occasion.

Weapons & Equipment of Note: Native American U.S.A. SAMAS with TW modifications: Armor of Ithan, Impervious to Energy, and Invisibility Superior, all at 10th level strength.
Money: 16,000 credits. Psythe doesn't have much interest in or need for money.

Ban

Captain of Infantry

"Well you know what soldier? I don't care. Because there's people in that town that need our help or they're gonna die. So you can pout about it being too dangerous all you like, but you're gonna go in guns blazin' just like the rest of us or you're gonna find my boot in your mouth!"

Brandon awoke one morning in a seedy hotel in Silverno with no idea of who or where he was. The room he occupied was empty except for a dusty backpack filled with clothes and a few other miscellaneous items, and a laser pistol tucked carefully under his pillow. After a few minutes of pacing around his room, Brandon found a wallet and set of keys locked in a drawer. Inside the wallet was a Coalition ID with his face and the name "Brandon Marshall."

Gathering up the pack and ambling downstairs, Brandon turned his room key in to the clerk and was stunned when she pulled a suit of armor and a heavy laser rifle from the storage room and gave them to him. Not to appear uncouth, Brandon took the armor and weapon and walked out onto the street. After several failed attempts at using the keys he found, Brandon finally found the vehicle to which one belonged, a bright red NG-Rocket.

Before he even had a chance to pull out into the street, he heard the shouts behind him just before a laser blast blew a pillar next to him in two. Four Coalition soldiers down the street were racing towards him, weapons blazing. Without a thought and much to his amazement, Brandon slammed the accelerator on the hovercycle and fled into the streets, and eventually out of the city and into the wilderness. Running scared, Brandon eventually stumbled into Arzno. Low on food and supplies and in an apparently safe community, Brandon decided to stay and relax for awhile before moving on.

All of this occurred over six years ago and Brandon still has no idea who he is or what he was doing in Silverno. All he knows is that his stopover in Arzno has turned into a successful mercenary career and that it's a life he's perfectly comfortable with. As captain of infantry, Brandon is in his element as a down and dirty ground pounder.

Brandon now knows that he's a Crazy, and that the implants in his brain may well be the source of his memory loss. They are undoubtedly the source of some of his other "quirks," such as his terrible temper and fear of enclosed spaces. It is also likely the reason for his delusions that he is a True Atlantean instead of an ordinary human being. Without an identity to call his own, and being surrounded by them, it wasn't much of a stretch for Brandon to convince himself that he was one, despite his diminutive stature.

Recently, some psychic researchers visiting Arzno suggested that it may be possible to penetrate Brandon's memory block and determine who he was and what happened in his past, once and for all. Brandon adamantly refused their offer and drove them off in a bout of frustration, seriously injuring one. Though the psychics have long since left Arzno, Brandon is beginning to regret his decision and is having second thoughts. He isn't even sure why he refused their offer in the first place. It's a lost opportunity now, however, and Brandon's thoughts are turned back to the task at hand — Xavier's vampire army.

Real Name: Unknown; he presumes it to be Brandon Marshall (fake CS I.D.). Goes commonly by the nickname of Ban.
Rank: Captain
Alignment: Scrupulous
Hit Points: 51
S.D.C.: 153
P.P.E.: 20
I.S.P.: 46
Attributes: I.Q. 12, M.E. 10, M.A. 11, P.S. 25, P.P. 20, P.E. 26, P.B. 7, Spd. 24
Experience: 8th level Crazy
Weight: 142 lbs (63.9 kg)
Height: 5 feet, 8 inches (1.73 m)
Sex: Male
Age: 28
Disposition: Brandon is a rough and demanding commander who has no patience for cowardice or inferior work. He's a hard worker who expects the same from every man under his command. It's important to note that Brandon doesn't believe that women are suited for the battlefield, and feels uncomfortable around them on a personal level. He's a pure professional when it comes to his duty.
Insanities:
1. Believes he's a True Atlantean

2. Claustrophobic
3. Obsessed with Cleanliness
4. Frenzy: Anger/Frustration
5. Obsession: Hates Gambling (even being caught playing games of chance for fun will result in absurdly harsh penalties)

Natural Abilities: Standard fare for a Crazy.
Magic: None, though he respects and admires it.
Psionics: Sixth Sense, See the Invisible and Clairvoyance.
Bionics/Cybernetics: None
Combat: Hand to Hand: Martial Arts: 5 attacks per melee, +9 to parry, +9 to dodge, +5 to strike, +10 to damage, +11 to roll, +2 initiative, critical strike on a natural 18-20, paired weapons.
Bonuses: +2 vs psionics, +6 vs magic, +6 vs mind control, +10 vs poison, +32% vs coma/death.
Vulnerabilities/Penalties: Well, he's nuts. In particular, his tendency to fly into a frenzy when extremely angry/upset more than slightly clouds his judgement. Brandon also refuses to sleep inside tents or ride in vehicles due to his claustrophobia, which also keeps him outside of vampire lairs, instead directing the action from outside and trying to flush the demons out into the open.
Skills of Note: Acrobatics, Climbing 90%/80%, Prowl 80%, Boxing, Athletics, Body Building, W.P. Axe, W.P. Sword, W.P. Energy Pistol, and W.P. Energy Rifle.
Allies of Note: Other than the members of the AMC, Brandon doesn't know of anyone who he could call an ally or friend.
Enemies of Note: In addition to the legions of vampires, Brandon also appears to be wanted by the Coalition, though he doesn't know why.
Appearance: A stocky but short man with dirty blond hair in a crew cut, Ban isn't the most attractive or intimidating guy around, even less so when he claims to be a True Atlantean.
Weapons & Equipment of Note: Brandon has access to all of the AMC's armories, but tends towards heavy weapons with a high rate of fire.
Money: Brandon has amassed a small fortune of 158,000 credits.

Sir Tyrone

Captain of Intelligence

When no news of Sir Tyrone's expedition into the vampire kingdoms came back to Lazlo for over ten years, Erin Tarn and the Council of Learning feared the worst. It wasn't without a great deal of sadness that Erin accepted the sad fact that her loyal protector and friend was likely dead. Now, over twenty years later, Sir Tyrone and his expedition are little more than statistics and rarely enter anyone's minds, though Erin occasionally reminisces about the old times with the Cyber-Knight.

Unbeknownst to anyone outside of Mexico, Sir Tyrone is still alive, through nothing but a miracle of strength and determination.

Though the majority of Sir Tyrone's expedition was eradicated by the vampires of Mexico, he and a few others were spared and taken to the blood pools of Muluc. The blood pools were insidious places where human cattle were restrained and hooked into advanced life support equipment so that they could produce and be drained of blood for the vampires for years.

Most of Sir Tyrone's companions succumbed and died, burnt out after an agonizing five to eight years, but the Cyber-Knight, with his tremendous strength and hope, clung to life for an incredible twelve years before a slave riot released him from the vampires' clutches.

Years of being hooked into life sustaining equipment and being drained of precious blood took a tremendous toll on Tyrone's body and mind. Even after years of working to rebuild his lost strength and dexterity, Tyrone is still only a shadow of his former self. Despite his feeble condition however, he pushed on to complete his mission with newfound determination. He must reveal the truth about the vampire kingdoms to the rest of the world.

Despite the objections of his saviours, Sir Tyrone set out on a one man mission to the north and out of vampire territory, back to human civilization. His and Erin Tarn's worst fears were confirmed; the vampires were prolific, well organized and powerful. He had to contact Erin and warn the world of the monsters that dwelt in the deserts of Mexico. Numerous times during his voyage, Sir Tyrone narrowly avoided recapture and certain death. Eventually, struggling from exhaustion and dying of starvation, Psythe came across the destitute Cyber-Knight on one of his patrol runs. Sir Tyrone was rushed to Arzno and, thanks to speedy medical attention and magic, was saved from death.

After discussions with Onra and Lanis, Sir Tyrone has decided to remain with Arzno for a time before leaving to find Erin Tarn to tell her his tale. Onra and Lanis are skeptical about Sir Tyrone's claims, as is just about everyone else in the city. Sir Tyrone has learned to accept others' doubts and no longer speaks about his past or associations with Erin Tarn. His priority at the present is to prove to Onra, Lanis and anyone else who will listen that the vampires are a greater threat than anyone had imagined. Now that Xavier has made his presence known with his well-organized vampire forces, Sir Tyrone's words are beginning to take on more weight.

Real Name: Dorian Tyrone
Rank: Captain
Alignment: Aberrant (was scrupulous)
Hit Points: 68
S.D.C.: 29 (was 93)
P.P.E.: 23
I.S.P.: 54
Attributes: I.Q. 10, M.E. 19, M.A. 14, P.S. 8 (was 24), P.P. 9 (was 14), P.E. 10 (was 20), P.B. 11, Spd. 9 (was 39)
Experience: 12th level Cyber-Knight
Weight: 188 lbs (84.6 kg)
Height: 6 feet (1.83 m)
Sex: Male
Age: 58
Disposition: Sir Tyrone is quiet, serious and forlorn. Few have ever seen him smile, and even fewer have seen him laugh. The years he spent in the heart of the vampire kingdoms have forever jaded him into the cold and calculating man he is today. While he still holds the beliefs and values of the Cyber-Knight above all else, he has become increasingly obsessed with the destruction of the vampire infestation, driving him to "bend the rules for the greater good."
Insanity: Phobia: Crypts and underground places.
Natural Abilities: None

Magic: Lore only.

Psionics: Empathy, Sense Evil, Summon Inner Strength and Psi-Sword: 5D6 M.D.

Bionics/Cybernetics: Cyber-Armor (A.R.: 16, 50 M.D.C.)

Combat: 4 attacks per melee, +1 on initiative, +2 to strike, +8 to parry, +4 to dodge, +3 to roll, jump kick, leap attack, paired weapons, entangle, critical strike on a natural 18-20. Sir Tyrone's fighting prowess was once much greater than this, but old age and the years spent in the blood pools have taken their toll. Even with a strict exercise regime and extensive medical treatment, Sir Tyrone's body has never fully healed.

Bonuses: +2 to save vs psionics and insanity.

Vulnerabilities/Penalties: Sir Tyrone's obsessive desire to see the vampire kingdoms destroyed can prevent him from seeing the big picture. Even so, Tyrone is a brilliant and observant man with years of experience, and won't let his emotions overly cloud his judgement. Sir Tyrone's old injuries from the Muluc blood pools also sometimes reassert themselves when he tries to push himself too hard, dropping his attacks per melee, bonuses and speed by half until he can recover himself.

Skills of Note: Lore: Demon 98%, Paramedic 98%, Horsemanship 98%, W.P. Sword, W.P. Blunt, W.P. Energy Rifle, and W.P. Energy Pistol.

Allies of Note: Sir Tyrone is no longer in contact with anyone south of the Rio Grande. All of his allies and friends are within Arzno, though should he ever return to Lazlo he will be greeted with a hero's welcome.

Enemies: Vampires, Xavier's vampire army in particular. Sir Tyrone was also on the Coalition's most wanted list, but has long since been removed.

Weapons & Equipment of Note: Sir Tyrone has been a warrior and adventurer longer than many weapons manufacturers have been in business. He's somewhat out of touch with the times and is suspicious and resistant to new technology. Consequently, he tends to stick to the weapons he used in his day, a JA-11 and a Wilk's 300 (precursor to the 320, 1D6 damage but only a 750 foot/228.6 m range and 8 shots per E-Clip).

Money: Sir Tyrone virtually ignores his finances, only dipping into his savings to buy things he needs, when he needs them. Incidentally, his savings have swelled to 88,000 credits, and he'd be as surprised as anyone to find out he had that much tucked away.

Rumble

Captain of Mechanized Forces

The lights in the mineshaft were no more than dark globes that reflected the light of Rumble's chest spotlight and shone like raindrops in the dark. Rumble turned his head slowly, surveying the mine walls around him, the powerful servos in the borg's neck surprisingly silent. He switched his eyes through several different optic modes, from infrared to ultraviolet, and turned back to the other three miners that had accompanied him down the shaft.

"Doesn't appear to be any damage. No signs of a cave in. Must be something further down," he said. The others behind nodded and the group pushed on toward the pump room. The mine's power and other systems had mysteriously died the night before without warning. Rumble and several other experienced miners had been assigned to survey the mines and fix the problem, if possible. After three hours below the surface they had made little progress, though it was looking more and more like a deliberate act of sabotage than an act of nature.

"This was no accident." said Rumble, his voice trembling with irritation or anger, it was difficult to tell which. He was clenching a batch of severed wires in his vice-like bionic hand. The pump room, oddly enough, was still fully operational, though every other system from lighting to communications was forcibly disabled. Rumble released the cable and turned toward one of the many adjoining tunnels.

"Whoever did this is still here. We're gonna teach 'em to mess with Rothwell Mines." Rumble's focus was broken by the shout of one of his comrades. He turned to see two spike-covered human forms emerge from the darkness carrying a third, obviously wounded.

Rumble raised himself from inspecting the damage and rose to his full seven foot height, nearly touching the stone ceiling. The other miners gathered around him cautiously, eyeing the newcomers as they came into the light of their helmet lanterns.

"Are you responsible for this?" Rumble bellowed, his bionicly enhanced voice echoing through the otherwise silent passages. The three spiked men stepped into the chamber and halted. The spikes, part of their bizarre armor, cast long, sharp shadows on the walls and down the tunnel behind them. One of the men in the spiked armor lifted the injured man and left him in the arms of the other. He stepped forward a single step and rose his arms in a gesture of peace. Even so, Rumble noticed the sword scabbard around the man's waist and the rifle slung over his shoulder.

"I am Onra, this is Psythe and my injured comrade is known as Vincent, and I assure you we are not responsible in any way for the problems in this mine," the man explained calmly. Rumble eyed him carefully. He sounded sincere, but it was difficult to trust a man with such gear.

"Then why are you here? Onra."

The man lowered his hands and returned Rumble's cold stare.

"We have been on the trail of a band of dangerous vampires. The trail led here, to your mines. We encountered a group of them a short time ago, down this shaft from which we just came. That is how Vincent came to be injured," he said, looking in-

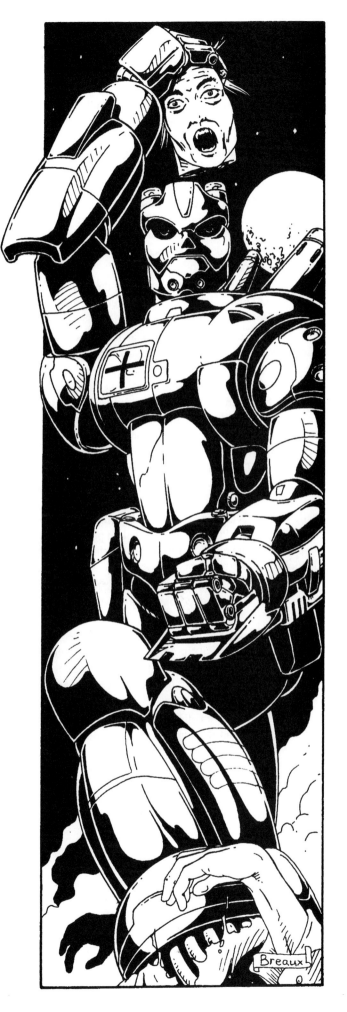

93

tently at the Borg still standing defiantly in the center of the chamber. After a few tense seconds that seemed like hours, Rumble decided the man's words rung with the sound of the truth.

"Very well then. We can't return via shaft four since that's where you came from. We have to assume they know where we are, the only way to go is forward. We can get out through the old shaft from the original mine. Okay," Rumble looked at the frightened faces around him and then to his new comrades and their unusual weaponry. "Let's go."

Onra lit the last flare and tossed it into the tunnel behind them where it erupted into a brilliant globe of white light. He dropped the satchel that he had carried the Techno-Wizard flares in on the ground and gripped his crystal-laden rifle tightly in his hands.

"That's the last of 'em. It should keep them at bay for a while longer." he turned to Rumble and gestured down the tunnel with his rifle. "How much farther?"

Rumble turned his head, looking as far as his spotlight would illuminate before the inky blackness of the tunnel again took over.

"A quarter of a mile, maybe a little less." he responded. Onra shook his head and the others exchanged frightened looks. Rumble turned back to look at the globe of daylight that hovered in the center of the tunnel a short distance behind them. He smiled as only a Borg can.

"The rest of you go on ahead. I have an idea."

A previously concealed compartment in Rumble's left leg opened and Rumble began to pull an assortment of wires and small white blocks out of it. The other miners exchanged worried glances; they knew what Rumble had planned. Onra and his mercenary companions simply watched him confusedly. Rumble looked directly at Onra.

"Don't worry. I'll catch up," he said. "Now hurry up. There should be an access ladder that leads upward not too much farther."

Onra, still unsure as to the Borg's plans, nodded and the three mercenaries moved on, the three miners right behind. Several minutes later, after Rumble and the globe were lost in the distance, the group came to an old steel ladder just as Rumble had told them they would.

Just as Psythe began climbing, their ears were assaulted by a violent "bang," and the tunnel shook around them as dust and small stones fell from the walls and roof. Onra and Psythe, eyes wide with terror, looked to each other with horror as the miners simply lowered their heads. Leaving Vincent with the three miners, Onra and Psythe dashed down the tunnel, guns at the ready. After a short distance their helmet lights caught sight of a large humanoid form.

"Egad!" exclaimed Onra, running forward to help the mighty Borg stumbling along, leaning on the tunnel wall for support. His previously shining bionic body was charred and covered in soot with numerous dents and gashes. "Are you alright?!" Onra asked, at a loss to help the mechanical man if he wasn't.

"Monsters won't get past that for awhile. I just wish I had better timing." Rumble said in an irritated voice. *"Lets get out of here and then blow the whole place, vamps 'n all."*

Ferdinand Merris started out the same as many young men in the mountains of what was once Colorado. Young and impoverished, but with lofty dreams for the future, he went to work in the silver and coal mines that dotted the rust colored peaks throughout the area. After several years of hard work, Ferdinand was finally afforded the break he had been waiting for. He was offered the opportunity to undergo a full bionic conversion into a mining Borg in exchange for three years of service. After that he was free to go and do as he pleased in search of his fortune.

As a young man of twenty-four with no other prospects presenting themselves, Ferdinand readily agreed. Once the conversion was completed without a hitch, Ferdinand worked for the prescribed three years in the mine, and was housed, fed and maintained by the mining company. When his contract expired, he thanked his previous employers and went on his way. A small but prosperous mining outfit known as Rothwell Mines quickly picked him up. Ferdinand's experience and skill with explosives, in addition to his bionic body, made him a prized catch for the small operation and he quickly rose in ranks to become the mine's foreman.

Unfortunately all good things must come to an end, and when vampires infiltrated the mine shafts it became necessary to collapse the entire complex and shut the mine down. Ferdinand's courage and skills impressed Onra, who was all too pleased to accept Ferdinand's request to accompany them back to Arzno. Ferdinand, who more often than not goes by his nickname "Rumble," has adjusted to mercenary work surprisingly well. His mining experience has proven indispensable in deep vampire lairs, as has his knowledge of heavy machinery and explosives. It is for this reason that he's joined the company's mechanized forces. His mining Borg body has been modified and upgraded, adding additional armor and weapon systems while keeping many of the mining implements Rumble has come to rely upon.

Real Name: Ferdinand Merris
Alias: Rumble
Rank: Captain
Alignment: Principled
M.D.C.: 240, plus 420 for heavy infantry armor
P.P.E.: 2
Attributes: I.Q. 14, M.E. 14, M.A. 11, P.S. 30 (bionic), P.P. 22 (bionic), P.E.: 14, P.B.: 6, Spd.: 66 (45 mph/72 km)
Experience: 6th level Mining Borg, 3rd level Military Borg
Weight: 1200 lbs (540 kg)
Height: 7 feet, 6 inches (2.29 m)
Sex: Male
Age: 31
Disposition: Generally serious and single-minded when on duty, Ferdinand is still a bit too formal in non-combat situations as well. Ferdinand likes it when things are running smoothly and orderly, and hates surprises.
Natural Abilities: None
Magic: None
Psionics: None
Bionics/Cybernetics: Full bionic conversion for mining with additional military/combat enhancements. Universal headjack, amplified hearing with sound filtration system, multi-optic system, modular hands and arms with access to

all attachments from **New West™**, all bionic lung features as well as large and small concealed compartments in both legs.

Combat: Hand to Hand: Expert: 3 attacks per melee, +7 to parry and dodge, +6 to strike, +4 to roll, +1 on initiative, +4 to pull punch, +15 to damage, critical strike on an unmodified 18, 19 or 20.

Bonuses: +3 to save vs Horror Factor.

Vulnerabilities/Penalties: Despite his training in Arzno, Ferdinand is still more miner than soldier at heart. Consequently, he sometimes has difficulty with military etiquette and command structures. He is also unwilling to command his armored forces from behind the lines, instead pushing his way right up to the front with his troops. His bionic nature also obviously prevents him from using any kind of magical or psionic enhancements.

Skills of Note: Underground Tunneling 65%, Underground Architecture 55%, Underground Sense of Direction 65%, Metal Working 65%, Radio: Basic 80%, Demolitions 95%, Basic Mechanics 65%, Pilot: Tanks and APCs 70%, Fortification 50%, W.P. Knife, W.P. Energy Rifle, W.P. Heavy Energy.

Allies of Note: Ferdinand is well known as a loyal and hard-working miner who will stand by his fellow workers and employers through thick and thin. He has been asked on more than one occasion to leave Arzno to become foreman of various prestigious mines in the region, all of which he has politely refused.

Enemies: Ferdinand also made a few enemies within the mining industry, particularly with cruel and exploitative mining companies who don't treat their workers with respect. Ferdinand hates nothing more than irresponsible management, since it puts the miners at risk.

Weapons & Equipment of Note: Ferdinand still has all of his old mining gear and bionics, as well as several new pieces of military equipment. As head of the Arzno armored division, he has access to just about any heavy weapon or vehicle he may need. He personally prefers large APCs and transports, and high explosives.

Money: 240,000 in universal credits and precious metals. Ferdinand amassed most of this during his mining years and has been living off of it for a long time.

Patria Nemesio

Leader of Delta Squad

Patria never knew her mother very well, though she has heard countless stories about her from both her father, Lanis, and other citizens of Arzno. When Patria was only 11 years old, her mother was killed in a massive vampire raid on the town in the early years of the AMC.

Over the years following her mother's death, Patria's life was filled with anger and confusion. Her father, who had always been somewhat distant, found himself at a loss when it came to raising his young daughter. Though he tried, he was unable to replace the void left by Patria's mother. In fact, he ended up pushing her farther and farther away, as he tried to make up for his own loss by pursuing the vampire threat with a new passion, leaving Patria to find her own way in life. Unfortunately, it was not the way Lanis had hoped she would chose. Patria's mother was an accomplished wizard, a lover of life, freedom and happiness. It was these things that Lanis had loved in her and he

imagined these things becoming a part of his daughter, that she would carry on where his wife had left off. To his disappointment, Patria turned out to be quite different from what he had hoped.

The years of awkward silence between the father and daughter had a profound effect on Patria. Though she was young when her mother was killed, she could still sense the incredible loss and change of personality in her father, a change she couldn't help but make herself. Patria became increasingly militant and aggressive, joining the Arzno militia rather than studying the mystic arts like her father wished. When Lanis expressed his anger to Patria and demanded she leave the militia to study at the magic college, Patria fled from Arzno and her father's demands. Eventually, Patria ended up joining a group of fighters for good who called themselves "The Crusaders," with members across the Megaverse including Cyber-Knights and Atlantean Undead Slayers. For the first time since her mother was killed, Patria felt that she belonged. In the following years, she underwent the arduous process of acquiring the tattoos and training of an Undead Slayer. Shortly afterwards, Patria returned to her father and Arzno, ready to do what she could to rebuild her father's dream.

When Patria returned a tattooed warrior, Lanis wept tears of anger and regret. His hopes that his daughter would become like her mother were shattered. Not only was she a warrior and destroyer probably destined to die on the field of battle, she could now never practice the magical arts like he had hoped. Patria was equally disappointed when she met with her father's tremendous disapproval.

Today the two have scarce little contact with each other. Lanis feels that he has lost not only his wife but also his daughter to the vampires forever. Patria hopes that one day her father may realize that she isn't her mother and that she must follow her own path. All she seeks is her father's approval, which is not yet forthcoming. Until then, she continues that which she sees as her duty, slaying the beasts that have caused so much pain for her and her father.

Real Name: Patria Nemesio
Rank: Lieutenant
Alignment: Unprincipled
Hit Points: See M.D.C.
M.D.C.: 289
P.P.E.: 258
Attributes: I.Q. 21, M.E. 22, M.A. 24, P.S. 30, P.P. 15, P.E. 18, P.B. 22, Spd 28
Horror Factor: 13 to monsters and practitioners of evil.
Experience: 6th level Undead Slayer
Weight: 153 lbs (68.9)
Height: 6 feet, 3 inches (1.91 m)
Sex: Female
Age: 32
Disposition: Patria is a tough and self-reliant warrior who is willing to put her life on the line at the drop of a hat. She has suffered disapproval and disappointment in the past and has come to rely on herself more than anything or anyone else. When things get tough, Patria remains steadfast and will take action when others back down. Ironically, though she remains distant from other troops, she inadvertently inspires many to push themselves further and to test their limits.
Natural Abilities: Increased P.P.E. recovery, cannot be meta-

morphosed or otherwise transformed in any way, impervious to vampire bites, sense the presence of vampires within a 1000 foot (305 m) radius, and recognizes vampires by sight. In addition, she can sense ley lines and dimensional Rifts the same as a Ley Line Walker, as well as ley line phasing, and can operate dimensional pyramids. Also see combat bonuses.

Magic: A general understanding of magic tattoos and how to use them. As a True Atlantean Undead Slayer, Patria has the Marks of Heritage plus the following 23 tattoos:

Weapons, Animals & Monsters: Flaming Sword, Flaming Bow and Arrow with Wings, Dagger, Staff, Flaming Shield, Flaming Spear with Coiled Snake and Wings, Animal: Wolf, Animal: Eagle, Monster: Leatherwing, Monster: Grigleaper, Animal: Cheetah, Whip.

Power Tattoos: Protection From Vampires, Turn Dead, Invulnerability, Control the Forces of Air, Healing: Basic, Healing: Super, Knowledge & Reading, Chain with a Broken Link (strength), Chain Encircling a Skull (psionic save), Lightning Bolts (shoot lightning) and Third Eye (supernatural vision).

Psionics: None

Combat: Hand to Hand: Martial Arts: 3 attacks per melee, +3 to parry and dodge, +2 to strike, +3 to roll with punch/fall or impact, critical strike on a natural 18, 19 or 20.

Bonuses: +4 to save vs psionics, +6 to save vs magic, +2 to save vs poison, +6% vs coma/death, +8 to save vs Horror Factor, 70% to trust/intimidate, and 60% to charm/impress.

Vulnerabilities/Penalties: Patria's rugged independence and lurking anger at her father have resulted in her having great difficulty with figures of authority. On numerous occasions Patria has disobeyed direct orders, instead doing what she has felt was best. She has accomplished great heroics this way, but also puts herself and others at great risk. Sir Tyrone is the only senior figure she listens to and respects, primarily because he treats her more like a person than anyone else does. In a sense, Sir Tyrone is the father she no longer has.

Skills of Note: Languages & Literacy: Dragonese/Elf, American, and Greek 98%, Languages: Spanish, Euro, and Faerie Speak 97%, Intelligence 69%, Tracking 72%, Wilderness Survival 77%, Lore: Demons & Monsters 82%, Lore: Faerie Folk 67%, Swimming 87%, W.P. Archery & Targeting, W.P. Knife, W.P. Sword, W.P. Energy Pistol, W.P. Energy Rifle, Hand to Hand: Martial Arts, Prowl 62%, Horsemanship 77%, Escape Artist 72%, First Aid 87%, Pilot Hovercraft 92%, and Detect Ambush 72%.

Allies of Note: Apart from the citizens of Arzno and the members of the Arzno Mercenary Corps, Patria is also on good terms with the Cyber-Knights and others amongst The Crusaders.

Enemies of Note: Vampires and the Splugorth.

Appearance: A tall, slender beauty with flowing blond hair, deep green eyes and outstanding grace. Patria has been the object of many a man's affection, but is too dedicated to the crusade against the undead and the disdain of her father to be distracted by love.

Weapons & Equipment of Note: A wooden cross, a dozen wooden stakes and mallet, a TX-5 Pump Pistol, a JA-11, 3 silver plated knifes, a longbow and quiver of arrows, and a

TW Water Shotgun. Rides a male Psi-Pony named Thunder. Thunder wears cavalry barding when entering combat or traveling (90 M.D.C.).

Money: 13,000 in universal credits. Patria donates most of her money to the poor and to the war effort.

Gerra No'ta
Head Field Mechanic for
the Arzno Mercenary Corps

The advance team was cornered, pinned down by the adult Hydra and its nine ugly heads, laying in wait just outside of the cave entrance. The team had been sent to investigate some vampire activity in the canyon, and got a little more than they bargained for with their hungry serpent friend. Gerra looked around and assessed the situation. They had only lost one man, but several of the twenty or so were injured. The troop transport lay fifty yards behind the leering head of their monstrous foe. Thus far, any attack on the beast did nothing but unleash a hail of attacks through the cave entrance, which burned, froze and poisoned all inside. They were in a pinch and were all looking toward their Techno-Wizard mechanic for help.

He was way ahead of them. For the past hour of the standoff, he had been busy cannibalizing parts from weapons and hurriedly lacing them with stones and gems from his trusty field pouch. The result was half a dozen hand grenades armed to distract the monster while they made their escape. They weren't pretty, but they would do.

He handed the grenades to six healthy troops and made the count to move. As the troops ran from the cave, the grenades were thrown. The crystal-laden spheres soared upward, then detected the evil presence of the Hydra and were drawn toward it. The troops shielded their eyes as the blinding flashes ignited in the many eyes of the beast. It reared back, firing its various breath weapons randomly as the last of the soldiers reached the transport. In another moment they were fleeing hurriedly from the scene and patting Gerra on the back.

Gerra is a relatively new member of the Arzno Mercenary Corps, especially for his high status. His position was given directly by Lanis, the Corps' sponsor who found him to be far above the simple manufacturing of the TW items sold at Arzno Weapons Manufacturing. His ability to think on his is feet amazing, and with his skill as a Techno-Wizard coupled with his mechanical knowledge and psionic abilities, Lanis declared and Onra agreed that he was perfect for the job of field mechanic.

On the field of battle, Gerra is a cunning magical tactician and a ruthless warrior. Off the field, he is the brilliant mind behind the TWA-1250 Imitator armor, the TWW-2000 Vamp Killer and many other unique inventions. Gerra is a non-commissioned officer in his position, and is most commonly sent on reconnaissance missions (where quick thinking is often critical) as the team co-leader. His troops respect him for his abilities on and off the battlefield and few are troubled by his unusually alien appearance.

Real Name: Gerra No'ta
Rank: Chief Sergeant
Alignment: Unprincipled
Hit Points: 29

S.D.C.: 51
P.P.E.: 105
I.S.P.: 79
Attributes: I.Q. 17, M.E. 10, M.A. 11, P.S. 12, P.P. 12, P.E. 14, P.B. 7, Spd. 10
Experience: 5th level Trimadore Techno-Wizard
Weight: 211 lbs (95 kg)

Breaux

Height: 7 feet, 7 inches (2.31 m)

Sex: Male

Age: 25

Disposition: Gerra believes strongly in the cause of the people of Arzno, and fights diligently for them. The fact that he is respected and well paid doesn't hurt either.

Natural Abilities: Like all Trimadore, Gerra has perfect vision and excellent hearing, a strong mechanical aptitude and a superior sense of touch.

Magic: Blinding Flash, Globe of Daylight, Ignite Fire, Fuel Flame, Fire Bolt, Call Lightning, Energy Bolt, Energy Field, Impervious to Energy, Telekinesis, Armor of Ithan, Fly as the Eagle, Create Wood, Create Water, Invisibility: Simple and Superior, Sense Evil, and Teleport: Superior. It is important to note that in addition to these, Gerra has access to the spells of all of the mages at Arzno for the purposes of TW devices.

Psionics: Mind Block, Speed Reading, Object Read, and Tele-mechanics. Considered a major psionic.

Bionics/Cybernetics: None

Combat: Hand to Hand: Basic: 4 attacks per melee. +2 on initiative, +2 to parry and dodge, +1 to strike and +4 to pull/roll with punch, fall or impact.

Bonuses: +2 vs magic, +7 vs Horror Factor, +1 vs disease and sickness, and +1 vs possession.

Vulnerabilities/Penalties: The Trimadore is clearly inhuman, making disguise impossible.

Skills of Note: Language: American and Spanish 87% and Techno-can 73%, Literacy: American 63% and Techno-can 53%, Mechanical Engineer 48%, Weapons Engineer 48%, Armorer 63%, Robot Electronics 53%, Robot Mechanics 43%, W.P. Energy Pistol, W.P. Energy Rifle, W.P. Heavy Energy, Hand to Hand: Basic.

Allies of Note: The few fellow Trimadore on Rifts Earth, and the people of Arzno.

Enemies: The vampires and other menaces fought by Arzno, and he isn't too fond of the Coalition.

Weapons & Equipment of Note: Specially designed Rhino Imitator Armor with an extra-heavy force field (100 M.D.C.) and an extra-large P.P.E. battery (100 P.P.E.). His weapon of choice is a silver or standard rail gun. He also carries a pouch with a dozen each of the most commonly used gems and crystals.

Money: 90,000 in hard credits, and another 120,000 or so in gems.

Fidel

Sergeant in the AMC and rogue CS Dog Boy

The smell of the supernatural filled the air and the nostrils of the hefty mutant Rottweiller as he swung his neuro-mace at his seemingly invincible foe. For the hundredth time, the club found its mark, discharging its stunning energy and sending it coursing over the pale white body of the attacking creature. Still, unfazed, it leapt forward and literally took a bite out of the shoulder of the Dog Boy's riot armor with its massive fangs. The Dog Boy grabbed the demon and threw him across the room, sending him into a wall. He took the moment to look over at his shoulder toward his comrades to see how they fared. To his dismay he saw only corpses, bloody and dismembered, each with one or even a couple of the pale demons crouched over it, siphoning the rich fluid from the veins of the fallen through jagged breaches in their armor. Only then did the CS soldier realize what he was up against, and that all of the terrible stories were true. Vampires. Quickly he estimated about eight of the demons, as they one by one lifted their eyes to him. He became suddenly aware of his heart pounding in his chest as he began to pant in fear. At that moment the CS Dog Boy veteran, Fidel, turned tail and ran.

After narrowly escaping his first encounter with vampires, Fidel returned to his CS outpost to report the incident and the true presence of vampires in the south. He was given a mental examination, found unfit for combat, and reassigned to the Lone Star ISS. His report was never officially filed and dismissed without examination. After about a month with ISS, Fidel bugged out and went AWOL. He hired himself out as a mercenary and bounty hunter in several of the larger towns in the southwest, until he stumbled upon a poster for employment with the AMC. When he saw the chance to learn more about vampires and how to fight them, he took it. He has now been with the Corps for eight years and has emerged as a real veteran and leader, especially in the areas of reconnaissance and seek and destroy.

Fidel would be somewhat happy to know that his report, though officially ignored, did not fall between the cracks. His story has happened a dozen times, to many CS troops from all walks of the service, from Juicers to decorated officers. A research team has been assembled and will soon be released into the wastelands of the southwest to study the many legends of vampires, and document the truth. If Fidel learns of this team it is likely that he'll at least find them and see what they're doing about the problem. Right now he's happy in Arzno and would not likely leave, even for his former masters.

Real Name: Fidel

Aliases: None, other than typical slang for Dog Boys.

Rank: Sergeant

Alignment: Unprincipled

Hit Points: 48

S.D.C.: 82

P.P.E.: 12

I.S.P.: 93

Attributes: I.Q. 11, M.E. 13, M.A. 12, P.S. 25, P.P. 18, P.E. 28, P.B. 8, Spd. 41

Experience: 6th level Rottweiler Dog Boy

Weight: 160 lbs (72 kg)

Height: 5 feet, 10 inches (1.78 m)

Sex: Male

Age: 11

Mutant Abnormality: Full color vision.

Disposition: Fidel is a fun guy to be around, and loves the AMC. He feels that he has found a place to belong, both with his (somewhat) human masters and his fellow misfits. His experiences now have only accented the lies and mistreatment he experienced with the CS, yet something inside him still longs for it. He accounts for this as a genetic program and does his best to dismiss it.

Natural Abilities: Has the abilities and senses of any Dog Boy. Sense Psychic and Magic Energy (75 feet/22.9 m if dormant, 650 feet/198.1 m if active): 16% to recognize a specific psychic scent, 65% chance to track if powers are in use. Sense Supernatural Beings (100 feet/30.5 m if dormant, 1500 feet/457.2 m if active): 72% to sense or identify the type of creature. Tracking these creatures by scent is 55% if dormant or 82% if powers are active.

Magic: None, but loves using TW weapons and armor.

Psionics: Sixth Sense, Mind Block, Sense Evil, Sense Magic, and Empathy. Considered a master psionic (rolls 10 to save).

Bionics/Cybernetics: None.

Combat: 5 attacks per melee, +2 initiative, +7 to parry and dodge, +5 to strike, +10 to damage and +6 to pull/roll with punch, fall or impact.

Bonuses: +1 vs psionics, +7 vs magic, poisons, and toxins, +26% save vs coma/death.

Vulnerabilities/Penalties: Ley lines disrupt many natural abilities of the Dog Boy. See **Rifts®** or **Lone Star** for details.

Skills of Note: Language: American and Dragonese 90%, Prowl 55%, Intelligence 58%, Radio: Basic 80%, Radio: Scramblers 65%, Pilot Hovercraft 85%, Read Sensory Equipment 65%, Weapon Systems 75%, Land Navigation 66%, Wilderness Survival 55%, W.P. Energy Rifle, W.P. Energy Pistol, W.P. Heavy Energy, W.P. Blunt, and Hand to Hand: Martial Arts.

Allies of Note: In addition to Arzno and its citizens, there are still several Dog Pack soldiers who are friends of Fidel and would help him if they could.

Enemies: Vampires and other supernatural evils, plus he's wanted by the CS, especially by many of the Dog Boys. Some may understand his motives for bugging out, but few condone it.

Weapons & Equipment of Note: Usually wears TWA-900 Light Armor (he loves the spikes) or occasionally his old riot armor for show. His favorite weapons include a Neuro-Mace, a TWW-1300 Lightning Mace, and a TWW-3500 Water Rifle.

Money: Keeps a modest amount of cash nearby for emergencies, roughly 35,000 credits immediately available in Arzno.

Samantha
Sergeant and resident werebeast
of the Arzno Mercenary Corps

The half-human creature crept in the shadows cast by eerie green street lamps, in the main square of the small southwestern town, her eyes focused on her prey across the street. Her keen vision saw every movement of the three demons, as they crawled from the cellar of the small pub and made their way toward the hotel next door, full of unsuspecting, heavily sleeping travelers on their way to El Paso for the weekend festivities. Samantha watched as the three vampires started to make their way across the alley, like snakes entering the crib of a child.

It was then that she made her move. Her inky black coat bristled with excitement as she all but flew across the street and pounced on one of the demons, slashing with her claws and biting with her deadly fangs. Her pride rested largely on the fact that she didn't need fancy weapons or magic to fight these creatures, only her natural gifts. As she clawed through the flesh of one beast, another struck her from behind. Leaving the first too damaged to fight back for the time being, the werejaguar turned, grabbed the next creature and threw it into a nearby horse trough. The demon screamed as its skin burned, and the third beast began to metamorphose into a giant wolf, taking flight. Samantha's fangs found the creature's neck and held on tight. She whipped him around and drove his body over a hitching post. As her attention shifted back to the second creature, she pounced and held it under the water, and pumped the handle on the faucet above. The creature's screams were muffled by the water, but they soon enough ceased.

Just as she was about to turn back to the first of her victims, her sixth sense alerted her. It was too late; he had found her first. Samantha was caught off guard for once, and the regenerated demon jumped at her, wailing and screaming. She winced, preparing herself for the impact, but the demon fell short of his mark, blood spewing from his chest and a giant wooden stake protruding from his back.

The werebeast looked up, panting and coat glistening with sweat, to meet the veiled face of the huge armored figure before her. The voice boomed from behind the helmet, "I need your help."

Samantha caught her breath as she looked upon the pearl-white, silver spiked armor and didn't question her instinctive answer for a moment. "I owe you more than that," she whispered.

After meeting the Mage Onra and hearing of his mission, Samantha could be happy nowhere else besides the Arzno Mercenary Corps. She was the first inhuman member of the Corps, and therefore spent most of her time in her human facade, and continues to do so out of habit and for the comfort of others. Still, she is most comfortable (and formidable) in her natural form, and does not hesitate to use it when hunting or in combat. Despite her insecurities, she is fully accepted as an indispensable member and leader of the Corps. Still, she has declined having a unit under her command on numerous occasions, because she feels that she wouldn't receive the proper respect. Perhaps someday she'll realize how much she is needed.

Samantha's history is nothing special. She grew up in a loose affiliation of werebeasts in Mexico, and through her hunting of the vampires, ended up north of the Rio Grande where she met Onra. She hunts vampires for different reasons than most. Some do it for revenge, others for the money. Samantha does it because it's fun and it's in her blood. Werebeasts (especially werejags) and vampires are natural enemies, and often hunt each other just because it's what they're expected to do. She doesn't need any other reason. Samantha does, however, like humans more than she wants to admit. Before her AMC days, she would routinely find some small town on the Rio Grande and appoint herself its protector. She would live in an abandoned building, sleeping during the day and secretly hunting the vampires at night. Once she had killed them all and the town was safe, she would move on. For this reason, about half a dozen southern Texas and New Mexico villages and towns have myths about a feline protector saving them from the vampire threat. She has heard the stories but is too self-defeating to believe that they could possibly be talking about her. She avoids the areas that her legends are known, just to be safe. The last thing she wants is hero-worship.

Real Name: Unknown, goes by Samantha

Aliases: Playfully (or seriously by some less-tolerant people) known as Demon, also Cat, Jag, or Sam (she hates that nickname). Known by some villagers as the Gata Negra, or Black Cat.

Rank: Sergeant

Alignment: Unprincipled

Hit Points: 54

S.D.C.: None, see natural abilities.

P.P.E.: 70

I.S.P.: 23

Attributes: I.Q. 9, M.E. 11, M.A. 13, P.S. 20, P.P. 21, P.E. 19, P.B. 13, Spd 28

Experience: 5th level Werejaguar

Weight: 240 lbs (108 kg)

Height: 6 feet (1.8 m) in human form, 5 feet (1.5 m) long or tall in other forms.

Sex: Female

Age: 25

Disposition: Samantha is a brilliant fighter and hunter, but a little bit self-defeating when it comes to her own impact on those around her. She is well liked, but would never consider herself "one of the gang."

Natural Abilities: As per any werebeast. Has three forms, the natural being a half-woman, half-jaguar. Can also appear as a giant jaguar or humanoid. Basically impervious to all forms of common weapons. Nightvision (300 feet/91.4 m), bio regenerate 2D6 Hit Points per hour, plus naturally psionic with magic abilities (see below). Also see skills and vulnerabilities.

Magic: Tongues, Chameleon, Astral Projection, Repel Animals, Heal Wounds, Metamorphosis: Animal, and Metamorphosis: Human.

Psionics: Sixth Sense, Mind Block, and See the Invisible. Considered a minor psionic.

Bionics/Cybernetics: None. Not compatible.

Combat: 5 attacks per melee in natural or jaguar form, 2 in human form. +1 on initiative, +5 to parry and dodge, +5 to strike, +5 to damage and +3 to pull/roll with punch, fall or impact.

Bonuses: +2 vs psionics, +4 vs magic, +6 vs Horror Factor, impervious to poisons/toxins. +8% save vs coma/Death.

Vulnerabilities/Penalties: Weapons of silver do double damage. Wolfbay and garlic will hold a werebeast at bay.

Skills of Note: Language: Spanish 98% and American 75%, Prowl 82%, Swim 60%, Climbing 90/80%, Acrobatics 80%, Track by Smell 60%, Land Navigation 90%, Math: Basic 70%, Demon and Magic Lore 50%, Track Animals 70%, Hunting, W.P. Knife +1 thrown, +1 strike, +2 parry, W.P. Archery and Targeting 4 attacks, +2 strike.

Allies of Note: In addition to Arzno and its citizens, several small villages in the Southwest view Samantha as a savior and would gladly help her in any way.

Enemies: Vampires and other supernatural evils. No contact with the CS, but would quickly find trouble with them as well.

Weapons & Equipment of Note: Doesn't usually use weapons and doesn't own many, but she owns half a dozen silver throwing knives, which she often uses through the first round of combat, and she is starting to like them as she improves.

Money: 58,000 from several years of service with the AMC, but she doesn't really think about it.

Hank Payne

Distributor

"I don't know what you're talking about!" Hank exclaimed violently at the Coalition soldier's accusation. "I've never seen

these weapons before in my life! How in the world should I know where they came from?" he blurted in frustration, pointing an accusing finger at the unusual looking rifles stacked upon each other in the open crate on the ground beside the soldier. Hank turned his gaze to the red eyes of the soldier's dead boy armor, trying to imagine the human eyes that peered out from behind them. His face didn't betray his fear; he already knew from the way the soldier had spoken to him that they didn't have any evidence against him, but even so, one couldn't help but be afraid of someone packing the firepower of a twentieth century tank.

"Sir, if you continue to make such a big deal out of this, I'll be forced to take you into custody." said the soldier, his voice trembling ever so slightly. Hank picked up on the soldier's insecurity and refused to back down.

"This is ridiculous! I'm a loyal citizen of the Coalition States. I have rights, you know. You can't just threaten and accuse me of something like this! I'd like to speak to your superior officer about this, right now!"

Hank clenched his teeth, trying to keep a stern face despite his fear. For a moment he wondered if the soldier was going to call his bluff, but in the end Hank's instincts were right as usual. The soldier fidgeted with the rifle in his hand and leaned towards Hank's face, twitching with anxiety.

"Um. Well, Sir that won't be necessary. There's obviously been some kind of mixup. I'm sorry for any inconvenience," he stuttered. Hank imagined the expression of fear that must have crossed the young soldier's face at the thought of being grilled by his superior officer. He struggled not to smile and keep a straight face.

"Darn right you're sorry. Now if you don't mind I think I've spent enough time at your stinking checkpoint," he growled, as he turned and proceeded through the gates of the blockade. He mumbled to himself under his breath just loud enough so that the soldier could hear. Now, he thought, the only problem was getting those weapons back from the dead heads...

Nobody knows exactly who Hank is or where he comes from, but rumors abound and most paint him in a less-than-savory light. Some say he's on the run from a big gambling debt, others say he's in trouble with the CS, and some say he killed someone in Tolkeen, amongst a multitude of other stories. If any are true, Hank doesn't say.

Looking at or talking with Hank, one would never think he was capable of any of the things that he's supposed to have done, according to the rumors. He just seems like a perfectly nice guy, the sort of fellow you'd like your daughter to marry. In truth, Hank is a master showman, and you can never tell whether that handsome face is telling you the truth or stabbing you in the back. That's why he's so good at what he does.

Hank first got involved with Arzno and the AMC when a group of vampire hunters, trapped in a vampire controlled town, managed to contact Lanis to ask for supplies. Getting the weapons and other equipment into the town would seem to be impossible, and Lanis was at a loss as to how he could get the desperately needed supplies to the vampire hunters in time. Somehow, through his various connections, Hank heard about Lanis' predicament and offered his services. Two days later the weapons were in the hands of the vampire hunters, and Hank had established the beginning of a long business relationship.

Hank would prefer to think of himself as an independent operative who just happens to do a lot of work for Arzno. In truth, smuggling Arzno manufactured equipment has formed virtually all of Hank's business for the past three years, and it shows no signs of slowing down. Lanis is impressed with Hank's ability, even if he feels somewhat uncomfortable with the mysterious smuggler.

Regardless of Lanis' unease, Hank has proven his loyalty on numerous occasions and has truly become a part of the Arzno team, even if he won't admit it. Hank has truly taken to the people of Arzno and their cause, and while he can't help his more unscrupulous tendencies at times, he feels that he belongs there, much to his chagrin.

Real Name: Hank Payne

Rank: None, civilian contractor

Alignment: Anarchist

Hit Points: 39

S.D.C.: 16

P.P.E.: 5

Attributes: I.Q.: 11, M.E.: 13, M.A.: 25, P.S.: 7, P.P.: 10, P.E.: 9, P.B.: 21, Spd.: 8

Experience: 8th level Smuggler

Weight: 134 lbs (60.3 kg)

Height: 5 feet, 10 inches (1.78 m)

Sex: Male

Age: 35

Disposition: Hank is a notorious prankster and smooth talker. He's always got a smile on his face and a joke on his lips, at least when around people he knows. When "on the job," Hank can assume any demeanor that will get the job done. Hank likes to assume different guises almost as though it were a game, but he knows when the game is up and when to get off the field.

Natural Abilities: None

Magic: None. He thinks it's useful and more importantly, profitable, but has no interest in it himself.

Psionics: None

Bionics/Cybernetics: None

Combat: Hand to Hand: Basic: 3 attacks per melee, +2 to parry and dodge, +1 to strike, +2 to damage, +2 to roll with punch/fall or impact, critical strike on a natural 19 or 20.

Bonuses: 84% to invoke trust or intimidate, and 55% to charm/impress.

Vulnerabilities/Penalties: Though he would never admit it, Hank genuinely cares for the people of Arzno and will do what he can to help and protect them. Hank is also a notorious risk-taker who likes to tread a thin line in order to get that extra bit of profit. One day he's sure to miscalculate and find himself in serious trouble.

Skills of Note: Literacy: American 98%, Languages: American, Spanish, Dragonese and Euro 98%, Detect Ambush 85%, Detect Concealment 75%, Escape Artist 55%, Disguise 55%, Impersonation 60/40%, Concealment 46%, Palming 50%, Streetwise 52%, Cryptography 60%, Computer Hacking 35%, W.P. Energy Pistol, W.P. Knife.

Allies of Note: Hank has contacts and people who owe him favors throughout the southern states. Plus there are those who Hank could easily blackmail for assistance, though calling them allies might be a bit of a stretch. Then of course there is Onra and other members of the AMC, and similar clients throughout the region.

Enemies: If people realized it was Hank who ripped off, blackmailed, bribed and snuck right under their noses, he'd be in real trouble with a lot of people. Fortunately, Hank seems to have managed to get off pretty much scot-free every time.

Weapons & Equipment of Note: Hank seems to go through weapons and equipment (often rare or exotic) at a tremendous rate, and never seems to have the same gear from one day to the next. Two things that are constant, though, are a tweed vest and a pocket pen/flashlight. In truth, the vest is a suit of Triax plain clothes armor (A.R.: 10, M.D.C.: 10) and the pen a concealed laser (two shots, 1D4 M.D. at 30 feet/9.1 m). How Hank got his hands on them, only he knows, and they're his best-kept secrets.

Money: 1D6×100,000 in universal credits, plus 3D6×100,000 in contraband items at any given time. Hank's finances are in a constant state of flux since he's always wheeling and dealing, trying to trade up for more profit.

Other Personnel

The Corps also has the following personnel:

15 Techno-Wizards, levels 4-6 (serve as field maintenance and combat)

5 Ley-Line Walkers, levels 4-7

3 Battle Magi, levels 4-5

3 Mystics, levels 4-6

4 Undead Slayers, levels 3-6

8 Gunslingers and Gunfighters, levels 3-8

7 Wilderness Scouts, levels 3-6

9 Power Armor soldiers (1 is a Techno-Wizard, 3 are RPA Elite, and others are Headhunters and Bounty Hunters), levels 4-8

6 Borgs (4 Full, 2 Partial), levels 5-7

6 Cyber-Knights, levels 4-7

3 Psi-Stalkers, levels 5-6

6 Dog Boys, levels 3-7

3 Crazies, levels 4-5

2 Juicers, level 4

1 Lyn-Srial Cloud Weaver, level 6

2 Lyn-Srial Sky Knights, levels 4 and 6

12 Soldiers with tactics and military training (i.e. Grunts, Special Forces, CS Tech Officers, etc.), levels 3-8

Any additional 2-10 at any given time, mostly 1st and 2nd level Vagabonds/Headhunters/pilots/grunts

Non-Combatants: Up to 40 tech, medical, and other personnel are on the road with the active squads, and an additional 75 at the headquarters (many of the support team members are low level Techno-Wizards or those with limited combat skills). Members of the AMC are not allowed to take any family on the road with them, and generally maintain their own equipment and cook their own food, thus lowering the need for excess personnel.

Weapons and Equipment

Generally one half of the squad will be outfitted with TW equipment, and the other with mundane gear. Other equipment is available upon assignment, and teams sometimes mix and match mundane and Techno-Wizard equipment to best suit the needs of the mission.

Standard Issue Equipment for
Anti-Vampire Missions (TW equipment)

- TW Metal Water Pistol (2D6 H.P.)

- TW Converted Wilk's 247 "Hero" Dual Pistol (two settings: 4D6 S.D.C. and 5D6 M.D.C.; being magic energy, both settings do half damage to vampires but aren't lethal)

- TW Full-size Water Rifle (4D6 H.P.); one in four will have a Water Grenade Launcher as well (1D4x10 H.P.)

- One in ten will carry a Water Cannon (3D6x10 H.P.) in place of the rifle

- A suit of TW body armor or mundane armor with 1D4 TW enhancements (generally 60 to 80 M.D.C.)

- 3 silver fragmentation grenades, 2 high-explosive grenades, and one smoke grenade (all may be TW or mundane; occasionally water, steam, or wood fragmentation grenades are substituted)

- 2 Globe of Daylight Flares

- A mundane or TW knife, flashlight, silver cross, wooden stakes and mallet, rope, and other miscellaneous equipment

- Standard Issue Equipment for Anti-Vampire Missions (mundane equipment) (12 pt)

- Metal Water Pistol (2D6 H.P.)

- General Officer's .45 with standard and silver rounds (4D6 S.D.C./H.P.)

- A JA-11 Juicer Assassin Energy Rifle with silver S.D.C. rounds (5D6 S.D.C./H.P.)

- One in four will carry an assault rifle with silver rounds (4D6 S.D.C./H.P.) and a grenade launcher (2D6 M.D. explosive or 1D4 M.D./4D6 H.P. silver fragmentation standard) in place of the JA-11

- One in ten soldiers will carry a Portable Water Cannon (6D6 H.P.) in place of a rifle

- Each soldier generally supplies his own suit of body armor (typical M.D.C. from 50 to 80), but CS Light Dead Boy armor (50 M.D.C.) is available if desired

- 2 silver fragmentation, 3 high-explosive, and one smoke grenade

- A survival knife, flashlight, silver cross, six wooden stakes and a mallet, and other miscellaneous equipment

Non-Vampire Missions

For missions not involving vampires, Mega-Damage weapons and equipment will be provided if necessary, but most of the members of the Corps are mercenaries with their own equipment and armor. Regardless of the mission, the water pistol, silver cross, and stakes are always carried, just in case.

Vehicles

The AMC uses vehicles built by Arzno Weapons Manufacturing, and many were designed by the Techno-Wizards at the Corps. Vehicles are used in transport of troops as well as combat.

- 3 "Demon Beetle" Troop Transports

- 1 "Annihilator" Assault Vehicle

- 12 TW Scout Cycles

- 6 Sandstorm Hovercraft
- 6 "Whirlybird" Personal Helicopters
- 1 "Smiley Chopper" Gunship
- 2 "Kamikaze" one-man fighters
- 9-20 various robots and power armor, including one Glitter Boy, a couple of old-style SAMAS, and several suits of Samson power armor, all with TW retrofitting. There are always at least 9 (owned by AMC), but many employees have special training in robot combat, and sub-contracting to local mercenaries is common.
- Many mercenaries own their own ATV's, motorcycles, and hovercycles, which they are occasionally allowed to take on missions. There are typically 10 ATV's, 15 hovercycles, and 12 motorcycles that are available if necessary, plus a number of S.D.C. trucks, cars, and vans.

Places of Note in Arzno

1. Arzno Weapons Manufacturing. AWM is the life's blood of the city and territory of Arzno. It employs over a thousand of the town's inhabitants, and supplies the Arzno Mercenary Corps with most of its equipment, weapons, and vehicles. On top of that, the city has contracted AWM to provide the vast majority of power, water, and what magical defenses the city and Civilian Patrollers employ. In addition to the TW items listed in this supplement, equivalents to most other Techno-Wizardry items from the **Rifts®** main book, **World Book 14: New West™**, **World Book 16: Federation of Magic™**, and **Rifter™ #2**, as well as most other TW items from other supplements are available at 60 to 70% of the listed price (the black market price). See the section on Arzno Weapons Manufacturing for more details.

Two huge factories are owned by AWM, one for vehicles and the other for armor, weapons, and miscellaneous items. The vehicle plant is a giant hangar with a 40 foot (12.2 m) ceiling, and the other building is three stories tall, each full of work space and offices. A large showroom and office building is in front of the factory buildings. Tours are available by appointment.

2. The AMC Compound. The base of operations for the Arzno Mercenary Corps is a large, walled complex that actually makes up the northeastern side of the city walls. It serves as the training center, armory, business administration site, and all-around headquarters for the Corps' leaders and soldiers when they're not on assignment.

The compound is surrounded by thick M.D.C. walls (20 feet/6.1 m tall and 10 feet/3 m thick, 35 M.D.C. for every 25 square feet/2.25 sq. m) with three weapons towers — one by the gate, one at the northeastern corner, and one on the east side of the compound. Each has a Starfire Pulse Cannon and a mundane machinegun, and each guard carries his own energy rifle. The guards (two per tower) are always in armor, and each carries a sidearm and three grenades (could be TW or mundane).

Through the front gates (enter from the west) is a large, four-story M.D.C. building (1500 M.D.C.) that serves as the headquarters. All company business is conducted in this building, as well as the Corps' briefings, debriefings, training, and many survival and weapons classes that are offered to the public. Offices, the lobby, conference rooms, and other business-related facilities are on the first floor. On the second floor is the communications center — the "mission control," so to speak — and the mini-hospital. The third floor houses briefing and conference rooms, plus emergency weapon and armor storage. The classrooms and gun range are on the fourth floor. A helipad and two missile launchers (10 short range, 10 medium range, and 4 long range each) are located on the roof.

To the north is the armory and vehicle bay, where armor, weapons, and vehicles are issued, repaired, augmented, or in some cases built. The armory is built around a small pyramid that controls the small nexus there. The P.P.E. from the nexus and pyramid are used in the creation of the complex and magic-costly items that are built and worked on in the hangar.

To the east of the armory are 6 barracks, each of which houses 30 soldiers. There are two community bathrooms in each (men and women share bathroom and shower facilities) and fifteen sets of bunk beds. Each soldier has a footlocker and a standup locker for personal items and clothing. Officers stay in five houses, just south of the barracks, two to a house except for Onra and Psythe, who each have their own. To the east is the mess hall and laundry.

There are three silos on the southwest corner of the compound. One contains emergency water and one is an emergency power generator. Both are Techno-Wizard devices and can supply up to 500 people for 3 days with no P.P.E. cost, but each day past the third drains 750 P.P.E. for the water and 500 for the electricity from the pyramid. The other silo generates an emergency energy field around the compound (1000 M.D.C.) that can be held for an hour before it shuts down. When it has been used for an hour, the batteries need an entire week to recharge, or twice as long if the energy field is completely destroyed.

Under the tower on the northeast corner on the east wall, is a small gate (15 feet/4.6 m across and tall) that leads out of the city walls altogether. Outside the walls is a fenced-in, one square mile (2.56 sq. km) maneuver field. The fences are fifteen feet (4.6 m) tall, electrified, and have barbed wire on top. Surrounding the large battlefield is a microwave fence and several surveillance cameras, to further aid in the detection of intruders. The terrain has been altered using various kinds of magic to make it very unique. The grounds range from steep ridges and boulders to dense forest. The battlefield is used to train troops, practice maneuvers, and help keep veterans' skills sharp.

War Games

One of the most popular games is what the soldiers call "Stunners," a game using TW devices that simulate combat by "zapping" and restraining targets. Such features include varied damage, range, and accuracy. These mock weapons are generally rifles, but include land mines, grenades, and even blades. Magic restraining spells are sometimes allowed, but combative psionics and other magic are not. In the spring of every year a tournament is held on the battlegrounds, pitting teams of ten against each other. The games last for a week, and are open to anyone who can get ten men or women and the entrance fee of 200 credits per team together. The victors get medals, and defend their championship in the final round of the tourney the next year. The past two years have seen the AMC's own "Chameleon" commando squad the victors. Rumor is that this year they are going to give up their championship, break into five teams of two, and challenge any full teams to a two-on-ten, twenty-minute game. Whoever has the most men left at the end wins. The Civilian Patrollers are putting together a crack team to "eliminate" the Chameleons two at a time, or so the local joke goes. All proceeds go to the city hospital.

3. Moonshine's, a local pub. Moonshine's is located at the crossroads just south of the AMC complex, and is frequented by members of the Corps. It's a nice place that serves good food and better booze, but has a nice rustic quality that appeals to soldiers. Shows include tasteful dancing girls and other USO-style entertainment. They have poker night every Thursday and an all-you-can-eat buffet Mondays and Wednesdays. The owner, known simply as "Moonshine" to most, is a quiet, reserved, handsome man who likes to sit back and watch his guests have a good time.

Unknown to most everyone, Gannon "Moonshine" Cullen is secretly a Secondary Vampire. He was turned by Xavier himself, but was able to escape the vampire's control after about a year of almost unbearable servitude to the evil general. Moonshine thinks he's fooling everyone, and is in fact fooling himself. He is unwittingly a servant of Xavier, who let him "escape" and return to his home in Arzno. When Xavier needs him again, Moonshine will certainly bend to his will.

Psythe and a nurse at the hospital are both aware of his demonic nature. The nurse smuggles him blood, and Psythe has decided to let sleeping dogs lie. Psythe doesn't know that it was Xavier who created the vampire, and if he somehow finds out he will probably quietly report it to Onra. Lucky for Moonshine, Onra, Lanis, and the other handful of True Atlanteans don't frequent his bar. If they did, he would be discovered and in desperate trouble.

4. The Arzno Territory Hospital. In the middle of the city of Arzno is a large hospital that serves the city and surrounding communities. There are magical healers, TW-using doctors, and conventional Body Fixers available for family and emergency care. Limited repairs and treatment can be done on cybernetics, but very rarely bionics. There is a staff of 30 doctors and twice as many assistants, plus secretarial and administrative personnel. There are 500 beds in the three-story complex, but close to a thousand wounded could be treated in an emergency, though it would be a disorganized mess. Practical treatment couldn't exceed 700.

5. The Arzno Government Building. This building is located next to the hospital and houses most government offices. The wings are two stories tall and the main section is three.

The Civilian Patrollers Headquarters

In the east wing of the government building are the Civilian Patrollers' main offices and headquarters. The wing has two stories, the first being the temporary detention center, criminal processing center, and some conference and interrogation rooms. On the ground is also the garage, which holds fire-fighting equipment and some police vehicles. The fenced-in lot outside houses most police vehicles. The second floor holds Patrollers' offices, more conference rooms, communications, and the arsenal.

The Jail

The west wing serves as the prison in Arzno. For crimes punished by long-term incarceration such as manslaughter, grand theft, minor conspiracy, blackmailing public officials, or other moderate to severe crimes, the perpetrator is held in the jail. Less serious offenses such as drunkenness, brawling, criminal mischief, and other lesser offenders (jail time of a month or less) are held in the CP temporary detention centers. Two cellblocks (one per floor) hold 100 criminals each (two per cell), or up to 150 (three per cell) if necessary. In times of severe need, four men could be crammed into one cell, but that would be borderline inhumane and avoided if possible.

City Hall

The bottom floor of the main building serves as the office space for the Chief Elder, city offices such as utilities, transportation, and justice. A large part of this is the Council meeting chambers, where the public comes to voice opinions and hold hearings. Directly behind the hearing room is the Council's deliberation room where they can discuss matters in private.

Office space, conference rooms, and the modest city library take up the second story. Plans to expand the library are in the works, and it's only a matter of time before the Council of Elders votes to build a library building and research facility. Most books are technical manuals, old encyclopedias, contemporary fiction novels, and children's books.

The third floor is the courtroom. Arzno employs three judges, appointed by the Council, who rule on criminal matters and civil cases, or oversee a jury and administrate punishment on more serious cases (innocent or guilty by 3/5 majority). The three take turns doing city duty, leaving the other two to travel to other villages and towns in the territory to rule on cases there. Both in the territory and in the city, trials are swift since the accuser and defendant represent themselves. The wait is rarely over a week. Judges serve until the Council removes them or they step down. Usually, a judge serves for five years and then removes himself, nominating a successor for consideration by the Council. Current judges are Quintin Mebrinto (9th level Justice Ranger, Human), Ixnalis Wucnasta (8th level Sky Knight, Lyn-Srial), and Valis Smithton (10th level Rogue Scholar, Human). It is the policy of the Arzno courts to uphold the judgement of Cyber-Knights and Justice Rangers unless proven false.

Other Notes on the Government Building

The government building has four silos similar to those at the AMC compound, though smaller and less sophisticated. Two hold a three-day water supply and the other two can provide three days of electricity in an emergency. After the three days, water and power are gone. It takes roughly three to four weeks for the P.P.E. batteries to recharge. The water and power are supplied to the government building and the hospital next door. No energy shield is present.

5. The Brotherhood of Silver and Water. This vampire-hunting guild's headquarters is located within the city walls. Guild members can often be persuaded to perform extermination jobs free of charge if it will aid the common folk of the area. The building is on the south side of town and is little more than a safehouse with a few offices.

6. Other Magic and Weapon Shops. Magic and weapon shops are common in the city and territory of Arzno. Anything from magic herbs, spells and scrolls, to TW weaponry, talismans, and amulets are all readily available at 10% lower than the black market cost. There are many magic healers and herbalists in the city as well. Mundane weapon shops are just as common as magical ones, and all prices are reasonable. The black market doesn't operate within the city walls, but can be found in the surrounding territory. The same goes for chop-shops and crooked arms dealers.

To be continued

In Rifter #10

WEATHER... OR NOT?

An Optional Guide to Mother Nature in Role-Playing

By Owen Johnson a.k.a. Uxmal13

As a G.M., I would often describe the scenery, setting and mood of a game, but rarely the weather. Only if it had a major bearing on the game did I give consideration to things like: In a heavy rain storm, visibility is reduced and negative modifiers apply to tracking by scent, or in cold weather conditions, sound travels better. Weather conditions really did not concern me until my **Heroes Unlimited™** campaign.

In that campaign, one player character's armor is solar powered. I thought, with the campaign set in our home town (sunny Miami, Florida), this should be no problem for him. Then I really thought about it. We have our rainy season, humid scorching summers (with heat waves in the high 90s F/high 30s C), and mild winters (it's mid-December and today's high temperature is in the low 80s F/high 20s C). Then I sent the group on missions into different parts of the country and even Alberta, Canada. Weather conditions across the country suddenly became important. I have had the benefit of living across the U.S., and I put that knowledge to use. Mississippi has hot summers and really cold winters, but very little snow. Oklahoma gets very cold and snowy winters, tornadoes in the warmer months and summer temperatures that soar into the 100s F (37-43 C). Washington State has bitter cold and heavy winter snowfall, but rain falling for months straight during warmer periods of the year. Most of the players had never even seen live snowfall before. They were surprised to encounter difficult winter conditions. Freezing rain, road salts (eating away the undercarriage of their vehicles three months later), snowblindness, negative modifiers for prowling in snow eight inches (20 cm) or more deep, and black ice patches on the roads, brought on surprising and hilarious results.

Before long, I realized that weather is very important to game play. Weather change can be a powerful tool to gaming. The presence of weather, good or bad, will influence the actions and decisions of player characters and NPCs alike. Simple, random changes to the game environment can add realism to the experience. Ask yourself, how many of your planned activities were delayed or canceled entirely because of bad weather? In cases of extreme weather conditions, such as severe floods and drought, hurricanes, blizzards, killer winter storms, or tornadoes, seeking shelter for survival or evacuating the affected area are the only choices. Without the help of a major deity or elemental, player characters do not have the power to control or negate weather systems of that size. At best, elemental magic will temporarily affect a limited area. This is because the energy state of weather phenomena is so dynamic and extensive that affecting an entire weather system, stretching across hundreds of miles, would be impossible. Some storms, like tornadoes, require two weather systems, with high and low temperatures. For the solar powered armor character, I designed a simple table to come up with random weather conditions for most game "days." If the day was rainy and/or heavily overcast, he was dependant on an eight-hour power supply and outside electrical power sources.

The more detailed tables below can be used in most game settings, applying general weather patterns to climates that essentially have all four seasons (unlike South Florida). Game Masters should feel free to modify the conditions or duration rolled on the tables due to the local environment and circumstances. Example: Western Washington State has much more annual rainfall than the eastern half, in part because the Cascade mountain range forces more cloud moisture from passing weather systems. Other conditions to consider are: How far away is the equator? How far does the jetstream dip across the continent (usually accompanied by a drop in temperature)? Is the game setting in a temperate zone or rainforest? Are desert conditions (any place with an extremely low annual rain or snowfall) suitable for ice or sand? Changes in weather can occur day or night. When the season does change (even South Florida gets cold temperatures in the winter), roll on the applicable table. If no extreme summer or winter conditions are possible (like here in South Florida) use the table that applies most for the season and reroll results of 86-100%. Some seasonal results cannot possibly happen naturally. Winter in South Florida can be cold, with nighttime temperatures into the 40s F (4-9 C) with frost, but blizzards are unheard of and spring frost in the middle of a summer heat wave would make headlines. If any table result seems inappropriate, choose the conditions that fit best. High temperatures are during the daytime and low temperatures are at night.

Rolls of 86-100% represent extreme weather conditions, which can kill if not incapacitate most character races. It is assumed that characters are wearing normal clothing for their current weather conditions, not environmental body armor. As a general guide, light exposure (10-20 minutes) to these conditions mean characters risk a 5% chance of succumbing to heat stroke or hypothermia. Moderate exposure (20+1D4x10 minutes) to these conditions means characters risk a 30% chance of succumbing to heat stroke or hypothermia, with a +10% increase for each additional half hour. Severe exposure (more than two hours without relief or medical care) to these conditions mean characters risk a 60% chance of succumbing to heat stroke or hypothermia, with a +10% increase each additional fifteen minutes. A failed roll means the character will fall unconscious for 15+1D6x10 minutes before slipping into a coma. Without immediate medical attention (psionic, magical, or otherwise) the character will die after their length of a coma expires (hours equal to P.E. attribute). The chance for sunburn or frostbite is something else for G.M.'s to consider, and can affect characters at a rate of 4 points of S.D.C. damage per hour of exposure. In any case, sunburn or frostbite severity increases with extreme weather conditions. Of course, characters and races with special abilities to withstand these temperature extremes (technological, magical, or psionics) are unaffected, just as those with weaknesses to temperature extremes are more at risk.

Spring/Summer weather conditions:

1-5% Late Spring frost for 1D4 nights. Temperature lows in the 40s F (4-9 C) with possible crop damage.

6-15% Mild days/cool nights for 1+1D4 days. Temperature highs in the 70s and lows in the 60s F (16-25 C).

16-25% Rainy and overcast all day for 1D4 days. Temperature highs in the 70s and lows in the 60s F (16-25 C).

26-75% Sunny and partly cloudy skies for 1D6 weeks. Temperature highs in the 80s and lows in the 70s F (22-31 C).

76-85% Downpour for 4+1D6 hours with 2 inches (5 cm) of rainfall per hour. Possible flooding with temperature in the high 60s F (18-21 C).

86-95% Hot days/warm nights for 2+1D4 days. Temperature highs in the 90s and lows in the 80s F (27-36 C).

96-100% Heat wave for 1D4 weeks with drought conditions. 98+2D6 degree temperature and lows in the 80s F (27-43 C).

Fall/Winter weather conditions:

1-5% High winds/cool nights for 1D4 days. Temperature highs in the 70s and lows in the 60s F (16-25 C), wind gusts up to 30 mph (48 km).

6-15% Indian Summer for 1D4 days with 25% chance of light rain. Temperature highs in the 60s and lows in the 50s F (11-20 C).

16-25% Sleet or freezing rain for 1D4 days. Temperature highs in the 40s and lows in the 30s F (0-8 C).

26-75% Cold and clear skies for 1D6 weeks. Temperature highs in the 50s and lows in the 30s F (2-13 C).

76-85% Overcast clouds and snowfall for 3+1D6 days with 4 inches (10 cm) of snowfall per day. Temperature highs in the 40s F (5-8 C).

86-95% Freeze out for 2+1D4 days without snow, just bone chilling cold. Temperature highs in the 20s F (-4 to -1 C) and wind gusts up to 30 mph (48 km).

96-100% Blizzard conditions with 1 foot (.3 m) of snowfall for 3+2D4 days a day and 50+ mph (80+ km) winds. Temperature highs in the 20s and lows into the negative numbers Fahrenheit (-20 to -3 C).

Benefactors

A Rifts® Scotland Short Story
By Christopher Jones

Robyn Campbell died quietly; only the soft thump of his head striking the ground, and the low hum of a Vibro-sword, marked the assault on his unsuspecting neck. The surprise was so complete that his decapitated body stood erect for ten full heartbeats before it began its final tumble to the ground. The quick hands of the assailant assured that the Campbell's body made this descent without a sound.

Angus didn't like the Campbells, and he felt no remorse for his actions. The Campbells were traitors, every last one of them. They had betrayed their own people to side with the invading Fomorii. For that, Angus believed, they deserved to die, every black-hearted one of them.

But Angus MacFie was not here to kill traitors; he was here to spy on them. With a low, almost inaudible whistle, he called to his companions. Even his keen ears, sharpened by twelve years in the highlands, could not detect their approach until they were within a few feet. The captain, however, was able to get right behind him before Angus realized he was there.

Kalin MacGregor was like that, always demonstrating to his men just how vulnerable they could be. It would have been more annoying to them if he had any idea he was doing it. Kalin was simply more quiet, more alert, and more precise than anyone else. He was a born woodsman, and a born leader. And his men loved him.

Of course, to keep up with such a man, his company were all excellent warriors in their own right. Travis Keith was their combat engineer. He took care of the big guns and the explosives, and he had nerves of steel. Harris and Francis MacDonald were brothers. Expert trackers, they were also deadly with a rifle. Moira Munro was the scout. It was her job to spot the enemy before they had a chance to spot them. William "Big Will" Grant was a giant of a man. His job was being big, burly, and strong, and he did it quite well. And Angus... well, Angus was good at killing, up-close and personal.

It was Angus' skill with a blade which had secured them their current station. The company was positioned on a cliff top overlooking a small canyon. Lying on their bellies, to avoid being spotted, they inched their way to the edge, and looked down upon the gathering below.

Their intelligence had been correct, below them there must have been thousands of Scots, all from traitor clans. There were also Fomorians. At first glance there appeared to be just a few

From this distance, the company could not make out exactly what was being said, but they caught the general drift. The leaders were stirring their troopers into a frenzy, a blood frenzy. Kalin knew that meant the big push was coming. Ten years of uneasy truce was finally about to be shattered. The big question was, what would their target be.

The Lowland Kingdom, and its capital of New Caledonia, was the focal point of Scottish defenses. If the Fomorians could take the city, they would crush virtually all resistance in the country. This seemed the most likely target, however, there was another. The MacLeods of Skye had created a powerful fortress in New Dunvegan. In fact, they had already fought off two minor invasions. It was the easier target, too, as the MacLeods lacked the numbers of the Lowland Kingdom. Also, if he didn't neutralize Skye, Bres would have to worry about an assault on his flank.

With two such tempting targets, Kalin needed to know where the attack would come. Despite the extreme danger, he prepared his unit to creep forward for a better look. That's when the gunfire started.

Their first thoughts were that they had been spotted. Soon, however, they realized that the shots were coming from some distance to their left, along the same cliff edge. With potential danger so close, they quickly moved to investigate.

As they approached, they could make out the unmistakable forms of Fomorian warriors. They were fighting what looked to be other clansmen. It appeared as though these men had also been observing the gathering. Unfortunately for them, they had been discovered.

One of the defenders looked out of place. He was wearing a uniform which was definitely not Scottish. From his insignia, Kalin realized that he must be the German officer he had been hearing so much about. The last time he had visited New Caledonia, the city was abuzz with the news that an observer from the New German Republic was coming to determine whether or not the Scots needed assistance.

Kalin knew that the Scots could use all the help they could get, and a dead foreign agent was not likely to secure them much. All thought of the gathering left him as his new duty became clear. Instructing the MacDonalds to provide covering fire, he and the rest of his troops joined the fight to protect the NGR agent.

The fight was short, just like Kalin had planned it. It wasn't his goal to defeat the Fomorians, but to knock them off balance long enough to rescue their victims. The German officer was still alive. Impressively, he was holding his own against the giants. Unfortunately, he was the last survivor of his team.

With the Fomorians surprised and confused, Kalin grabbed the German and ordered his men to retreat. Under the covering fire of Harris and Francis, they were able to break free. Then, it was a race for their lives as they tried to put as much distance as possible between themselves and the giants.

Feeling it to be his duty as leader, Kalin took the most dangerous position, the rear. From there, he would be the first to face any Fomorian pursuers. That they would catch him, he was certain. The giants were fast, faster than the Scots, and they would recover quickly. Normally, he and his men would simply disappear into the highland mist, but he doubted that the for-

dozen, but careful observation revealed that there had to be a few hundred. No doubt the giants wanted to remind the traitors who the dominant partners were.

eigner's woodland skills were sufficient to evade the Fomorii, and the woodsmen among their Campbell allies.

As they fled, they were so fixated on escaping that they did not notice the great stag as they passed it by. Only Kalin managed to catch a glimpse of the noble beast, but even he doubted his senses. He dared not turn around, for fear he would stumble and make himself an easy target for the giants. Instead, he, and his men, ran on.

The great stag, half again larger than any known deer, stood watching the fleeing Scotsmen. He could smell the Fomorians coming, and knew they would be close on the heels of the clansmen. With grace which belied his size, the beast moved into the path of the pursuers. As he waited for them, an eerie yellow glow began to surround him.

The sight of the glowing beast stopped the pursuers in their tracks. They recovered quickly, however, and with weapons drawn, they cautiously advanced. The stag greeted them with a snort of defiance, pawing the ground in contempt. Yellow sparks began to dance around the creature's antlers, growing and growing until finally a ball of golden lightning burst forth, slamming into the giants. Again and again the stag brought forth his lightning, until the last of the giants lay dead.

From deep in the woods, Herne the Hunter watched the stag with curiosity, the Hounds of the Hunt lounging lazily about him. They could sense the nature of the stag, and were uncon-

cerned. Herne was a little surprised to see the beast. He knew that Lugh was wandering the Highlands, but had not expected to run across the ancient deity. He pondered the bright god's actions. His animal form suggested he was attempting to avoid scrutiny. His actions, however, had just the opposite effect.

Herne turned to watch the rapidly retreating forms of the mortals, his sharp eyes picking them out even at such distance. For these humans, Lugh had risked discovery. He was not the only Tuatha Da Danaan to value bravery, however. Without a word, the Hounds rose and loped after the humans, their master close behind.

Lugh watched The Hunter and his pack depart. Such was Herne's stealth and woodcraft that even one of Lugh's power had not detected him until the packmaster had moved to leave. If he had known of The Hunter's presence, perhaps he would have acted differently, choosing not to reveal himself, and leaving Herne to deal with the Fomorian giants instead. But then again, probably not. Men of such spirit and valor as those Scots deserved his help, and he was glad to give it.

Now it was time to leave, before the Fomorii re-appeared, en masse. He no longer feared for the safety of the mortal warriors. With the unseen escort of the Wild Hunt, they were out of danger. Still in the form of a stag, Lugh bounded away, disappearing once more into the Highlands.

Palladium Fantasy Hook, Line & Sinkers™

By Shawn Merrow

These Hook, Line & Sinker™ adventures are written with the **Palladium Fantasy RPG™** in mind, but some of them can be very easily adapted to the many other games by Palladium Books.

Can you do me a favor?

Hook: The characters are traveling through the Lower Barraduk region of the Western Empire, when they are contacted by a wealthy merchant who needs some help.

Line: He tells them an important caravan of his cargo was hijacked by a rival merchant, and he needs the characters to steal it back for him. This is very important to him, and he will offer the characters 5,000 gold each to do it. He has one condition, however: they must not look at the cargo. He says it is of a private nature and he wants it to remain that way.

Sinker: The caravan should be well guarded, but not to the point where the characters can't capture it; just make them work for it. What the characters may eventually discover is that the merchant was lying and this is not his caravan at all. He just duped the characters into stealing it for him. The nature of the cargo is up to the Game Master, but it should be something of great value or something to test the morals of the players (like

slaves). If and when the characters discover what's going on, they'll have to decide what to do with the caravan and the merchant who tricked them. Note the rightful owners should also be after the characters and in a rather bad mood about the whole thing.

Cargo of Pain

Hook: When traveling through the countryside, the characters come across the survivors of a recently attacked merchant caravan. They look to have been attacked by Orcs, but there is no sign of the attackers other than a few dead bodies.

Line: None of the merchants were killed in the attack, but their armed escort was almost completely wiped out. Several of the survivors died from their injuries, and the remaining few are too injured to protect the caravan. The merchants will try to hire the characters for extra protection, and offer a nice cut of the profit if they make it to where they are selling their cargo safety.

Sinker: The cargo is Orc slaves that were captured from a village up in the mountains. The Orcs who attacked were just trying to free their people from the slavers. This should put the players into a dilemma on what to do. That should be even worse if there are any members of the monster races in the party. Something else to keep in mind is that in most kingdoms, slavery of the monster races is perfectly legal and not considered wrong. It's up to the G.M. if more Orcs attack along the way to the city, if the characters take the job, but if they free the slaves they may also make some new enemies of the merchants.

Herb Hunt

Hook: The characters come across a small village that has been struck by a plague. The older and sicker members of the village have already died, and more will die soon.

Line: The real tough part is that the village healer knows how to cure the plague, but is to weak to go and gather the herbs that she needs. She will beg the characters to go and get them for her. If the characters agree, she will describe what the herb looks like and some nearby areas that may have some.

Sinker: The nearest place where the herb grows is two days away from the village. The problem is that the area has a large Faerie population, and they do not like trespassers on their land. They will at least make the whole visit very rough on the characters, and it will go downhill from there if the characters react violently to them. The characters also only have five days to get the herbs before the next group of villagers start to die.

Coyle Trouble

Hook: While staying in Ophidia in the Western Empire, the characters start to hear news of a growing number of attacks by Coyles on the outskirts of the province. So far the attacks have only been small and swift, but the public is getting very nervous.

Line: Overlord Troj Belopo is desperate to get more news on what's happening on his border, but does not want to spread his military forces too thin. He is willing to pay good money to groups of adventures who will help with the scouting of the border.

Sinker: The pay is good, but he also needs good hard info. Coming back and just saying "We saw Coyles" won't cut it. It needs to be hard numbers, info on their plans and locations of base camps. Though of course the Coyles won't be too pleased with the characters getting this info.

The enemy of my enemy is my...?

Hook: This HL&S works in conjunction with Coyle Trouble. While on the border of the Ophid's Grasslands Colony checking on Coyle activity, the characters come across a Wolfen in a desperate fight with some Coyles.

Line: If the characters act fast enough, they should have no trouble beating the Coyles and saving the Wolfen. He will introduce himself as a scout for the Wolfen Empire, sent to check on recent Coyle activity, and he thanks them for their assistance. He says he knows where the Coyles' base camp is, and he'd like to go in for a closer look, but figures he'll need help.

Sinker: If the characters were to join him, it would be about the right number to safely sneak up on the camp and still have some chance of survival if caught. The camp will have rings of guards around it, but with care the characters should be able to get close. In the camp is a new Coyle warlord, who is getting ready to lead his people into a new period of war against the Western Empire colony, and the Wolfen Empire if it gets in the way. The location of this camp and the warlord's plans are important info. It's now up to the characters to return with the info, so an army can be sent in time to stop the Coyles before they are fully ready. Quick thinking players maybe even able to work out a deal with the Wolfen to work together on this.

Finder's keepers, loser's blessing

Hook: While traveling through the countryside, the characters find a sword in the road. It looks like it was buried there for some time and some recent rain uncovered it.

Line: The sword is a magic one (it's up to the G.M. what type and bonuses), and will give the character who wields it powerful magic.

Sinker: The sword has one problem — it's cursed. The curse doesn't kick in for several weeks, but then it hits the characters with a vengeance. Any bonuses the character had from the sword before are reversed (+1 to saving throws vs magic becomes a -1). In addition, the character has a 20% chance each week of developing a random insanity. To get rid of the curse, the character will need to find someone else to take the sword. Just dropping the sword somewhere will not end the curse, until someone else has had it for a month.

It's just a simple cargo delivery

Hook: While the characters are in Epiphany (Western Empire) for one reason or another, they are offered a job by a member of the government.

Line: The job is to take a small box to House Valocek in Colfax (Western Empire). The nature of the cargo makes it too sensitive to send through normal channels. The box will be heavily warded to prevent the characters from snooping.

Sinker: Within the box are papers outlining the first steps in a formal alliance between House Kaze and House Valocek. The characters will no doubt face problems delivering the box, as bandits will assume it most be worth a fortune. Also, any of the other noble houses may get word of it through their spies and try to intercept it for their own purposes.

Ryan Beres '99

Adventures in Dragon-sitting

Hook: The characters are traveling through the wilderness when they come across a small town. The residents are in a uproar about a giant lizard that has been terrorizing the local wildlife.

Line: The townspeople offer the characters a small reward to deal with this lizard. The amount should be no more than 50 gold per character. They would offer more, but they are a very poor town.

Sinker: It shouldn't be to hard for the characters to find the lizard. The catch is, it's not a lizard but instead a very young Dragon. It's only a few weeks old and was just having fun chasing the animals. It had no idea of the harm it was causing. To make things worse for the characters, the Dragon takes an immediate liking to one of them and follows that character everywhere. What happens next is up to the players, but they now have a very young Dragon who will follow them and knows nothing about the world (Game Masters should have fun with that).

The joys of free enterprise

Hook: While the characters are traveling through the Lower Barraduk region of the Western Empire, they are contacted by a merchant who needs a escort for a caravan.

Line: It sounds like a simple escort mission of a rather boring cargo, but the pay is decent: 1,000 gold for each character.

Sinker: It is of course no simple cargo. The merchant is trying to flood the market and cause prices to drop. This will cost him a bit, but it will hurt a major rival even worse. If the rival hears of this (and of course he will), he will try to stop the caravan from ever reaching the city.

Monster Trouble

Hook: When traveling through the wilderness, the characters come across a small town.

Line: The people of the town approach the characters, saying they are being terrorized by a savage tribe of Orcs in a nearby valley. They will pay the characters to drive the Orcs away.

Sinker: The Orcs have never bothered the village. They just want to live in peace. The villagers want the Orcs' rich farmland and are using the characters to do their dirty work. If the characters kill the innocent Orcs, another group of heroes will certainly hear about the massacre.

She ain't no lady!

Hook: While traveling on a major road, the characters come across a coach that was attacked by a well armed force. There are dead bodies everywhere. It appears the defenders won, but it wasn't much good since what survivors there were died shortly afterwards.

Line: Well, they didn't get everyone. There is a woman hiding in what's left of the coach. If and when the characters get her to come out, she will identify herself as a noble woman of a local ruling house. She was on her way home from Caer Itom (Western Empire) to meet her future husband. She doesn't know who attacked her and will offer the characters rich rewards if they can safely escort her home.

Sinker: If the characters take the job, they could make a hefty haul getting her home safely. Not long into the trip, the characters will also find out she gives spoiled brats a bad name. She has had a very pampered life, and was given everything she ever wanted. It shouldn't be long before the characters start having fond flashbacks of past jobs, like dragon slaying. If the characters get too rough with her, she will throw a tantrum and at the very least threaten to lessen the reward, if not have them arrested.

Trophy Hunt

Hook: When visiting one of the cities in the Western Empire, the characters come across notices offering employment to Rangers and Warriors.

Line: The local lord is an avid hunter, and is need of extra help on some of his more dangerous hunts. Pick any creature from **Monsters & Animals** and this guy will hunt it. He will even give a go at a dragon if given the chance.

Sinker: The reason he needs outside help is that he is in direct competition with another lord. They have even gone so far as to have members of each other's hunting parties killed to slow each other down. The characters will have to deal with the dangers of the hunt as well as the competing lord.

We've been what?!

Hook: This one is mainly for Game Masters who have players who do large amounts of collateral damage in their fights. About a week after the last time they destroyed half a town to save it, the characters are approached by a tall man with something for them. And he won't take no for an answer.

Line: The item in question is a summons to court for damages. It seems someone was upset by the overkill used in their last adventure, and expects the characters to pay up for damages. So he is suing the characters.

Sinker: The characters have two weeks to show up before the court and tell their side of the story. If they do not show, the court will put a bounty out on their heads for failure to appear. Note: This will probably work best for players adventuring in the more civilized areas, like the Timiro Kingdom or the Western Empire.

Troubled Waters

Hook: While traveling by sea, the characters have to set into a small port town for some reason. This can be anything from repairing damage to the ship to picking up some supplies.

Line: It's a small town, but it has what the characters need. The characters should also notice that the people of the town are very nervous when they talk to the characters, as though they fear they are being watched.

Sinker: When the characters try to leave, they discover the trouble with the town. A powerful Water Warlock lives in the area, and considers the town to be his. He demands a stiff tax (several thousand gold, usually determined by how much he thinks the travelers in question can afford) from all who try to leave his port. If travelers don't pay, he turns his magic on them and sinks their ship. It's up to the characters if they pay, but if they don't they will have a fight on their hands.

"Fantasy Role-Playing" is our middle name

The Palladium Fantasy RPG® is a world of magic. A place where magic has helped to shape an entire world.

The Palladium Fantasy RPG® offers a world of diversity and adventure.

A place where humans stand at the pinnacle of power, and where nonhumans, like Wolfen, Coyles, Melech, Gromek, Giants, Ogres, Orcs, Goblins and many of the so-called "monster races," await their downfall (and the opportunity to dance on their bones).

Meanwhile, races like the multi-limbed Rahu-Men, Titans, Elves, Dwarves, Gnomes and others have joined forces with humankind in the hope that man may learn from their mistakes.

Then, there are those found on the fringes of human civilization or those who seem to have their own agendas. These include the shapeshifting Changelings, Dragons, Faerie Folk, Lizard Men, and Kobolds, among many others.

All available as player characters.

Creatures of evil are also afoot. Vile beings dedicated to the propagation of treachery, sorrow and death — or their own dreams of power.

Heroes. The player characters are the heroes in this expansive world of magic and adventure — be they Knight or Wizard, human or the farthest thing from it. They are adventurers, freebooters, explorers and champions who dare to take a stand and do what's right.

Rules enjoyed by over a million gamers. The core rules to *The Palladium Fantasy RPG®*, and all of Palladium's role-playing games, have been enjoyed and played by over a million gamers.

- Rules that enable the players to create memorable and fun characters that truly come to life in their imaginations. Over 25 different player characters are described in the basic rulebook alone, and over a dozen different races to choose from (many more are available in sourcebooks like **Monsters & Animals™**).
- Magic that makes sense with rules that take a plausible approach to magic. Several different types are available — spell casting, circles, wards, elemental magic, clergy and psionics.
- Over 300 spells, 60 wards (magic symbols), and 50 circles plus rune weapons, magic potions, scrolls, and magic items.
- Rules that offer incredible flexibility and diversity.
- Rules for realistic and fast paced combat.
- Rules that are easy to learn.
- Rules that link the player to Palladium's infinite Megaverse®.
- Demons, Giants, Faerie Folk, and world information.
- Game Master and Player tips too.
- Everything you need to play, except for dice and imagination.
- And fun! Lots of fun.
- $24.95 retail — 320 pages.

Adventure Sourcebooks

Old Ones™, 2nd Edition: Over 50 different cities, towns and forts. The Timiro Kingdom mapped and described, plus adventure galore. $20.95 — 224 pages.

Adventures on the High Seas™, 2nd Edition: Ship to ship combat rules, the Necromancer, Sailor and many other character classes, six adventures and over 20 islands to explore. $20.95 — 224 pages.

Monsters & Animals™, 2nd Edition: Over 100 monsters, nearly 200 animals, more world information and details. $20.95 — 240 pages!

Dragons & Gods™, 2nd Edition: Over 40 gods, 20 demonic lords and their powers, priests and magic. Plus 14 dragons, their habits and history, holy weapons and more. $20.95 — 232 pages!

The Western Empire™, 2nd Edition: An in depth look at the "Empire of Sin." 18 cities, 13 provinces, new herbs, magic items and adventure. $20.95 — 224 pages.

Baalgor Wastelands™, 2nd Edition: The hostile land mapped and described, new monsters, new player races, adventure and adventure ideas. $20.95; 216 pages.

Mount Nimro™, 2nd Edition: The war between the giants and the monstrous, winged Gromek. New player characters and monster races, history, world information, and adventure. $16.95 — 160 pages.

Island at the Edge of the World™: Crystal magic, the Ghost Kings, the secret history of Changelings and the Circle of Elemental magic that threatens the world! Still $15.95 — 160 pages.

Coming in 2000: The Eastern Territory™, The Land of the Damned™, Phi & Lopan™, and more.

Palladium Books – 12455 Universal Drive – Taylor, MI 48180